The

Wisdom

of the

Willow

The

WISDOM

of the

WILLOW

A Novel

NANCY CHADWICK

SHE WRITES PRESS

Published 2024
Printed in the United States of America
Print ISBN: 978-1-64742-652-1
E-ISBN: 978-1-64742-653-8
Library of Congress Control Number: 2023915804

For information, address:
She Writes Press
1569 Solano Ave #546
Berkeley, CA 94707

Interior design by Stacey Aaronson

She Writes Press is a division of SparkPoint Studio, LLC.

For those who seek conversation while meandering through the woods under the canopies of any forest, or when sitting in stillness beneath the limbs of any single tree

TABLE OF CONTENTS

"The green reed which bends in the wind is stronger than the mighty oak which breaks in a storm"

—THE OAK AND THE REED, AESOP'S FABLES

1998

Prologue

For the past thirty-five years, I've sat mornings here at this old wooden kitchen table. I run my hands over its dings and stains while gazing through the glass doors to the back porch where the life of each Dowling has opened. The yard's depth pulls me to it, whether during a sobering rain or a joyful sun, unconfined with no property line. If I sit quietly in my favorite chair, a yard-sale find from over thirty years ago that rounds one end of the rectangular porch, I can hear conversations blossoming as I recall the stories we've shared over the years. On the other end of the porch, facing me, is the squeaky glider with well-worn indented cushions that fills quickly with the squiggly young bodies of four girls. Not one could ever have it to herself. Each fought for space, but in the end, they snuggled in there tight while swinging into a comfortable rhythm together. Dowling history unfolded there, where we breathed air into our family's lungs and learned a thing or two about ourselves along the way.

This is my story of family and home, of sharing memories as a mother to Debra, Rose, Linney, and Charlotte, and as a wife to Joe. If it weren't for them, I wouldn't be sitting here looking out at a backyard defined by a wooden fence, yet undefined by where life would take us. Every spring, Joe and I would pack each corner and curved space with lilacs and hydrangea, dogwoods and boxwoods. We worked the earth on hands and knees in the flower beds, then filled empty dirt spaces with lavender and roses and anything else fragrant I could think of to adorn our surroundings with colorful finery. We created open invitations to butterflies and bees and finches and hummingbirds to feast on the blooms, and I listened to the girls' unceasing laughter as they chased chipmunks and squirrels and butterflies. Throughout the summer days, Joe wrapped me in smiles while he tinkered in the garage with a saw and hammer. He sifted through an old Folgers coffee can of nails and a wheelbarrow full of scrap wood to create a clever reinforcement for the sagging fence or to strengthen a weakened picnic table leg while listening to Lou Boudreau call the Chicago Cubs games on WGN radio. Joe had his space and so did I, and I think the girls did, too. Though separate in worlds that made us content, we shared a home that made us content together.

I remember when Joe and I first moved into this house, and I was pregnant with Debra. Joe didn't waste any time planting a tree, as if he felt it an obligation, soon after we settled, and the last piece of furniture was in place. He explained his thinking while we were seated on the glider one spring morning, looking out onto our sparsely landscaped yard: "Ya know, Margaret, we need to plant a tree," he said, slapping a hand on my knee as if he had the answer in final *Jeopardy*.

"Just a tree?" I sighed. I hoped my expectations of decorating a yard in colorful flowers and plump shrubs weren't dashed.

"Margaret, they're not 'just' trees." Joe's caterpillar brows sprung as he turned to me, adjusting his Cubs baseball cap on a bushy head of chocolate brown hair. "Did you know that they're connected?

Nutrients flow up from the roots and back down, communicating from one tree to another through their systems in the ground. And the one we will plant will not be an exception. It will be strong and stable and stand firm, and its branches will be flexible and bend without breaking." Joe gave our nearly empty back lot a hard stare, as if envisioning our new tree in its fullness. "Think of it as a safe place to be; a place to feel belonging, to learn from; a place to nurture us as it grows, like we will do with our family." His eyes grew tight in concentration. "And I think I have just the right tree in mind."

The next morning, when I went to grab the morning newspaper from the front stoop, Joe was easing the station wagon out from the garage. "See ya in a bit. I won't be long," he yelled, waving an extended arm through an open window. I couldn't be certain where he was headed, but I had a pretty good idea after yesterday's chat. And sure enough, while I was at the kitchen sink rinsing breakfast dishes, I looked out the window to see Joe dragging a burlap-wrapped root ball, young branches bouncing all over and hitting him in the head. I scurried to the other side of the counter with the dish towel still in hand, past the kitchen table and through the sliding doors to the backyard, to Joe and to our new tree. He ambled in circles, making soft imprints with his work boots in the grass, then looked up to find the sun hazy in the southwest sky. He wanted to pick the most open spot in the yard, where the rains collect in a bowl. "It'll have room here to grow, and we'll be comfortable sitting under it. Like home," he said.

I stepped aside to give Joe space to work as he stuck the young, wispy willow into the big hole in the ground and filled it with dirt. He patted the root ball in place, first with his hands, like a squirrel tapping the earth to bury an acorn, then with his foot, flattening the loose ground with a stomp or two. He then rubbed his hands together as if to free himself of the task, to let go, to say, *My job here is done—*

now grow and be free. I think Joe felt that he had given us a place to belong because he got us a house and filled it with nice things inside and out. Joe is a lot like that tree, providing us a place to grow.

We threaded our arms through each other while staring at our new willow and grinning in satisfaction. I think it was happy, too, with its skinny leaves jiggling in the breeze as if in laughter. Joe gave my baby bump a tender pat. "Don't worry, Margaret," he said, pulling me closer. "There's still plenty of space to plant all those flowers you love so much."

My wish is that I have given the girls the wisdom of the willow to guide them in finding their places.

PART I

"*Life is but a day,*
A fragile dew-drop on its perilous way
From a tree's summit."
—JOHN KEATS

OCTOBER

Charlotte

Ma stayed in the red brick Colonial because home was everything to her. Her place was in that house—and she felt it—deep in the marrow of her bones, where connections threaded through her body like veins to the heart. And one Sunday, she was ready to lie in a pillow of peace and walk with Jesus.

I was on my way, on a fifteen-minute drive to the only home I ever knew. I lived the nearest and was the youngest, so by default I was Ma's primary caregiver, my sisters reasoned. There was no arguing with that. To do so would be a confrontation, and that would make me nervous. And my sister Linney, the organic titanic, would plop a handful of crystals into the palm of my hand to bring forth calmness and deep breathing from within me, as if calling attention to a deficit she felt I had.

It was my favorite time of year, when Mother Nature can fool us, offering late summer heat and sun despite the early fall calendar noting otherwise. My Beetle windows were open to the last vestiges of late October, a montage of maple and oak leaves in burnt orange, crimson, and green apple, with autumn's spicy scent hitching a ride. I've never lived far from here, and I've never wanted to. My home gave me what I needed—an open landscape, beaches, access to city life, and seasons that are as pronounced as temperatures during a Chicago winter. My familiar surroundings gave me security.

As I neared the house, it appeared dwarfed now among the newer, larger homes around it, but it had loomed large to me as a child. My parents gave us a foundation here to take root and to connect, nestling into the curve of a cul-de-sac, one of many in the middle class of the tree-lined streets of Wilmette, a North Shore suburb of Chicago.

I turned on Birchwood Court, as I had done countless times before, more frequently during this past summer. Pulling into the driveway, my tires dropped into gaps in the cement, then rolled over chunks of uneven concrete before I came to a stop. Life had shifted here, for all of us. The once white siding on the top floor was now dull and gray, and the black paint on the shutters was chipped. Landscaped beds, once packed with pink and blue hydrangeas, red roses, and deep lavender, were now faded and folded into the earth from which they grew. But the house's redbrick foundation appeared to be holding on, maybe because of Dad's great care of its bones over the years in obligation to its integrity. When I would return for a visit, I'd automatically soften into its folds, becoming a piece of the Dowling fabric once again.

The outside had become a worn blanket with holes and frayed edges, as if with the passing of years; an essence of what home truly meant had been weakened where it was no longer how I remembered it. I couldn't see home clearly.

I opened the creaky front door and stood still in the foyer, blending into the silence, my body cutting the weight of thick air. The grandfather clock's ticking echoed, and the oak floors still popped, especially in one spot when heading upstairs, setting off an alarm when my sisters tried to sneak in and up to their rooms after coming home later than they were supposed to. I would hear Rose first. "I heard you last night," I'd whisper to her the next morning from across the kitchen table. She would flip her straight kohl-black hair away from her high-cheek-boned face to show a slight upward curve of her mouth, her hazel eyes peeking from underneath a curtain of bangs. I would never say anything to Deb because, as the oldest, she knew best, better than I, anyway. Oftentimes she was Ma's spokesperson, an instant messenger when we needed direction. "Go wash up for dinner and make yourselves presentable. Dinner is ready," she'd tell us with a cutting wave of her hand. Otherwise, I'd head to the dinner table as is, unkempt with dirty hands from working the Schafers' jungle gym next door, a sure disappointment to Ma and Dad.

Threading down the hallway, I skimmed past our lives hanging framed in photos, to the rear of the house where Dad was sitting slumped at the kitchen table, though not in his usual seat. He was where I used to sit, staring out through the glass doors to the backyard as if in defeat. Jingle, our golden retriever, newest Dowling, and angel, lay under the table undisturbed at his feet, offering comfort. My parents rescued him when they needed rescuing from their empty nests, after my sisters and I had left home to pursue our best selves. I stood in the doorway to see Dad's longing eyes move to his wife's gilded-framed picture on the sideboard, taken well before I came along. I wondered what Dad was thinking. Was he trying to recall all his memories with her so he wouldn't miss her more than he already was?

"Hey, Dad. I'm here," I said, sidling up to him at the table. "How are you doing?" I squeezed his rounded shoulders. "You okay?" His shirt and khaki pants looked as worn out as he did. His face was void of the bright eyes and lively engagement he had before Ma died.

"Fine, fine, dear," he said with a quivery smile.

We sat together, our elbows touching, staring out at the yard, under the spell of the willow branches pushed by easterly winds. Our eyes followed shriveled dead leaves, rambling along a thinned lawn and leftover from a fall landscape cleanup. I didn't know what to say. Maybe just being together was enough?

I thought of how we would no longer "carry on," as Dad used to say at a filled Dowling table at the end of meals, yet my sisters continued to deliberate about the dilemmas they faced in school. From Linney thinking about joining the pep squad in junior high, or Deb debating whether to go out for the debate team, or Rose considering trying for the part of Maria in *West Side Story*, Dad would hear us out, his head turning back and forth as he weighed the pros and cons of each side, and end it by folding his hands on the table and telling us, "Do what you have to do." Well, I could have argued I had to quit speech class as it turned my insides upside down, knowing I had to stand in front of the class to talk about something as boring as the value of pocket protectors.

The wind rushed quicker through the yard and the skies dimmed. I told Dad I needed to go into the attic. "You go do what you need to do, Char. I'm headed for a stroll out back." I watched him get up from the table, step over Jingle to reach the glass doors and pull them open. Jingle sprang out the door first, and Dad followed. I waited to leave until he settled into his favorite chair on the porch, next to Ma's, to visit her in the memories of their lives.

Cobwebs clung across the corners of the attic's door at an unlit narrow landing, as if to block any trespasser of the past. When I was little, I believed Santa Claus hid our presents in the reclusive place, something no one else knew. My parents entrusted me to keep that knowledge private, saying it was a secret only I could keep. And as a grown adult now, I can say I had been a good secret-keeper because of what Ma had asked of me that day last May.

The door resisted my pull, perhaps a sign I wasn't supposed to be there, but I knew it was because of rust-coated hinges and infrequent use. A final tug, and it gave way. I waited for stirred dust to clear and warm air to settle to see where I was going. The midmorning sun offered light through a tiny square window to guide my footing, marking life in the dormancy of dust and dirt. I thought that was Ma's old dresser straight ahead. I remembered when she told me about it, the first piece of furniture she ever owned, front drawers inlaid with cherry and pine. When Ma and Dad moved into this house, he told her she didn't have to take her old bedroom furniture; she could get a whole new set. But there was something about hanging on to the familiar; Ma couldn't part with it. A tarnished wrought iron headboard leaned against a near wall. Children's dolls in various states of undress sat propped askew in an opened, broken suitcase under the window, trains were derailed from their dismantled tracks, and shoeboxes of disintegrating cardboard held their shape as if undisturbed. Though I had no understanding of what I was seeing and thought it all to be insignificant, I understood they must have been important to someone at one time. And who was I to label any object as having no meaning?

And I saw what Ma must have been whispering about to me. The steamer trunk. It sat alone in a far corner, tucked under the rafters. As I neared the remote spot, the dank and musty odor signaled a travel back in time. As old as it appeared, it was a part of this house's foundation and its origin. It was large enough to keep best secrets and long memories and strong enough to hold tall tales. My hand skimmed across the ruts and scrapes that were evidence of a well-traveled wooden box, darkened with age, and held by tarnished metal straps that ran along each side. When I opened the cover, a mixed odor of lacquered wood, mildew, and mothballs struck my nose and itched my eyes. Wrinkled, stained silk that covered the lid's interior showed tears at the edges from small, rusted nails holding its place. Nestled atop the tidy stack of dated men's white shirts and work trousers, women's black pumps, and a collection of scarves in every color of the rainbow was a large cardboard box, newer by the looks of its stiff, square shape. I opened a time capsule that brought the past into the present. When I released the box's flaps, a cotton rug, a silk tapestry, and a linen tablecloth freed themselves of darkness. I pulled the treasures from their tomb and held the fabrics of our lives.

PART

II

"The wonder is that we can see these trees
and not wonder more."

—RALPH WALDO EMERSON

MAY

Debra

Seeing old college friends on this Memorial Day weekend will be a celebration, a coming together, as we have tried and often failed to do because of our busy schedules. The day will reawaken a time when those relationships meant everything to me. The bonds among us, like anchors, have defied forces of nature such as a breakup, a failed class, or a new roommate who threatened our stability. Sure, we had our clashes, but nothing a night out at O'Donohue's couldn't smooth out. We've come a long way, from serving ourselves beer from a pitcher into plastic cups, to pouring wine into glass goblets from corked bottles wearing classy labels. It's all about the packaging, the presence, not that I equate myself with an attractive wine bottle.

Awakening to an overcast chilly morning, I must recall where I am—alone, without Dennis. I am relieved to have this weekend free as a holiday grants me permission to be away from work, and to slow down. I'm usually in implementation mode, making corporate events happen, checking this and that, and asking questions to ensure I have a happy client. Wandering the bedroom, my familiar that is filled with "D&D" monogramming etched in picture frames nestled in deep nooks, stitched along the hems of pillowcases, and scripted in chocolate brown on throw pillows now feels unfamiliar. The scent of Irish Spring soap is faint when it's usually strong, as Dennis carries it into the bedroom after a morning shower. I can almost hear his voice, now softer and in the distance, telling me, "You'd better step it up," when I was late for work. It was years in the making for Ma and Dad to turn their house into a home for us Dowlings, and I question if I have done that with Dennis and this home.

After a refreshing shower, I slip on a pair of white linen pants and a black tunic, wrestle my wayward hair into a ponytail, then grab a pair of hoop earrings and bangle bracelets. I check myself in the full-length mirror hanging on the inside of the closet door, before slipping on flats and heading downstairs and into the kitchen.

I'm already in a misty sweat during early preparation for lunch. I think the last time I wore this outfit was on a business trip overseas to Shanghai. Who goes to Shanghai in August, anyway, with the excruciating humidity and heat? Well, apparently, Kinsey and Moore, the corporate event planning company I work for, does. Thankfully, Memorial Day weekend in Chicago is no August weekend in Shanghai. The cool spring breezes haven't yet given way to hot summer air.

I pull wineglasses from their racks in an upper kitchen cabinet and luncheon plates in a lower one, anticipating the chatter among us as we catch up and pick up where we left off—as younger adults who hadn't yet mastered the art of bullshitting. It seems the older we get, the more we feel we must hide flaws and faults, as if perfection is synonymous with wisdom and aging. Chopping, slicing, and dicing lettuce, red onion, bacon, and hard-boiled egg go into a seven-layer salad prep, and I take a break to open the dining room sliding doors and the windows in the front living room. I breathe in the sweet spring scent and feel the cool cross-ventilation. Goose bumps travel throughout my body as if awakening a new, calmer self.

After I've cleaned the kitchen, I set the table where I anticipate the coming together of us in friendship, recalling midday meals we once shared in the dorm's cafeteria. We'd check out a table of graduate students nearby, their books open and studying while they plowed through a pepperoni pizza, and how we never opened a book until later at night.

Camille's voice taps me into the present, her singsongy tone arriving before the doorbell's chime. "Heeelllooo, anyone home?"

I open the door to a set of perfect white teeth and dimples and hands waving frantically.

"Your hair! You cut short that gorgeous head of auburn," I say.

"Sassy, now, aren't I?" She swings her head from side to side, giving her locks a fluff and her bracelets a dangle. What a sashay she does through that door, her flouncy yellow blouse waving with each shimmy. That's Camille, always making an entrance.

"Wait . . . Deb," Lisa yells from the driveway. "I'm coming, too." She makes her way in black heels while pulling down a short white pencil skirt. A red halter top fits her well, showing off an ample bosom. Her slender figure hasn't changed a bit since college.

Camille and Lisa were never in competition, but rather were a complement to each other. I liked that about them.

"Here, for you," Lisa says, pushing a bottle of Beaujolais into my chest as she steps inside. She's always had a sense of urgency.

"Welcome."

I usher the ladies into the living room where the sun has brightened a seated corner filled with a sectional sofa in crème with dark stained pine end tables, floor-to-ceiling white bookcases on either side of a brick fireplace. Camille pulls off her sunglasses, and her green eyes widen. "Nice place you got here. I knew you'd do well, Deb, but not *this* well." Lisa remains occupied with adjusting her skirt and top. They stop talking and turn their heads in unison to have a look around. Camille places a hand on the back of one of two armchairs patterned in gray and tan, then picks up a wedding photo of me and Dennis on a console table separating the living room from the dining space. I think how Dennis and I have *our* friends and Dennis always meets *his* friends somewhere. Sure, I talk to them on the phone, but rarely do we go out with them or have them here. I think it's peculiar, and sad. It's as if my home here is separate and private from my home with my best friends from college or the ones I have made in the neighborhood.

We march into the kitchen and gather around the island in the middle where I've readied all our luncheon pleasures. "Here. Grab a platter," I say, handing Lisa a plate of Swiss cheese and Club crackers and Camille a bowl of Planters cheese balls. I pick up a Crate and Barrel serving platter, a wedding shower gift, with colorful crudités. Event planning details are innate: whether for work or for a social event, they give me a sense of accomplishment, which, in my business, doesn't always get recognized. "C'mon, this way." I motion us back to the living room with a bottle of wine in hand.

I settle the platter next to a tulip and daffodil floral arrangement on a round coffee table, and I note my attractive handiwork on the colorful food presentation and spring bouquet. Before we sit, I notice how plump the couch's cushions look, still so creamy and new, so not broken in. It's as if no one lives in this house.

"So, where've you all been lately, huh?" I blurt in sarcasm remembering "Grace" is not my middle name. You know how that goes—no filter sometimes. I hold up my glass. "Let's toast," I say to change the subject, deflecting a weakness I have of not trying harder to keep our friendship going. I admit my infrequent check-ins with a phone call don't replace in-person gab fests that are sure to rekindle the spark in our friendship that has dimmed over the years.

It's a matter of draining that first glass of wine, or beer, our drink of choice at college, and the ride becomes more carefree, and we begin to talk like college women all over again with salty language and critical thinking about others. Eventually our conversation becomes adult-like with more critical thinking about ourselves, and our language more politically correct.

It isn't just these two friends, though. Our group used to be a foursome. When we would try to get together, Tracey usually had plans or said, "Maybe next time?" She'd make us believe we could expect her, and then she wouldn't show up. I can only think back to college when she started dating some guy in Western Civ. She never noticed him until he noticed her, staring at her during class. It was about that time when she stopped going with us to our regular Friday nights at Cleary's for happy hour. And then she'd show up after a few months because, well, as she would sadly announce, "It just didn't work out." We concluded her absence was because of a guy who took our place. It was a pattern. No happy hours with Tracey, we assumed, meant she was having a very happy hour with a new guy.

I consider this get-together more of an exercise in connecting to something "other," another life I had before marriage. I missed my friends, who admittedly I had shifted to different places, by no fault of theirs, when I declared "I do." When I was younger, I was determined that marriage would no way in hell interfere with a life I had made for myself. Yet here I am now, extending a mea culpa with this luncheon for not getting together as much as my conscience was calling me to.

I borrow time by grabbing the open bottle of pinot and pouring what remains into my glass. And then I have a look at its label. Anderson Valley. Dennis and I used to take trips to San Francisco, plotting our winery stops, for long weekends. Our last drive was to Mendocino, where we stayed at the Mendocino Farmhouse. It was secluded and quiet, with no distractions from an outside world we felt was overloaded and overloading us. That trip was different from the others. We couldn't help but be forced to speak with each other when conversation was once organic and free-flowing. Marriage is a lot of work.

"How is Charlie?" Camille says, reaching for a newly opened bottle. "How's the stepparenting thing going?"

"Charlie is finding his way. I think it's hormones. Who knew being a spouse and a stepparent is like being a project manager—of your husband and children?" I sit back and smooth out the creases embedded in my tunic's linen realizing what I might be really saying. Has married life and co-parenting become like work? Are they like tasks on a to-do list with no choice but to complete them? I take a controlled breath and let out a sigh.

"Knock it off," Lisa says, diving into the stuffed mini peppers as if that were lunch. "We've all known each other for a long time. And if there's anyone here who would win most likely to keep it together, it would be you, Deb. You're the strongest one of all of us."

All eyes meet mine.

I've heard that before. From Ma. She used to tell me that because I was the oldest, I was also the strongest, and she deployed me to keep my younger sisters in line, as if they never had self-control. But each does have a will of her own, a common thread that started with Ma and has continued to run through the Dowling women.

I have a difficult time with what to say next. "Thank you, Lisa," or "Oh, gee, I'm not really. It only looks that way," and I sound too vulnerable. So, instead I say, "C'mon, let's grab plates in the kitchen and have lunch."

"Nice presentation, Deb. You remembered," Camille says, carrying a bottle of Chardonnay to the dining room table. Dennis and I spotted the set, handmade in oak and cherry, on a trip to New England earlier in our marriage. With sturdy legs supporting an elegant top, the table reminded me of us—strong and smart. "Seven-layer salads sure have been our thing since our post-college days. Whenever we'd meet for lunch in the city, we'd all order the seven-layer because all the other businesswomen in the restaurant were eating them, and we wanted to be just like them."

"And now we are just like them," I say, filling our wineglasses while mini baguettes nestled in a cloth-lined basket are passed around.

The Matanzas Creek was Dennis's aunt's favorite wine. When we visited her and her husband, Tom, in San Francisco, Tom would disappear to the wine "cellar," a white locked box in the garage, and reappear with a bottle of Cakebread and one of Matanzas Creek in hand, much to Aunt Joan's delight, who would clap her hands and squeal, "The perfect choices and one of my favorites." Sharing dinners with Dennis's family over California wine was as much a part of home as being married to Dennis.

"Let's toast," I say, directing us to hold up our glasses. "It feels kind of odd . . . missing someone."

I think of Tracey. Her effervescent personality reminds me of the bubbles in the flutes of Domaine Chandon that Dennis and I served at our wedding. She always was able to make friends easily, especially men, captivating them into conversation.

"Oh, Deb . . . are you and Dennis . . . in trouble?" Lisa says, covering her mouth politely as if she's asked a no-no.

I put down my fork and shake my head. "No, not Dennis! I'm talking about missing Tracey. This is the longest we've gone without hearing from her. Right? And no return calls either."

"Maybe she thinks our friendship has run its course, and she's found new friends," Lisa says, stabbing lettuce leaves and chunks of celery.

"She started to travel with work . . . I think," Camille adds.

"Sounds like Dennis. He's been gone a lot. When he isn't traveling to meet clients, he's got weekend gigs." I mumble this through nibbling torn bites of bread.

Suspicion and silence roll into the room like afternoon fog over the Golden Gate. The sheers billow excitedly as if an omen.

"Do you think he's having an affair?" Camille asks, her raised eyebrows peeking over the rim of her glass.

Heads swivel; eyes pin on me.

"Oh, God, really, Camille?" Lisa punches the air with an open hand. "Why in God's name would you even say such a thing?"

"No, it's okay to say what you're thinking, Camille. The idea of infidelity never crossed my mind when I said 'I do,' but, honestly"— I quiet my voice—"sometimes I do think about it now."

Conversation pauses and I stare out to the backyard, like Ma used to do when something bothered her, as if the answer lay hidden in the spring landscape. "Sometimes you can figure things out by talking with the trees and the flowers and the birds," she'd tell me. I wondered how she could be talking when I never did see her mouth moving.

"Maybe Tracey has a new job and it's keeping her away from us?" Lisa says.

Camille interjects. "I thought we were talking about Dennis."

"We are," Lisa continues, "and I was changing the subject to someone else who seems to be MIA lately." She uses her fingers to air-quote "MIA."

"I think she's still at that marketing firm," Camille pipes up.

I ask, "Which one?"

"The one she got after we graduated: C . . . M . . ."

Camille looks at me. "CMG. Hey, I think Dennis's agency pitched that firm. Do you know if they got it?"

"Don't know," I tell her, shrugging my shoulders.

I usually don't keep up with the ad agency business and who is pitching whom for what business, but I know since I took on the BMT Worldwide Advertising Agency as a client and met Dennis, the "T" in BMT, it was all about the agency business, what clients were hopping to what agencies and who was going with them.

Lisa asks, "And how is it that you know this?"

"Must have read it somewhere . . ." Camille murmurs, looking off into the distance, trying to recall.

I question the bond we made in college, one that was supposed to last forever. One thing we promised each other was to always tell the truth, to never have secrets among us. We sealed our promise with a white macramé bracelet. If any one of us thought of not telling the truth, we'd roll the tight knots with beads between our fingers and find strength in doing the right thing. I think of my bracelet and wonder if they're thinking of theirs now.

Learning to trust myself with anyone is the ultimate lesson in understanding my vulnerabilities. I vaguely remember Dennis mention that BMT was pitching a new marketing firm. I never did ask him, and though he usually tells me about new business pitches, he failed to mention this one's outcome.

The room cools, and it isn't because the morning sun has moved from the living room, and for that reason, our afternoon ends soon after lunch.

ᘇᘏᘇ Rose ᘏᘇᘏ

Mornings, while the coffee is brewing, I like to lean over my kitchen sink to look east, north, and south, out the bay window at pockets of wonder and discovery that beckon me to join. Seeing in all directions feels like a metaphor for the ways of my life as if I were a vagabond, moving from place to place, from one character to another, from one relationship to the next. I sound like my sister Linney, except for the "all directions" part, as she operates in just one. "Just the present moment," she'll say, taking a deep, yogic breath.

My older sister, Deb—Debra to her business acquaintances—is busy over Memorial Day weekend with her old college friends. Linney, number three sister, has the shop to deal with, and Charlotte, number four and last sister, is with Ma, trying her best to come up with what to barbecue. Charlotte will get the job done, in her own way, and Ma will love any way Charlotte handles it. She's Ma's baby.

I've never really felt forced to do anything, but I have to force myself this time to show up for my neighborhood block party today here in Lake Forest, a northern suburb of Chicago. It's a yearly thing on this holiday weekend for a mix of young couples with no kids, couples with kids, and married-forever couples, to catch up with one another. We meet on a dead-end, private street with no curbs or sidewalks, which makes for a country road kind of feel—neighborly, too. My place is small yet big on comfort, painted in mellow yellow with white shutters and minty-turquoise flower boxes underlining the white-framed windows. Gracious oaks, hickories, and cottonwoods have grown into one another in their old age along the street providing a canopy of shade in the summer and a trellis of shadows in the winter. This is my rooted base, despite my many and lengthy absences from it because of work. It has been my anchor when I was adrift, which usually has come in waves commensurate with tides: what part of the country I'm in, what acting gig I have, or who I'm seeing.

I stash a couple bottles of pinot grigio, brats, buns, and a party fruit platter in a picnic basket. I think the last time I used this basket was when Ma carried servingware in it out to the picnic table in the backyard of our home. I smile to think that it's remained in the family, and now I have a chance to use it as a reminder and connection to where I grew up.

With the basket in a crook of one elbow and a folding chair slipped in the other, I leave out the back door.

On my way down the street, couples and children are gathering. Husky men lean over grills in preparation for cooking, women work together to pull out table legs tucked under card tables, and a bounce house wobbles gently while anchored to the Kenneys' front yard. A couple of teenage boys carry heavy coolers on their shoulders while watching their footing. I don't recognize many, but I do recognize Marcie's petite frame up ahead. As I near her, I see we are dressed alike, she in slimming Guess jeans, I in faded Calvin's, white T-shirts under jean jackets, white Keds on our feet. She's let her caramel mane grow longer. She's busy ushering her two kids over to their father while she unloads grocery bags filled with juice boxes, cheese sticks, and green grapes.

"Hey there, Marcie," I shout, waving in greeting. "This looks like as good a place as any to unpack." I join her at a long folding table covered in a red-, white-, and blue-striped plastic tablecloth, and set down my picnic basket and lawn chair.

I don't hesitate to say Marcie is my best friend because she was the first neighbor to ring my doorbell the day I moved in. And best friends are forever. Marcie is everything I'm not—down-to-earth, a real warm-and-fuzzy person any woman would want to bare her soul to. She matched a male version of herself and started a family like it was the easiest, most uncomplicated thing in the world, like she was riding her bike to the 7-Eleven for a cola slushie on a hot summer day.

"Rose? Is that you?" Marcie says, sliding her sunglasses atop her head. Her sky-blue eyes have a good look at me, and her arms outstretch to welcome a hug. "You mean you're actually in town for a whole weekend?" A wink punctuates her sarcasm. I break away first, perhaps because of a bit of shame.

"You're funny, and yes, I'm here and looking forward to enjoying my neighbors. I know, it's been a while." I evade her look, and get busy unwrapping the party tray, napkins, and plastic cups.

"We've been here all along, Rose, and we're not going anywhere." Marcie gestures to our gathering neighbors with an open hand.

"I see Doug over there, readying the grill with precision and organization. He doesn't miss a step with the setup. You sure can count on him, Marcie . . . and I don't mean just for grilling hot dogs and hamburgers—I mean for being a good husband and dad, too."

Marcie and Doug are committed parents of five-year-old twins, Jennifer and Benjamin, aka Jen and Ben. In the early days, we'd go out as a foursome, Marcie and Doug, me and . . . whoever I was dating at the time. When their kids joined, it became a different foursome—Marcie and Doug, Jen and Ben. How their lives changed after having children. I thought I'd find my answer to what I wanted to do with my life here in the suburbs, and as Ma used to say, "allowing yourself to discover what you have yet to see through the familiarity of your home inside and the one outside in the natural world." I'm not sure what all that meant, but I trust Ma's words, and I hope to figure it out soon. This is where Deb would chime in and tell me how, indeed, I am a drama queen.

I unpack what remains in my basket. It's difficult to look Marcie in the eye, not because of the rising high-noon sun, but because I know if I do, she'll see right through me, into a window to my troubles.

"You're awfully quiet," she says, arranging pitchers of lemonade and cola. "Drink?"

"Got anything stronger?"

"Ah, I see." Marcie slips out a bottle of Chardonnay from inside her tote bag. After she pours us each a cup, we fuss with the multiple tabletops, creating stations of soft drinks, potato and corn chip bowls, bottles of catsup and mustard, and jars of pickles. The "adult only" table is quickly stocked with red and white wines and coolers of beer that fit tightly under the tables.

We fiddle with our chairs to face the clearing skies and sit.

"So . . . taking a break from all the traveling?" Marcie asks, leaning her head back and her face up to meet the sun. This is her lead-in, an olive branch she is extending as a sign of peace and a safe place to be with a valued, trustworthy friend.

"I quit the magazine," I blurt, defiant, as if throwing up my hands, not in defeat but in spite. If the magazine isn't my place to be, then, so there, I'll leave you. "I used to think I wanted to travel with *Abroad* in search of undiscovered places, hidden gems on islands, and undisturbed earth, but now, I don't know. It was a fun ride with the magazine, writing articles that border on puff pieces with *National Geographic*–quality photos, without a lot of substance."

"You mean, meeting a variety of charismatic, wealthy men who were available to show you around those hidden gems and undisturbed earth, right?" I look away and watch the kids pile into the bounce house.

She has me there, digging deep into the vulnerable pockets of my soul. Marcie has always told it to me straight. Sure, I can be swayed easily by well-dressed, well-groomed men who enjoy a good cocktail, a fine dinner, and even finer after-dinner drinks. But where has that gotten me?

"What will you do next?" Marcie asks. "And I don't mean after this party."

"Don't know. No immediate plans. After this party or for the rest of my life." I let my self-pity show. I sip more wine and notice how the kids laugh and scream, bouncing unencumbered without a care in the world.

"Did something happen? I've never seen you like this." She reaches over and gently places a hand on my wrist.

It isn't what has happened—more like what hasn't happened. I tell her, "Julian and I were like peanut butter and jelly. We naturally stuck together, sweet and savory, only he wasn't a fan of any fruit that wasn't in its original packaging."

"So, you're feeling guilty because it didn't work out? Or . . ."

"No guilt. I just don't commit . . . to things," I tell her before dashing to the table for a handful of carrot sticks.

"And you're finding now in your more grown-up years that your younger ways have bitten you in the ass. Sounds like you're having an identity crisis."

I wonder if that is what's happening. My identity is in crisis? I stare at the plumbs of smoke erupting from the grills as burgers are flipped and hot dogs are rolled over the greasy grates.

"Why don't you take some time to figure things out? Take the summer off, Rose."

Therein lies the problem. Taking time off. I have never been idle for more than a few minutes at a time. And when I do get home, I am unconnected, restless. Maybe it's because I haven't spent much time here and I considered my surrogate homes to be wherever I was working. Was I avoiding being at home because of the very home I was afraid of making?

The cool air turns humid as storm clouds dance around the sun. I take off my jacket and hang it on the back of the chair.

"Take time for yourself, Rose. You've spent years asking the world how it sees itself. How about asking yourself how you see you? Hell, why don't you write a book about it all?"

"A book?" I chuckle at the absurdity. "But I can't write one if I don't know how it will end." I sober and pause. "Will I find my answers? Will I find my place to be?"

I've traveled the world, met strangers in undiscovered lands where I could be anybody, taking on a different character. Now, I want to get to the heart of who I am, and that means no longer being a writer for a travel magazine. This is where I have made my home, where it is about being yourself, and not about being someone you aren't. Home is the truth, to yourself, isn't it?

Linney

Early mornings are my favorite time. Waking up and peeking through the rails of the wrought iron headboard set against my bedroom window, I discover a new dawn. The kind sun rouses the sleeping. Birds wake in song, and the crimson leaves of the Japanese maple wave good morning in spring breezes; the early hours are ones of gratitude. I retreat to a cozy nook where I slip ceremoniously into asanas, sinking my bare feet to pose in mountain where I find my place in calm before I start the day's work.

A busy Memorial Day weekend kicks off another summer season at Magnolia, a small shop in Winnetka, near the shore of Lake Michigan, north of Chicago, where I work.

Magnolia inspires me every day, and helps me to stay rooted. I say that because of its bones, as it was built in the 1920s, and of its history as a carriage house. Bridget challenges me to make the shop inviting by extending the outside in, to give life to Magnolia. A butterfly garden is steps away from a small front porch set in flagstone, offering our guests tranquility and an occasional glimpse at finches and chickadees in the summer visiting the garden's blooms and frolicking in the birdbath. In cooler months, Bridget navigates guests to warmth and rest around the corner to a dimly lit firepit centered among circling Adirondack chairs. My soul is here, and I am indebted to Bridget for hiring me many years ago.

I, too, live in a coach house, just past the Magnolia grove. Actually, you could say it's outside my back door, a ten-minute walk up a narrow gravel path, through a meadow that isn't yet filled with waist-high lemon wildflowers, buttercups and cosmos mixed with honeysuckle, milkweed, and thistle. But in a few weeks, their heads will pop, and I'll be surrounded in a kaleidoscope of color and the spicy scents of wild prairie. In the meantime, I enjoy a Monet palette of daffodils, tulips, hyacinth, and crocus energizing the once dormant flower beds. Traipsing through this spring meadow to the Wedgewood-blue shop is food for my soul. I can't imagine myself living anywhere else as this is the best of both worlds, personal and professional.

Opening Magnolia's French doors, a concentration of lemon verbena, rose, and lavender from comingled soaps, sachets, and scented candles hits my nose. I rearrange delicate vases accenting place settings on round tables covered in French cotton cloth, before making my way down a short hall to the back office.

As I do each morning, I fill feeders outside the back door with a seed mix, calling the birds to a safe place, and a hanging glass ball with sugar water to bring the hummingbirds to drink. There's no door in this house that doesn't lead to a special place where I can experience moments that will never be repeated.

Back and forth with an old broom, I clear the brick walkway in a rhythm that seems to match that of the natural world. Working my way around the house doubles as a meditation on gratitude—the breaking through of bee balm, daisies, coneflowers, and black-eyed Susans in a warming bed—and as a security check. Suddenly, I hear a faint noise like grinding gravel, or footsteps? It stops. Must be Dottie, my beagle, chasing a chipmunk along the footpath. Dottie has the run of the place and makes for the best shop greeter and protector by punching the air with a hardy howl to notify me that customers are nearing. Wind chimes twirl and their notes break the day's tempo. I set the broom next to the door and look over my shoulder before turning the knob and stepping inside where Bridget's desk sits under a window, just inside to the left. I lean over it and peer through the smudgy pane for another look, and my hand sticks to a note on the desk's blotter. I don't remember seeing this when I closed last night. I pick up the lavender-colored paper.

"Good morning, Linney! I won't be in until later today. My spirit is strong, but my body is feeling a little weak. I know you can handle whatever comes your way. Enjoy it all, Linney. I'll see you soon."

There's something different about Bridget's words. Her voice sounds tired, which is strange since she usually has enough energy for both of us. Bridget owns Magnolia; she is Magnolia. She's shown me her love for this place by her care and devotion to its details, and through her, I have learned the meaning of having my own sense of place.

I put down the note. The oak wood floor creaks, a familiar sound I've come to recognize are footsteps, and I hurry to the front of the store, but there's no one there. I shift to dust a bookcase of ceramic knickknacks settled on bookcase shelves when the morning light dims on a sunny day. I peer through the square window. Outside, a dark figure startles me, then quickly leaves my sight. There is usually no one here this early, so my curiosity and sense of protecting Magnolia urge me to dash outside, nearly taking a nearby table covering and display with me. I circle the shop to the rear and stop at the firepit, where a well-dressed man stands in a white button-down shirt, with one hand in the pocket of his tawny slacks. With the other hand, he takes a drag of a cigarette while staring in the distance.

"Hi there. We open at ten," I yell and wave to catch his attention.

He turns to me, his navy sports jacket open to reveal a slender frame. I don't recognize him as any patron of Magnolia or friend of Bridget.

"I'm not here to shop. I'm here to look around." His voice is deep, his words accented, as his fingers navigate the scenery in the air. "I see you have a unique place . . . well-positioned off a side street . . . with an inviting walkway."

I walk closer. The morning breezes carry his male scent of spicy aftershave and nicotine to me.

"Old-world, Englishy-French charm, too. The grounds and this shop . . . this little house, are rather captivating . . . like you, I'd say." His face is observant, yet curious, like a child's standing in a new playroom. He exhales one last plume of smoke then throws the spent cigarette on the flagstone, grinding the butt with the bottom of his oxford shoe.

"Hey, do you mind? Please, no littering." I grab a rusted coffee can from a nearby potting bench and hold it for him while he retrieves the spent nub and deposits it in the can.

I watch his dark almond eyes survey the details of me: faded denim jeans, yellow-and-white peasant blouse, and a necklace of small stones with a charm centered on my chest. Goose bumps creep up my body.

"How can I help you?" I take a step back and set the can down.

Dottie comes racing from around the corner with an erect tail and a disturbed bark at the too-close stranger as if in protest, telling him he doesn't belong, not at this hour anyway. I watch her circle the man, give his shiny shoes a good sniff while together we check out the stranger from all angles.

"Alejandro Leone is my name," he says, the words sliding off his tongue like butter. He extends a hand to offer me his business card. "But *you* can call me Alex." He grins, then smooths his head of shiny black hair with an open hand.

"I like what you've got here . . ." He turns his gaze away from me to the landscaped distance where his eyes become small and his brows turn tight.

"Thank you, but what is it that I can do for you?" I speak louder in annoyance.

"Are you the owner?" He squints as if to find clarity on my face.

"No, I'm not."

"Well, I have a proposition."

"You'll need to talk to the owner about any proposition. She'll be in later this afternoon." I start walking away, assuming our conversation has ended.

"I don't think that will be necessary. Maybe you can help me. Is there somewhere we can talk?"

I don't respond right away but take a moment to consider whether I should be talking to him about business matters. But I know Bridget has financial worries on her mind—roof repair, replacing the air-conditioning, furnace inspection—and maybe I can help by deflecting any unsolicited business propositions.

"Follow me."

With Dottie at my heels, and then Mr. Leone, I hold open the door to the back office and we file in. It is tidy, free of used teacups and crumbly napkins, but stocked with a filled cookie jar surrounded by a wooden bowl of mixed dried wildflowers that has its place on the farmhouse table at one end of the room.

I stand tall. "Please, sit," I say, directing him to the table first.

The cool morning breeze turns hurried and carries with it through an open window lingering scents of damp wood and potted lavender. This is where Bridget and I have our meetings and our afternoon tea, in these familiar surroundings where I feel her presence, and with it the confidence to handle the ensuing conversation with Mr. Leone.

He pulls out a white business card and slides it across the table until my folded hands stop it. I pick it up, squinting to read the smaller print. "Shore Investments?" I ask. *What does a business like this want with a small shop off a residential street?*

"I represent a group of investors who are interested in an investment property. There are quite a few opportunities along this northern part of Chicago, and we choose *you* because we like the location—access to Lake Michigan and the city. This shop has old-world charm among the trees on a private, secluded spot that could attract many more visitors."

"Our 'visitors' are our guests, and we treat them with personal attention and catering. We know who they are and what they want," I counter.

"And I'd like to increase that sales appeal by offering to buy this . . . boutique." He emphasizes each syllable as he draws an imaginary semicircle with an open hand around a sitting area of stuffed chairs, end tables, and reading lamps at the opposite end of the room. I gasp quietly and sink back in my seat. *Buy the shop? My home for many years? Bridget's pride and joy, her life?*

I pull forward, unfold my hands, and firmly press them into the table.

"It's not for sale." I give the table an emphatic pat.

"Well, don't you think that's for the owner to decide, Miss . . . Miss?"

"Dowling. Linney Dowling. And it is, Mr. Leone. But let me be clear. This shop has been in the owner's life for more than fifty years. It is her life and has become mine as well. And its success is because it is personal. We are not a commercial property. We feel the house's history and respect its grounds through what it represents. And it would never be Magnolia if it were to change."

"I'm not looking to change a thing, Miss Dowling."

"Look, I know investors are driven to make money and they'll do anything and everything necessary to achieve their goal. I'll discuss it with the owner when she's available."

I stand tall and look down at him.

"Now, if you'll excuse me, I've got a business to take care of." I move to the doorway and motion him toward the way out. He follows me to the front of the shop.

"Good day, Mr. Leone." I open the door and offer him a curt smile.

"I'll be in touch again soon," he says before I promptly shut the door behind him, clipping his words.

I turn and see Dottie cock her head to one side, mirroring what I feel—that a change could be imminent. I want to ignore his proposition and hope he never contacts me again, and then it will all go away. I shake my head, sigh, and admit the meeting might not be our last encounter. I must tell Bridget.

❧ Margaret ❧

Joe and I usually spend Memorial Day weekend in the backyard, weather permitting, as a holiday in May in Chicago can be as cold and rainy as any day in October. We sit and envision what the summer will be like for us, wondering if the lilacs will bloom full, considering what we will plant this year to invite more bees and birds. Home takes root deeper into us with each passing month. We spent our early married years layering a place to nest, readying ourselves for the memories we were about to create with children. Now that the girls are grown women, home remains here on Birchwood Court.

We don't expect the girls to spend the holiday with their parents, as they are busy with their own lives. Deb phoned yesterday to tell me she is having her old college friends over for a luncheon. Rose is home and is going to a barbecue with her neighbors on the block. It will be a big holiday weekend for Linney and for Magnolia. But I do expect Charlotte to stop by early this afternoon. She always brings what she'd like her dad to barbecue. This time, she is looking forward to grilled hamburgers, and I can hear Deb chiding her sister about forgetting the gherkins . . . again. I like to think that it's the colder months Char favors, as it's a time for comfort food. She usually makes quarts of minestrone soup, her favorite and ours, too, and being single and alone in her apartment, she'll drop off a tub filled to the brim with leftovers to share.

Joe has pep in his step, something I'm glad to see, as sometimes I catch him plopped in his chair on the back porch and gazing into the distance, as if having a conversation with himself. He's always thinking about something: how to get better drainage in the yard, replacing the flagstone on the side of the house with larger step pads, or building out the back deck to give us more "walking-around room," as he calls it.

"Hi, Ma. I see Dad's out back, just sittin' and staring," Charlotte says, pulling open the kitchen screen door, her bobbed waves of honey hair losing their place with the forced breezes. I notice her petite frame, so different from her sisters who have their dad's tall, fuller build. But Charlotte is a well-shaped pear, and I'm more of a rounded-out apple. I had her figure once.

"I think it'll be us three," I tell her as we gather at the kitchen counter.

"Again?"

She shifts her weight to the other foot, as she often does when anxiety makes her unsteady.

"Your sisters have busy lives."

"Thanks, Ma." She unpacks Lay's potato chips, baby carrots,

celery sticks, and a jar of gherkins and places them on the white ceramic-tiled counter.

I notice the sarcasm in her tone, and I walk to her.

"And you do, too, Charlotte." I give her a smile while pushing stray ringlets away from her face.

I go to the pantry and fill my folded-up apron bottom with paper plates, napkins, and condiments, then drop the load on the empty counter.

"How's that job of yours going, by the way? I think they're taking advantage of you over there . . . Grab the burger patties from the fridge, will you, please?"

"It's fine, Ma. Everything's fine at work and no, they're not." Her voice is raised as she drops the burger packages on the counter, then fiddles with her hair, curling a strand around her finger. This has been her way to calm herself throughout her childhood, and as I see, now, too. She takes a step back.

I know Char works hard as an assistant account executive, whatever that means, sometimes putting in late hours. And when she's not there, she's here, checking up on me and Joe.

Charlotte dances around the square kitchen, boxed by a sink, long counter, and stove, anticipating what I'll need by grabbing the salt and pepper shakers while I add more mayonnaise to the potato salad. Such a nervous thing she is.

"I'm sure it is, honey, but any plans to move on . . . to a bigger company? You've been there for a while now, and I think you might be able to do better elsewhere. Ya know, aim higher for yourself."

"Why does everyone want what they think is best for me?" She stomps a foot and stands straight like a flagpole on the Fourth of July, as if bracing for a confrontation.

I rest my stirring spoon to give her my full attention.

"I was in that job for only a couple of weeks when Deb asked me if there was a path for me to promotion. 'Don't waste your time with that place if there's no way to move up,' she told me. And Linney asks me what I'm learning about running a small business, like she's quizzing me. I tell her, 'Nothing.' I wouldn't learn much yet from answering phones and filing and checking the accuracy of purchase orders. And Rose thinks since there's only one man in the office, who happens to be single but too old for me, that I should go where there are better male prospects. But I'm doing fine right where I am. That's where I belong."

"Your sisters are just trying to help you along."

"I don't need their help. Why don't they keep to finding what's best for themselves? I'm not like them."

She slaps the kitchen towel on the counter, then walks around it to the other side, bumping a kitchen chair out of place and yanking open the sliding door, colliding with Jingle who rushes into the yard to chase an unsuspecting squirrel. She pulls a porch chair from its mate, and plops down next to Joe. I resume stirring, then move to the other side of the counter where I'm close enough to overhear Joe soothing Charlotte with his words.

"I heard that," Joe says, looking away from the newspaper and peeling off his eyeglasses.

"Sorry. I didn't mean to raise my voice at Ma."

Charlotte settles and rests her feet up on the deck rail.

"I do it every now and then."

"Sometimes you need to speak your mind. Otherwise, issues fester, and you get to thinking things you shouldn't. You gotta let others know how you feel. I may not be much of a touchy-feely kind of man, but I'm always in tune with what's going on, though your mother may think not so much."

"Well, Dad, I'm feeling good today because I'm here with you two. Now it's time to light the grill. I got those burgers waiting for you to slap on."

I'm relieved to see a smile on Charlotte's face, and not rolling tears.

Their faces are soft, reflections of each other in their hazel eyes.

·ᢀᢀᢀ Charlotte ᢀᢀᢀ·

We call her Ma for no reason other than that it's informal. She thinks formalities represent a nationality of which she considers herself a member. During our young years, our deportment was a reflection on her, and if my sisters and I showed slovenly ways, "What would the neighbors think?" she'd say. Calling her Ma in public, we'd get a look from her that screamed blasphemy, using a slang for a more proper "Mother." But we did it anyway, and it stuck.

Ma would dress me and my older sisters in girly ways—white anklets and Mary Jane shoes in kindergarten, tidy dresses in middle school, matching pantsuits in junior high, ponytails and floral tops in high school, because I think she wanted to look like a good, caring mother. I admit, looking back at it now, Ma was teaching us to care about ourselves, to have respect and confidence, and she showed that by dressing herself and us well. Ma would never think of leaving the house without an internal checklist: lipstick, check; polish-on manicured nails, check; hair poufed and sprayed, check. And a circular spritz of Nina Ricci L'Air du Temps around her body showed us we needed to smell good, too.

Straddling a purple-and-white Schwinn bike seat while wearing a dress was more my style; it matched my carefree, go-with-the-flow attitude. Riding bikes with other kids up and down Birchwood Court also meant independence from my sisters.

My oldest sister, Deb, is the bossy one. She's half of Dennis and Deb, otherwise known as Double D. She's also all monograms, on picture frames, bedsheets, napkins and place mats, throw pillows, and even a lapel pin, though one could argue it stands for Debra Dowling. Why would she need to be well-labeled when she's got three younger sisters who know who is the oldest in the family? And Rose? Doesn't talk much but does appear to have a conversation, like in her head, just by observing. Some may interpret that as being shy, but shyness did not keep her from becoming an actress and then traveling the world. And then there's Linney, whose down-to-earth-ness I admire, right down to her composting, vegetarian, and yoga-posing ways, but I stop her when I'm told to embrace the crystals. I don't need to breathe; I need my sisters to connect with me occasionally. I'm not sure how they would describe me other than being a "nervous type." I think they'd also say I always do as I'm told.

It wasn't easy growing up as the youngest Dowling. From getting hand-me-down clothes to doing their chores, it all rolled downhill and stopped at the bottom where I was to catch it all. I could never admit this to my sisters, as they would say I had it easy. By the time I came along, six years after Linney was born, Ma had to start all over. She must have been relieved when all her daughters were in school, but not so much when she couldn't take off in the car to have lunch with Mrs. Cleary or any other neighbor.

The neighborhood was always important to Ma. She said everyone needs a community to belong to, and that's why it's important to reach out to those who you think might not feel as if they belong and to make them feel welcome. I didn't consider myself a reacher then, and I still don't now.

Growing up, I had to share a room with Linney. I didn't think we were a good pair back then, but looking at it now, Linney's natural softness balanced out Deb's bossiness and Rose's cultured superiority. I think the only time I might have had a little of Rose in me was on laundry day. It was a weekly ordeal, during which she would tell me to stop being so dramatic when no one else was hauling the dirty laundry into the basement. I admit I would purposely bang the full baskets through the doorways and clomp down the stairs.

Linney was all about balance, and she tried to show me how it was done, with help from her crystals, of course. She became a natural at everything, as in organic, of the earth, a yogi and grower of vegetables. One early spring, Ma asked Dad to set aside a corner in the backyard for Ma to grow her "edible things." Dad wasn't sure what Ma had in mind; I'm not sure if Ma knew what she wanted, but Linney and Ma ended up growing tomatoes, basil, zucchini, and peppers. With the kind of attention that vegetable garden received, Ma was able to make gallons of pasta sauce from its bounty, canning jars enough to feed the whole neighborhood with Mrs. Cleary receiving the first jars. And Ma delivered them personally with her face made up, hair poufed looking her best in her Sunday shoes.

When my sisters were in high school, I didn't see much of them as I think they considered me a dangling thread that needed to be pulled off. They would break from me, hopping on their bikes first thing in the summer morning, beach towels flapping over their shoulders as they rode to Gilson Beach, leaving me stranded. So, I would stay home and find my own amusement. I'd read more Judy Blume books or hop on my bike and ride in circles several times around the neighborhood. On each ride, I'd see something different— one time an open gate into the Holihans' backyard where their new puppy, Ginger, chased squirrels. Time made things change, and made gates open. From one hour to the next, you never had the exact same hour. And I would always be back home. A starting place once again.

I look back at it now and see how not having my sisters around was both a blessing and a curse. They modeled where I could take my life, yet I had to go my own way. And when we clashed, my anxiety was unrelenting. Living up to their expectations fought with my life decisions.

There was one time when Deb raised her voice at me over the phone. "What's next for you after high school?" I told her I wasn't going to college. "What do you mean, no college? How will you get a job, make enough money to support yourself?" Her fast words ran together.

And then Rose had to tell me what I would do in place of college. She concluded, "So, you'll travel, meet people, meet men, discover cultures in worlds away from here."

And Linney told me I needed a solid reason for not going, unlike she had. She simply said her advance studies were outside, with the natural world as her teacher, and not inside, within four walls. It was as if my sisters thought I couldn't handle my life without their butting in on what I should do. I couldn't bear to leave home to go to college anyway. I mean, how would that work? Alone with all those people in a big place with big buildings? I tried to shut off their voices in my head as I looked to getting myself out into the world, the Charlotte way.

Having a life like theirs—one that included college, big corporate jobs, and travel—was not for me. Staying close to home, and working for a small, local company, was.

So, I decided to take courses nearby in business administration at the community college. I finished with an associate's degree and started working part-time at OutSource Plumbing, a small company of five where I do the administration for the office. Hell, I *am* the administration, thanks to Georgia, the office manager, who gave me the opportunity. We clicked, becoming fast friends and teammates as she gave me the green light to revamp their filing system, which wasn't much of a system until I turned it into one. I organized from disorganization—misfiled papers to a new computerized filing system of purchase orders, freight receipts, and confirmation notices by client rather than by job number—and it has proven to be efficient and a time saver. I contributed on a small scale with big kudos from the president when I took on a few client orders, and it got me a promotion to assistant account executive. That's where I am today.

I also want to mention Pete, the single man in the office, and the only man in the office, who works in the back by shipping. When he comes up to the front, wearing dimples in his cheeks, tight, faded jeans on his athletic legs, and a too-small T-shirt that hugs his fit build, to say hello, I smile in return, blushing, no doubt, as I say, "Good morning," then turn and quickly walk away. The only thing I learn from these encounters is how right Rose is to suggest I need experiences with meeting the opposite sex. But feeling valuable to the company and seeing Pete each day keeps me calm and gives me a good dose of self-confidence. It works fine for me.

When word got around that there was a big company with millions of dollars that wanted to buy us, I got nervous thinking about what that meant. There'd be more people in the office doing more things, and people doing the same things. I could lose my job.

"Don't worry. There will be a place for you here," Georgia said.

I never thought when one company buys another, some employees would no longer have their jobs. I thought it all just merged. There's a lot about business I don't understand. And I don't want to. I'm not at all like Linney on this one.

"You can't stay there forever, Char. Small businesses like that get eaten up. The owners get old and want out. The industry changes," Deb said when I told her about the merger. I knew she'd have to put in her two cents.

I never thought about moving on. I have my work home there, and I have my real home on Birchwood Court with Ma and Dad. They're the two places where I belong.

❧ Rose ❧

As the second oldest, two years younger than my sister Deb, I could also be considered the third youngest after Linney and Charlotte or even the top half of the sisters-four. Talk about finding my place in the family.

In college, it was all about the theater. I couldn't wait to get there so I could get away from local productions and study for more serious roles. Mr. Hightower was a middle-aged Englishman and my freshman academic advisor. I saw him formally twice a semester, and informally in the academic office. His attire never varied from a grayish-white button-down shirt with sleeves that ended past his wrists, a vest of light wool or tweed, depending on the season, and dark trousers that were a bit too long on his short legs and too baggy in his flat seat. Central casting indeed.

When it came time to meet with him, I'd sit in a guest chair in front of his desk, but not before removing from the seat folders errant notepapers and books on the English Renaissance theater.

"Miss Dowling, I see you want to be in theater?" Mr. Hightower said, peering over his wire-rimmed eyeglasses. His smudgy lenses made his eyes large and fuzzy.

"Yes, I do. Not just to be an actress, though that's my goal, but to study the history of the theater, sets, characters, speech, costuming—the whole production. Theater is so . . . historical, capturing the times, the people; a pop culture of sorts. It's my chance at dramatizing the humorous and satirizing the absurd."

"Well, then, let's review the curriculum and requirements to get you on your way."

With a curt smile and a dash of eye contact, he opened what appeared to be my file. He shuffled papers, and brought a stapled packet to the top. With columns and lines, he began in pencil to make check marks in boxes.

"Where are you from, Miss Dowling?" he said, studying me as if trying to figure out the answer. His salt-and-pepper mustache twitched as he enunciated his words.

"I grew up in the suburbs, north of Chicago."

"I see. Any previous acting experience, local plays, working behind the scenes?"

"On summer breaks in high school. I took classes with my local park district and usually did get cast for end-of-summer productions. I think all that information is in my transcript . . . somewhere . . ." I leaned over and pointed to my bio.

I felt this was more like a job interview than any advisement of curriculum. Slight shifts in his chair elicited squeaks that added to my impatience.

"Yes, I see here. Very well. Did you enjoy yourself, Miss Dowling?"

Was this a question where my answer would prompt another check mark?

"I like being someone else for a while." His eyes remained focused on the paperwork. "I watch others and study them, their habits, the way they move, their speech. It helps me to be a better actor. I learn my characters through others."

Mr. Hightower continued to study the packet, carefully turning pages with plump fingers in a rhythm, as if he'd done this ritual a thousand times before. Finally, he came to the end of the stapled packet, and so did our question-and-answer session. My class schedule was set. I stood to leave.

"Miss Dowling," he said, looking up at me. "Do get crackin' on those books. There's more to life and to yourself than watching others."

One of my rewards for watching others was being with like-minded students. I found my tribe at the Jonathan Millroy campus theater where I hung out . . . a lot, finding inspiration amid an open space, surrounded by high black walls and long crimson velvet curtains. From *Little Women* to *Hamlet*, there was a place for me where out of the dark came stories and portrayals to tell those stories.

After graduation, I moved back home and got a job waiting tables at Gibson's steak house in the city, where the tips were great, the patrons many, and the tabs even bigger. I wasn't myself, but a waitress, dressed in a white collared shirt and black bow tie, who learned a lot about people by telling them what they wanted to hear. My free days allowed me to discover the larger theater district and to spot a small one hidden in the neighborhoods. I imagined my picture and my name on billboards, while wishing for a big break, a chance at being in the right place at the right time. I believed it would be a matter of time before I'd find a theater group, a new tribe I could call my friends. In the meantime, I continued to learn about different cuts of meat.

Growing up, Ma would repeat to me and my sisters that when one door closes, another one opens. I thought about doors opening and closing when walking onstage. As a door opened, another door would close, leaving Rose behind to step over a threshold to be someone else. Was this what Ma was talking about? Could I count on the real world to be so generous and open for me to find my place? I thought about Ma, especially during that time when trying to find my place to be. The city was a long way from family gatherings under the willow tree, where home was sure to be found.

With only one appointment booked in the city that day, I spent my free time in the theater district, using it to find any open door I could step through. Feeling inspired, I invoked a little of Linney and wandered a few city blocks to visit the most popular venues—The Chicago Theatre, The Goodman, and the new Lookingglass Theatre Company—before my appointment. Linney would tell you how thinking and walking naturally flow together like the breath with the body—one of those yoga ideas. Soon, I would need to come down in expectations, as my appointment was at a smaller theater, so small, in fact, that I unknowingly passed its unmarked doors while on my walking/breathing exercises. So, I backtracked, slowing down when I spotted in an alley a dark mustard-colored door with a dim light above it, my source of navigation given to me by the casting director.

"Looking for work?" he asked, standing against a sooty brick wall outside The Roxy's back door. I was startled, not only from an unexpected man, but also an unkempt one who wore a rumpled black leather jacket while sipping a Diet Coke.

"Here to see the manager." I avoided eye contact. I was a little creeped out, standing near a back door with a stranger in a dark, narrow alley littered with empty coffee cups and cigarette butts. The smell of urine watered my eyes and made me cough.

"You mean Jack? He's up the stairs, to the right. Second door. Good luck." He held the heavy metal door open for me, and I could feel his eyes on my backside as I took each step blindly in a dim stairwell.

I anticipated what was behind door number two. I assumed this meet and greet would be like all the others where I'd leave my re-sume and headshot and hear, "We'll get back to you as soon as we can." When I talked to my friend Jenny, who set me up to meet Jack Barnes, the director, she said not to count on anything. Apparently, he was *the* guy to meet, and if he wanted your tape, you had a good chance at getting a callback.

He waved me in with a stiff hand before I had knocked on the open door. The dank office looked to be a former janitor's closet—it certainly was the size of one, with a hungover smell of Pine-Sol. Three steps in, and I stood before him, while he remained seated behind a desk that appeared too small for him and too big for the room. The salt-and-pepper stubble on his face matched a tangled mess of thin, dirty hair on the back of his head. Wafts of body odor trailed as he moved back and forth on the cracked linoleum, from file cabinet, right, back to his desk, left, using the roller wheels fitted to his chair. A single desk lamp illuminated the room in a yellowish tinge.

"Book," he said, holding his hand out and his head down, revealing a shiny baldness. He waited for me to place a list of my life's accomplishments in written words and photos into his hands without looking at me.

"Here."

I figured if he was going to speak in single words, I would respond as such.

"Tape."

Tape? Scotch tape? Masking tape? I didn't have any tape. *What tape is he talking about?*

"No tape. Headshot," I said. *Three words, violation. I'm disqualified.*

"If you can get me one in two days, you're in. I can't help you much more, uh . . . Rachel . . ." he said, searching for my name on the resume.

"It's Rose. Miss Rose Dowling to you, Jock."

I knew his name wasn't really Jock, but it made me feel better to call him that. I figured he wasn't paying attention to me anyway. Sure enough, his dismissive tone said we were done. I didn't bother to offer him a handshake, ignoring previous directives from my sister Deb, to always end a business meeting with a strong and confident handshake, signaling a close of discussion, respect, and professional deportment. Well, we managed one out of three without a handshake. I wasn't as impressed with Jock as apparently Jenny was. But I do admit I was lucky to have gotten my foot in the door, even without a tape.

As I walked out the door to the street, I must have looked how I felt about the vision of Jack when the rumpled jacket guy and I crossed paths again. Only this time, we made eye contact.

"That was fast. Did you even get to talk to him?" he shouted as I brushed past him.

I stopped and turned. The light above the mustard door flickered.

"Sure did. You work here?" I asked, making my way back to him.

"Unfortunately. Some unemployed actors wait on tables; I wait on Jack. By the way, I'm Julian." He held out his hand to shake mine.

"Rose." I waved "hello" and stuck my hands in my coat pockets unsure of what was lingering on his.

"You have time to get a beer?" he asked sheepishly.

"Ummm, sure. Why not? Not a good day, especially ending with encountering that piece of work." I shook my head and pulled up my coat's hood, as a cold rain was steadily falling.

We hurried a few doors down to Curtain's Pub, a small, stuffy box of a place to meet if you didn't want to be found. The darkness inside obscured patrons' faces. I stood close behind Julian at the crowded bar. When I looked over my shoulder to see if a booth was free, Julian turned and bumped into me, never losing a drop from the beer-filled pint glasses.

"Uh, sorry," he said, holding his gaze on me. When I looked up at him, I noticed that the top of my head had slipped just under his chin.

We angled for the same corner spot and slid into a booth. I guess he liked to have people seated in front of him, just like me.

"To us, and to better days ahead." He lifted his dripping pint glass.

We clinked glasses.

"So, how'd it go?"

"Okay. Something about a tape, and coming back, and . . ."

"I can help you put something together. I see them all, and I know what gets Jack's attention."

"I would appreciate that. Thank you."

I squirmed in my seat, working my bottom out from sinking farther into a rip in the Naugahyde. I took a couple of chugs to quench an imaginary thirst.

"So, what restaurant do you work at, anyway?" he blurted, breaking an awkward silence.

"Gibson's." I narrowed my eyes and cocked my head. "And how did you know I work at a restaurant?"

"Rose, if you aren't waiting tables as an actor, you're independently wealthy and would have no reason to live like we do."

"And how is that? How do *you* live?" I said, patting a flat hand on the sticky table.

"Cheaply. I've got a studio on Sheridan in Edgewater. And you?" He chugged three swallows.

"Oh, I . . . I'm living at home," I replied demurely. "I just finished school a couple of years ago." I said this to give reason why I was still at home.

Why I was embarrassed, I don't know. Maybe because I felt like such an amateur, a newbie, as if looking at the acting world in Chicago with rose-colored glasses. As if I could get a gig in the big city my first time out. And Julian knew better than I, as he had been working in small theaters for a few years. He could spot the ingénue.

I looked over to a party of five seated nearby, quiet young males erupting into cheers that broke hushed conversations. Other tables were filled with male bonding. I felt like an outcast.

"I think you and I . . . we could be partners. Two out looking for work is better than working it solo."

My attention shot back to him. He leaned into the table, as if ready to tell a secret, while twirling his glass with what little remained. "We could kind of tag-team." I didn't know if this was a question or a statement.

"But I thought you work for Jack."

"I do, but first, I'm an actor. That's what I do. Not to assist a director, Jack style, as an errand boy."

Silence. I furrowed my brow and stared at him. *What's in it for him?*

"Let me think about it. I don't know. I don't know you and . . ." I told him, wiping with a cocktail napkin beer rings plotted on the table.

It could be a sign, one of the open doors Ma had told me about. To this day, I can still hear her voice in my head. While in the car driving me to local auditions, starting when I was about ten or eleven, she'd lean into the steering wheel and peer in the rearview mirror at me sitting in the back seat. "You'll do your best, Rose, I know you will. Be polite and gracious," she'd yell out the window to me after I'd jump out of the car.

"Meet me for dinner. Tonight. Seven? We can talk more about it," Julian said.

I was running late that night and hurried to dress. Mesmerized by a closet full of jeans and tops, I recalled how I had answered him quickly, almost eagerly, despite an initial hesitancy. Although this get-together might be all business, a flirty side was hopeful for getting personal.

I pulled from the closet black jeans tucked in a stack of blue ones and a glittery silver top buried in the back and slipped both on. I looked in the full-length mirror, and when satisfied, I covered myself in a favorite black jacket hanging on the closet doorknob, pulling down the side hems feeling as if I completed a business look. I gave one last shimmy in the mirror, catching the sparkle in the metallic threads of the shirt, while adjusting its straps and the straps of my bra, confirming I had both sides covered.

When I swung open the doors of Osteria Avanzare, Julian, who was standing just inside, was startled by the gust of wind. I didn't recognize him at first, freshly shaved, hair combed, and without his rumbled leather jacket, smelling of Zest soap when he offered me a kiss on the check. Following the bouncy hostess to a round booth, I eyed him from behind, head to unscuffed shoes, seeing a newly defined frame dressed in slimming gray pants and fitted button-down black shirt. We slid into the forest-green leather booth and quickly ordered a Peroni for him and a prosecco for me. We started right in with typical first-date chatter—the weather, where we were from, how we liked working in Chicago—before segueing into how our auditions were going or not going, which led me to rehash my conversation with Jack Barnes.

"So, about that tape . . ." he started, speaking above clattering dishes.

"Yes, again, I appreciate your help with it. I'm at your mercy." I tipped my glass to him and took a sip of the bubbly.

"Well, I will actually need *you*. My buddy has a postproduction studio not far from here. I'll need to shoot some video, headshots. If that's okay with you?"

This was the first time I really noticed his soft green eyes. His licorice curls bounced with each motion of his head.

"Whatever you need from me." I sipped, leaned in, and flipped back an errant section of hair, hoping business conversation would steer to maybe something more personal.

"How long have you been at this? And I'm not including your time working for Jock."

"Jock?"

"Never mind . . . just kind of a thing he and I had."

"I think I've lost count," he said, sinking into the leather. "Less time than it seems like. I had good connections with directors and theaters in the city while in college, but the older I got, the more disconnected I became as directors moved around. Working for Jack fills in the gaps until a new season comes around."

His words trailed, as if he were reminded of feeling alone when in constant battle for attention among his competition. We expose ourselves, giving everything we have, whether on tape or at an in-person audition, where we hope the door that closes behind us will quickly reopen to welcome us back to meet a new character. I wondered if I was meeting my mirror image.

"It is a struggle to be seen as a gem among the others, a one-of-a-kind treasure that needs to be grabbed and shown off," I told him. "But we persist, don't we?"

I stopped pressing my finger in the creases of the white linen table covering to look into his eyes, searching for our common bond. "Working our craft, auditioning, making friends in the business." I winked and took off my jacket, feeling warmed and more comfortable. "Shall we order?" I asked, opening the menu and giving it a read.

But I was distracted by my attraction to Julian, to his kindness and honesty. We talked as if we were friends picking up where we had left off. I know that sounds trite; if anyone were to tell me that, I'd give them an eye roll.

And that was the beginning of a complicated relationship.

Julian maintained a few connections among the smaller theaters in the city, and during our first year together, he didn't hesitate to invite me to his social get-togethers with fellow actors. "I'm not so sure," I told him over the phone when he extended one such invitation. "You all are probably way out of my league."

"Oh, no, you don't—don't go keeping yourself from meeting new people. It's all a part of what you do. We're all one family, and the more members, the bigger and better the support—and the net-working group."

Maybe I had falsely accused my competition of not being team players. I gave it more thought, and, with cautious optimism, I agreed to meet one of Julian's best friends, Ray, at our usual happy hour stop in Old Town.

"Hey, Rose, think small," Ray said. I noticed his jeans puddled at the ankles and plaid shirttails ending just above his knees. I squinted, looking down at Ray then up to Julian, trying to figure out if this was an inside joke between them. "Look to the smaller theaters, away from downtown to the north side. You can sharpen your craft, meet talented actors and influential directors who want the smaller stages to work their own visions, their way."

After listening to Ray's advice, I got to thinking that not all actors consider themselves competitors but rather are willing to offer each other direction. This new community made me feel comfortable and welcome. I was glad to have found them, a place to belong, a new home. My artistic world was expanding, and, thanks to Ma, I considered meeting Julian and his friends an open door—one that I walked right through. I nudged Ray affectionately. "Thanks for that," I told him.

I had been commuting for two years from home in the north suburbs to the city, and it hindered my getting work. I was often called to auditions quickly and had to be downtown in hours, and sometimes I couldn't get there in time. My overnight bag got bigger, and soon I was packing to stay at Julian's for weeks at a time.

"Maybe you should just move in here with me." He said this matter-of-factly at the kitchen table one morning over coffee where our files, tapes, and photos comingled. "It would make economical and logistical sense."

"Agreed." I continued reading the *Theatre Times*.

"I'll see you around seven tonight," he said, plopping a kiss on my cheek before leaving for work. "We can celebrate."

I thought of moving in with him as pure logistics, you know. Living part-time here was one thing, but having this as my home was another. I would need closet space, and the compact, four-room apartment would need a makeover, if that was even possible. And did I mention doing something with all this black? "This way, the chairs, tables, and curtains all match," he told me. Thankfully, there was a place for two on a well-lived couch in the living room. Yes, "but it's not just black, it's *midnight* black," he told me. Though the cushions sank to lows I've never experienced before with a couch, it was a place to stretch out unencumbered as it was the only place that remained clutter free.

Mornings when I'd awaken before Julian, I'd linger in the galley kitchen, catching whatever sunshine was available. The sun splashed light onto daffodil walls, then shone on a square table glossed in a grassy green. Though the table's disarray reflected the entire apart-ment of one bathroom, a closet-sized bedroom, and one living room, the kitchen was my favorite place. I relished time here as this was the only space that was in color.

Yes, moving in together was more of a business decision, an economical advantage, but having a roommate with benefits could not be overlooked. I admit, I was attracted to Julian's unassuming ways and offers to help me navigate my profession and my personal life by offering a place to be . . . with him. But I was unsure of making a commitment.

Until one night when he startled me. I think we had been together for less than a year.

It was more like a jolt of reality when his love confession spilled out. He stood tall in the middle of the apartment, commanding my attention as I sat on the couch. Muted lighting set the make-believe stage. This was my first time working with him, running lines in preparation for an audition. I was curious about his acting skills. How would he portray his character? Soft-spoken and timid, drawing from his own nature?

The scene, a monologue, required an emotional range, starting with anger, then sadness, slowing diction. But by the end of the scene, he was breaking eye contact with me. This is when he bent down on one knee, put down his script, and looked into my eyes.

"Could you ever surrender to someone whose flaws . . . could you ever love someone whose instability and insecurity might drive you too crazy?"

I looked down at my script and searched for my line, but was distracted, confused. That wasn't in the script. It didn't matter. My eyes locked onto his face.

"Are you asking me to love you?" I knew that wasn't my line, but it seemed logical Rose would ask it in that moment.

"I love you, Rose, and I hope you can love me, too," he said, sealing the scene with a kiss.

And I sure didn't know much about this "in love" thing. I had dated on occasion but nothing that was close to committed. I did know that coming home to Julian and sharing our days was a reward, a giving back to me for all the pieces of myself that I had given away with each audition and role I'd played.

❧ Linney ❧

In high school, I was a daydreamer. I'd stare out the classroom windows and search for a distraction in an outside world that would settle my fidgety self. I'd especially search long on a winter's day to connect with the extraordinary from an ordinary gray and off-white canvas. If I was lucky, I'd see a cardinal perched on a naked branch or a lone squirrel making hatch marks in the downy carpet of snow. I wondered why they hadn't migrated with their kind or hunkered down in hibernation. Were they simply trying to survive in their own way? I liked to think I, too, followed my own path to survival.

Perhaps my dreams were wishful thinking. After I graduated high school, I'd know what I was going to do next, and it excluded college. Though Deb and Rose knew for sure that they were going on to get their advanced degrees, I simply had no desire to spend another four years confined inside, encumbered by books, studying, and test-taking. After the pomp and circumstance, I wondered if I would feel at home someplace else as I did growing up on Birchwood Court. I knew Ma and Dad didn't mind having me around after I graduated, but with Deb's quick exodus soon after her graduation and Rose's move-out shortly thereafter, well, I felt I needed to go, too, wherever that might be.

On one particularly unsettled day, I got into the car and drove with no destination in mind. I'd never know all the possibilities of open doors out there unless I got out to see them. I remembered Ma telling us when we were young, something about doors and when one closes another opens, and I was hoping that I would come across an open door somewhere soon in the north suburbs of Chicago.

That day was effortless, the weather agreeable, with little traffic to negotiate. At a stoplight, I looked ahead and spotted a red clapboard barn and redbrick house to match. Cows were grazing in the distance. I turned off and pulled into a gravel lot adjacent to the barn, chuckling at the thought of a small working farm spread out in a tight upper-class suburb. I was in luck as the sign told me Wagner Farm was open to visitors. I got out of the car and smiled with pleasure while turning full circle to take it all in—a sprawling pasture of cows, a chicken coop, pig stalls, and draft horses nibbling from a trough against a sunny side of the barn. I set off for adventure, kicking up dirt with my Doc Martens, the air pungent with manure and dry hay, of earth and composting and the sweet scent of mums from the fall flower sale, odors that quickly replaced the dull suburban scents I had become accustomed to. These were inspirations.

Walking from direct sunlight into a dark barn, my eyes needed to adjust before I could inspect the tidy dwelling empty of livestock. My maxi jean skirt waved from large fans working to keep the air circulating in the stalls.

"Hi there, can I help ya?" A figure in silhouette stood in the open doorway, backlit by the bright outside and billowing dust.

"This is a wonderful place, and I can see it attracts many others who think so too," I told him, spinning to take in the surrounding view.

As the tall man, dressed in a green-and-navy-plaid shirt, khaki pants, and green rubber boots, moved into the full dimness of the barn, I thought he was a farmworker.

"We do have loads of visitors when we're open. And thanks for coming in. I can give you a tour if you'd like." His youthful voice matched his boyish grin.

"Yes, I'd like that."

We stepped out into a panoramic view. Patches of flocked geese occupied a bountiful grazing field.

"My ma and dad used to take my sisters and me, when we were little, to a pet farm in Wisconsin. We'd jump from the car almost before my dad brought it to a full stop. We'd return with gobs of manure dried to our shoes, hay stuck everywhere from our hair to our socks, and a cloud of barn odors following us. Mom would say, 'No harm in connecting with that which we are all a part of. Mother Nature has sustained us through thousands of years and, God willing, will continue to do so.' I liked doing some digging with dirt under my fingernails and mud on my knees to show for it. Working the earth is grounding . . . like connecting to home."

He smiled and nodded. I followed him to the chicken coop, where a volunteer was dropping lettuce and kale leaves from a torn cardboard box. Hens came charging and clucking.

"What do you do here?" I asked.

"I manage the place." His blue-gray eyes became even clearer as he stepped closer to me. "I'm Cole, by the way."

"Linney." His hand yielded to mine in a firm handshake. "And you look too clean to be working this farm."

"Been in the office this morning, book work."

I shaded my eyes and pointed over his shoulder to the draft horses, who had moved into the field. In a pair, they clomped rhythmically in straight lines, pulling a large wooden wagon filled with hay and spent cornstalks, stirring up the earth with their hooves and imprinting lines from the wagon's wheels.

"Looks like harvest time."

"It is. The farm keeps pace with the changing of the seasons."

I wanted to spend my days here, cultivating, nurturing, maturing with all other living things, even if it was to be a temporary stop along the way while I searched for a more permanent home.

I remembered when Deb used to ask me on a Friday afternoon after I got home from school, "You're not gonna leave that sad example of a schoolbag there on the bedroom floor, are you?" Of course I was. It was my room, too, and I wanted to feel at home in my space like she did. And she'd start in. "You need to take responsibility for yourself as no one else will when you get older. You can't forget to bring home your homework books or your sweaty gym clothes to wash after leaving it in your locker all week." Just because Deb had an office job lined up before she graduated from college didn't mean I had to have one, too, before I graduated high school.

"Wow, this would be a great place to work," I said, studying cows, horses, and grand trees popping up here and there in the fields. I remembered Deb telling me if I truly wanted something, I had to ask for it. "This is a place to take care of what provides for us. Milk from cows and eggs from hens, corn from the land. It's all connected, isn't it? Kind of cyclical." I watched the horses, now hitched to a plow, pulling effortlessly through the fields in the distance. "I'd really love to work here." My face turned pink as the words slipped from my mouth. I shied away from him to pat the flat heads of cows leaning their big faces over the fence. Their long pink tongues uncurled to give me a few good licks on my sweat-shirted arm.

I shadowed Cole for the next hour as he talked to the volunteers, a middle-aged married couple dressed in khakis and denim shirts, three moms who talked about their little ones, and a lone skinny teenager, inside the learning center. After they dispersed, we walked outside to the freshly harvested vegetable gardens where Cole shared with me a day in the life of a farmworker, starting in what seemed to be the middle of the night with milking cows, cleaning stalls and the coop, seeing to feeding schedules, and running programs in the learning center. Day after day, the work repeated, yet no two days were alike. From Spike, the fanciest rooster you'd ever see, to Daisy, the biggest draft horse I'd ever seen, the animals were family. Cole and the volunteers provided connections to comfort and familiarity as, together, they learned something with each new day.

"So, Linney, why a farm?"

"Where I grew up, in Wilmette, my dad planted a willow tree in the backyard soon after he and my ma moved into the house. My sisters and I weren't born yet, but he planted that tree as a part of his homemaking. Then, after my sisters and I came along, Ma would gather us around under the willow, where she'd read us a story, or tell us something about the birds we saw, the bumblebees we heard, or the value of growing rosebushes. And then there were the trees. She'd tell us how they communicate with one another and how there's an invisible web of connections underground, up through the trees to their crowns. And I see the many connections on this farm. It's like home."

He turned to me and announced with his hands on his hips, "Then working here is what you will do."

"Really? Just like that? I'd be so grateful for the opportunity." I giggled and smiled wide with happiness, grabbing his hand and giving it a good shake in delight.

"Yes, like that!" He winked, and I swear his eyes sparkled bluer and his smile grew bigger. Things were looking up, brighter and larger than I could have imagined. Taking responsibility for finding my place proved rewarding.

When I started working at the farm the following week, there were no two days alike. Some days, I'd greet visitors as busloads of kids visited, offloading one bus after another, or I'd work in the heritage center talking about the farm's history, or lead guided tours, clean the chicken coop, or sell seasonal harvests. I learned about making money and how easy it was to lose it. I developed relationships with regular visitors and offered my suggestions on business plans for development, thanking donors, and implementing fundraisers. I knew Deb would think I was wasting my time working on a farm; hell, she'd probably laugh at me. I can hear her sarcasm now, telling Ma on the phone, "Oh, what valuable skills she is learning, cleaning stalls and collecting eggs!" But Ma would defend me. "She's happy, Deb." And Ma used to tell us that being happy at whatever we're doing is what matters.

I called Ma soon after my first day of work. "I'm at home here, Ma. This is where I'd like to be."

⁕⁕ Charlotte ⁕⁕

Ma doesn't go to the doctor. Unless anyone in the family was in visible pain, bleeding, or unable to move, we just didn't go. Dad didn't have much to say when it came to treating his children's ailments, as Ma was the boss of medical decisions. Whether we skinned our knees or broke an arm from a fall, Ma called the diagnosis and would have the problem, a mere inconvenience, fixed with a Band-Aid.

A couple of days after Memorial Day weekend, I stop by the house to visit Ma and Dad on my day off. I barely get through the side door into the kitchen when Ma rushes to me from the hall and takes my arm.

"Where are we going?" I ask her as she snatches her sweater and purse from the kitchen table.

"To the doctor. I've got an appointment." She opens the door into the garage. I search her face for an explanation but she avoids my look.

I'm not alarmed that she has a doctor's appointment but rather by her covert, quiet urgency, as if she's telling me a secret. "Shhh, keep this one from your father."

It's unlike Ma to take me with her on a personal errand. Actually, I don't remember Ma doing anything personal. Her life to me was always an open book. I remember when my friend Margerie would come over and we'd pillage Ma's closet to play dress-up, digging for dresses and shoes and scarves and jewelry. When ransacking the closet floor looking for heels to match a red sundress, I came upon a light blue box with a slit open on the bottom. The stuff inside looked like tidy stacks of white padding. I didn't know if this was something I should wear, but since I didn't know how to wear it, I left it in the box. It was only later, when I was about thirteen and Ma reached into that box and pulled out one of those white pads and handed it over to me with a proud smile, saying, "You are now a woman," that I understood how to wear them.

Ma always got in the car to drive herself whenever she wanted and wherever she wanted to go. She might mention she was picking up a few things at the grocery store or going out for a while to get her hair done. But over the last year, when I'd call, Dad would tell me that Ma went out for a while, but he didn't know where she went or when she'd be back.

"Aren't you worried about Ma taking off like that?" I'd ask Dad.

"No. She's an independent woman, your mother is. She doesn't need to check in with me all the time," he'd say.

"Well, maybe she should," I mumbled.

"If your mother wants me to know something, she'll tell me. She always comes back, Char," Dad would say.

Ma's appointment is at the hospital. This doesn't concern me as her doctor's office is in a building on the hospital's campus. But she does not lead us there and instead punches the button of the automatic doors that open into the hospital lobby. Ma is ahead of me by a few paces, and she reaches the front desk to check in.

"Rose Dowling for a nine o'clock MRI," she said to the woman with a head of gray Brillo hair.

"Down the hall. Make a right, then another right to where it says 'radiology,'" she directs with two flips of her hand.

We arrive there, then sit in waiting. I distract myself from my overactive thoughts and study the people who are among us—a mix of old men staring into space, middle-aged women fiddling with their blouses and checking their earrings, and a sleepy teenager—to see what's wrong with them by how they look, and if they are getting this MRI, too. *What's an MRI, anyway?* Does Ma look like these people? I don't think so.

"Not right now, Charlotte."

She must know what I'm thinking, that she doesn't belong here. What exactly *are* we doing here? She's always been good at reading her daughters' minds.

An hour turns into two.

"What's happening with my mother? Please, where is Margaret Dowling? It's been two hours," I plead with the petite lady who appears swallowed behind her computer at the front desk, despite her smiles and giggles with those she talks with on the phone and who stand before her. I guess that's called customer service. Did she lose track of Ma since we've been here so long?

"It won't be much longer. She's in with the doctor now," she reports.

You can't imagine what is going through my mind. Is this some female test every woman has when she gets older? Maybe it's nothing, a checkup on a few things, like a blood test.

When Ma appears at the open automatic doors, she looks as if she has had an out-of-body experience. The backlight is fluorescent orange, and Ma is pale and gray. The muted shades blend in with each other, and it's difficult to see Ma. After a pause to focus, I hustle to her side.

"Not right now, dear," she says, hunched and staring at the floor.

I'm not going to ask questions, so she's wrong this time about anticipating what was to come from my mouth.

"Wait here. I'll get the car and—"

"No need, Charlotte. I'm fully capable of walking." She grabs my arm to halt me.

I steady her zombielike gait as we weave through the revolving doors into the fresh spring air, an immediate elixir for any person's ails. I pull down on her arm to get her to stop a minute and rest. And she does, taking the biggest, deepest breath I have ever seen anyone take. She does it again, and her cheeks pop pink splotches, her face becomes more open, her brow more relaxed. In silence, we make it into the car.

"I'm not pulling out of this parking space until you tell me what's going on," I say, becoming more impatient. If then wasn't a good time, now should be.

She stares through the windshield and watches hospital staff with tight eyes. They are dressed in white coats and green tops and bottoms, and hurriedly snake through cars as if they are enemies. Then she locks in on an elderly man in the car ahead, who is clutching a walker and being helped into the passenger side. Her green eyes soften. We leave for home.

"There's nothing that can be done about this thing growing inside my head." Her voice, commanding before we had left for the hospital, is now shaky when we pull into the garage.

"What? What 'thing'?" I shout, grimacing at the idea that there is something alien residing in my mother's head. "A tumor? You have a brain tumor, Ma?" I emphasize "brain tumor" as if I didn't hear her right the first time. "Well, clearly they can do something . . . like get it out?" I grip the steering wheel, though the car remains parked.

"That's all there is to know. And you will not tell anyone." Her head swivels to look at me, her voice defiant. "That is my telling, and only my telling, not yours."

"Fine," I tell her, angered. I want to override my mother's directive and tell my sisters as soon as I get home, reasoning the Dowlings need to rally to her side.

We sit in the garage in dark silence. My eyes dart back and forth in empty space; my thoughts in conversation about what to do.

I realize that keeping a secret between Ma and me, her secret, tells me that, though I may be the youngest, I can also be the wisest.

Debra

Standing in my bedroom at home as I neared college graduation, I realized the place looked more like a den than a place to sleep. Bookcases covered one wall like wallpaper. I crammed a small stuffed chair into a corner near my bed, a find from Grandma's house after she died. Double bookcases framed a window's sides, and a desk I'd had since fifth grade never moved from its place under that window. The room foreshadowed my next place to be after college.

"You're getting a head start on packing," Ma said, leaning against the doorway early one morning. She watched me sort girlhood belongings—patched denim jeans and novelty tees, well-read books by Stephen King and Erich Segal and a little Hemingway, a few Elton John albums, too.

"You don't have the job yet," she said.

My eyes widened. No comment from Ma was going to cast doubt on my plans for getting a job at Kinsey and Moore, an international corporate event planning firm that topped my job search list.

Her comment surprised me. She always encouraged my sisters and me to find our places, and now, she sounded as if I should put the brakes on. Surely, she understood that her firstborn was destined to leave the nest. I was leaving the home where Ma taught us under the willow about connecting and being in harmony with ourselves, wherever our home would take us. I expected her to follow her own wisdom and encourage us to break away from our first learned home to find our next places in the world.

"I'm getting organized, Ma. I can never start too soon, as the more I get into all this, the more time I have to figure out what to do with it all."

I pulled more stacked T-shirts from the closet shelves, letting a pile tumble to the floor.

"Slow down, Deb." Ma unfolded her arms and put a soft hand on my arm. "Take time to have a good look at the space you've made your own, one that you'll be leaving too soon. This is the only home you've ever known. Everything here is your connection to it."

I glanced at the piles on the floor that told me my life was changing.

"Come, Ma, sit." I pushed away worn college sweatshirts to make room for us on the bed. "And I'll remember this place, where I grew up, each time I look at what I brought with me. I'll think of the backyard where we played, the kitchen where you made dinner for us every night, and the family room where we ate popcorn and watched *Rich Man, Poor Man*. It will always be a point of reference, a familiarity and comfort. If I ever feel uncomfortable when I'm in the unfamiliar, I'll think of all the memories made here."

Looking back, I understand she would never have tried to hinder my career but rather needed to pause—to stop time, really—and to cherish the moments between her and her eldest. Ma and I hugged and breathed our memories into our souls. "Wherever I'm headed, and I'm sure it will be to K&M," I assured her, "the willow tree will always be in my mind, and I'll remember its stability. No matter how much it bends and sways, it doesn't break. But I'm also ready to leave home and to start a life I've been anticipating since college. I'm excited and hopeful for my future."

I didn't get my first job after graduation like my classmates whose dads got jobs for them. Camille and Lisa started working part-time at their dads' accounting firms even before they graduated. Camille started as a budget analyst, Lisa as an accounting clerk. I could picture her sliding nicely into a short pencil skirt. "And always, always, Deb," she'd tell me, "black pumps. You can't go wrong with them with any business attire." She ought to know, swinging her hips as her Garolini heels clicked on the linoleum office floor. Me, I couldn't possibly sashay; I'd look like I was about to tackle someone.

And then there was Tracey. She didn't know anyone and didn't know how to go about interviewing for a job, yet she had the most self-confidence and relied on her favorite bar as her place for networking. "Favorite" because the ad agency's account managers hung out there, and she hoped to meet one who could give her a job. And she did, and he did. He, leaning in and touching her hand: "I'm very impressed with your sharpness . . . and such charm." She, batting her heavily mascaraed eyelashes, licking her berry-stained lips, and turning on her dimples: "Well, thank you. I'm great with customers." Together, I don't think their IQs could have unfolded a paper bag.

But he did ask her to come in to speak with his boss. She was hired the next day as an account executive at CMG, a marketing firm in Chicago. I didn't blame her for her knack at getting what she wanted.

During my last semester of college, I set my sights on K&M as it was a sought-after, go-to company for entry-level jobs for college grads. I had the grades; I had interviewed well there. I had earned my way into their offices in downtown Chicago. I believed strongly in plan A, where the door to K&M remained open, and I'd be ready at a moment's notice when, not if, I got the call. In fact, I was so confident that I didn't make a plan B.

I can't remember where I was or what I was doing when K&M formally extended an offer. But when they did, my dry-cleaned suits, shined black pumps, and a ready-to-be-filled briefcase were lined up in the closet, waiting for the go-ahead.

"We received an excellent recommendation from a Mr. Kirby, the college dean. And we were very appreciative to be privy to the evaluation of your senior international business studies project. You demonstrated great management skills and a few unique problem-solving ideas. We think you'd be a great addition to Kinsey and Moore. What do you say, Debra?" the hiring manager asked me on a telephone call.

"I say thank you, and I'm looking forward to joining Kinsey and Moore."

I started working there the next month. I hardly slept the night before my first day. I lay awake with scenes that included pictures of girlhood: running through the sprinklers on a hot summer day, reading *The Great Train Robbery* in my early teens while listening to Elton John on the radio. It was all about me back then, and the moments my sisters and I were living. But now, it was about the future, planning for and envisioning a life I was meant to have.

Kinsey and Moore occupied the top ten floors of a nondescript, narrow building, just off the financial district in downtown Chicago. The good news was there was a dedicated elevator to floors ten to twenty. I'm not sure why I thought that good news; maybe because it made me feel I was in the big leagues now, with a great job, making good money in a city I loved with my own personal ride to the top.

A middle-aged receptionist with salt-and-pepper hair, fuzzy from that summer's humidity, sat low behind the reception desk with barely a smile on her coral-lipsticked lips. "Good morning. I'm Debra Dowling. This is my first day here," I said, capping my words with a bit of bounce.

"And who are you here to see?" she said, looking up at me through her heavy-lidded eyes.

"Mr. Cranston, please."

"I'll let him know."

A woman of few words, but efficient. *I'm sure we'll become good buddies*, I reassured myself, as this was the place where I belonged.

I used to loathe the first day of a new job. One summer in high school, I had a waitressing gig at an ice cream parlor. The screaming parents were endless, more so than the kids. The tips, adequate, and pooled. It was my first experience about fairness on the job, or lack thereof. I worked hard, turned tables, and thus made more tips. I had figured it out quickly. Andi, on the other hand, didn't get it. For someone who did nothing but check her lip gloss and hair in the bathroom, she got equal tips for doing unequal work. Now I was refreshed, thinking I'd be making good money here, for doing good work. I'd come a long way since the ice cream parlor.

I didn't wait long before the coral-lipped lady directed me through the double doors where KINSEY AND MOORE was emblazoned in smoky etched letters on the glass. The office floor was haphaz-ardly configured with tall cubicles, where I searched for a Mr. Cranston's nameplate on a door.

"In here, please," Mr. Cranston said, poking his head out from an office ahead and waving me over. He was dressed in an off-white oxford shirt held close around his neck, not by a button, but by a solid burgundy bow tie.

"Welcome, Debra." I sat in one of a pair of dark plaid-covered chairs in front of his large wood desk where, centered on the edge, was a traditional banker's lamp. On the credenza behind him, silver-framed photos of various sizes appeared grouped in chronological order: photos of births, graduations, marriages. An odor of stale coffee lingered. He slid into his cushy executive leather seat, then took a swipe with his left hand to clear away a stack of manila folders, paper clips, and disorganized pink message notes. "Now, tell me about yourself. I'd like to know more about you than what's on your resume. Why Kinsey and Moore?"

I crossed my legs at the ankles, smiled when looking at my black pumps, and then straightened my posture.

"Mr. Cranston, my passions are travel, accomplishments, and people around the globe. I bring my passions here as I believe we are a good fit for each other. I believe in organizing and implementing our clients' needs to produce an organic benefit—a happy client. Happy clients are infectious and build us a good reputation to position ourselves in promoting Kinsey and Moore globally. The key here is to be proactive, on the offense, offering options for our clients and the resources to deliver the best K&M experience."

"I like you, Debra," he said, pointing a finger at me and making a clicking sound with his tongue. His enthusiasm made one eye squint and hide behind an overgrown, bushy eyebrow. "You just grab 'em, don't you, and don't look back. I need someone who can steer us in the right direction. And we are all about people here, Debra. It's all about them and giving them a reason to return." His forcefully enunciated words tended to cause him to spit out his consonants.

"And please, call me Ken," he said with a wink and a crooked smile.

After we got the verbal pomp and circumstance out of the way, I believed KC and I would get along just fine. I wondered if, in time, I could call him "KC," as he had made me feel part of K&M's family.

For about six months, I was well into an office rhythm, keeping abreast of client news, sitting in on account meetings, completing reports, and answering client calls. I hadn't yet been given the opportunity to fly outside the US with the bigwigs as a liaison for a client event. I was about to talk to KC about that when he came to talk to me first.

"Debra, my office, please." Again, the poking out of his pudgy head from his office doorway. We sat at a round table for four in a corner surrounded by clean floor-to-ceiling windows with a view of Michigan Avenue. A sunbeam slipped through the vertical lines of high-rises.

I sat quickly and straightened a gap in my suit jacket. Folding my hands in my lap, I sat back and gave KC my attention.

"One of our clients, an ad agency here in Chicago, has its annual agency event, which we have organized for over ten years now, for its head office here and three satellite offices in London and Paris. The event should be a mix of local entertainment, client reviews, budget talks, and partner meetings. Essentially, it's a state-of-the-state address for Bates, Mather, Townsend Advertising Worldwide, but with fun time scheduled in for them, too. This is a big one for us, Debra, to show off our continued best for them." He pushed an overstuffed, hardbound binder across the table under my face. "We have a long-standing relationship with them, and we want to keep that partnership strong." He winked and smiled . . . again. "I'm trusting that you will listen to their needs and produce a successful event."

"I will not, Mr. Crrr . . . Ken, let you down. You can trust me to do an outstanding job." I flushed with adrenaline and felt as if I was on my mark and ready at the start line. KC was giving me the chance to create a successful event . . . and to not blow it.

My hands itched with eagerness as I studied the cover. When I opened the heavy black book, it would be full speed ahead, as my first opportunity to show them they could be confident in my ability to handle this client. The relentless sun shone on BATES, MATHER, TOWNSEND ADVERTISING in engraved gold letters on the black binder.

"If you need help or have any questions, ask John. He's our senior account manager and knows them well." KC leaned so far back, crossing his hands behind his head in the chair, I thought he was going to tip over.

"Thanks, Ken, I will."

I scooped up the binder, held it tight to my chest, and found seclusion in my office.

I knew little about BMT. I needed to know who their clients were. I needed to know everything about this ad agency, including the people who worked for it. I opened the overstuffed binder as if revealing a treasure. I had a lot of reading to do.

I glanced out the tall window to my right and noticed how high up I was, then looked down on dark spots, people scooting up and down the avenue. It felt corporate. I was ready for my new assignment.

On paper, Dennis Townsend looked like quite an accomplished man. As a creative director and partner, he was the "T" in BMT Worldwide, and responsible for all the creative ideas to be pitched to prospective clients, including development and execution. I admired his talent for creating clever mini stories to sell products. The agency was successful because of its winning advertising. Their staff would expect nothing but the best, and I'd show Mr. Townsend nothing but Kinsey and Moore's best.

I called a kickoff meeting with Mr. Townsend the following week. With about eighteen months to plan and execute the event, I needed all the time I could get from him. I wanted to get to know him a little, too. And what better way to do that than to meet for lunch outside the office?

"Hey, I'm looking forward to meeting you," he said, his voice confident and energetic with an emphasis on "you."

Maxine's, an old-time supper club with dim lighting, dark wood paneling, comfy chairs, `and, of course, white tablecloths, was a default spot for first-time K&M clients. It was conversation-friendly with impeccable service; the waitstaff knew exactly when to interrupt and when to leave guests alone. KC took me there for lunch on my first day of work, and I made a note should I need to bring clients there.

Though Mr. T was not a first-time client for K&M, I was a first-timer to him. I wondered if working with someone new and who would need to orient me would be frustrating for Mr. T. While waiting for him at a roomy table for two against a ceiling-to-floor bay window that looked onto hectic St. Clair Street, I divided my attention between the door and a notepad of talking points. My palms were sticky with sweat, and my heart revved in anticipation of a face-to-face meeting with this important client. I closed my notepad, and while making room for it in my bag, I was interrupted.

"Ahem . . . You must be Debra Dowling," he said. I shaded my eyes from the diffuse light coming through the grimy window and noticed a sapphire blue pocket scarf peeking from his suit coat. It was him, Dennis Townsend, just as John had told me, "Pocket scarf. He'll be wearing one," giving me the thumbs-up when I was leaving the office for the lunch meeting. It's funny how after talking with someone on the phone, you imagine how that person looks. From hearing Mr. T's youthful voice, I pictured him dressed in an ill-fitting suit, wrinkled oxford button-down, and a tie that hid stains well in its stripes. But this tall, handsome man wore a well-tailored midnight-blue suit with a shirt crisp as if spun from fine cotton, and a paisley tie that brought all of it and him together. He knew how to dress, and he also knew how to smile, I thought, as he showed off a row of white polished pearls.

"Oh, you snuck up on me." I exhaled, with one hand on my chest and the other hitting out of alignment the neatly set silverware centered on the folded napkin. "Mr. Townsend. How terrific to finally meet you."

He took my hands in his, and his cheerful eyes pulled me to him as we lingered over our introduction. I felt as if I were the sole person he needed to be with.

"Please sit. I'm so glad we could meet. Thank you for having lunch with me." *Is it warm in here, or are my nerves just exploding at the sight of this flawless-looking man?*

"Great idea to meet for lunch. Gets me out into a more informal, relaxed atmosphere, while doing business, of course." He pulled his starched white napkin, shook it, and placed it on his lap. I was mesmerized by his moves: slowly pulling down the cuffs of his shirt, jiggling the knot of his tie, moving the menu to one side. "I'm here for you, Debra. Whatever you need to make this event happen. I'm available. Just let me know." His eyes remained on mine.

"Good to hear, and thank you for that. I know you might have worked with John before, so I hope to get you up to speed quickly. If you don't mind, I've got a few quick—" Suddenly, I blanked at my talking points. "I, um . . ." I quickly rustled through my bag to find my file.

"No hurry, Debra, please. Let's talk first, have some lunch, and then segue into business." Smooth jazz playing in the background eased my nerves.

"Welcome back, Mr. Townsend," the short, stocky waiter announced. He cocked his head and held a small notepad and pen, ready to write. I was startled to see that Mr. T obviously was a regular here.

"What can I get you to drink to start things off?" The waiter looked at me with one raised eyebrow.

"White or red, Debra?"

"Um . . . yes . . . I'll have whatever you're having." I crossed my legs and sat back in my chair, eyeing him.

After a glass of Chianti and small talk over pasta primavera, our business conversation flowed easily. I couldn't have asked for a better first-time client meeting—and ultimately, I did hit all my talking points.

As we stood outside Maxine's doors, saying our goodbyes, he glanced at the darkening skies. "Looks like it might rain. Can I give you a lift back?"

"Thanks, but I prefer to get there on foot. And I always come prepared." I winked and pulled out an umbrella from my tote, ready to pop it open.

"Very well, then." He gave me a second look before turning and heading to his car. "I will talk to you soon."

"Yes, oh, yes . . . soon."

The office was just a few blocks from Maxine's anyway, and I

used my foot commute, chuckling at how my black pumps didn't let
me down, to take mental notes. The business discussion was quickly
fading due to the looks and sound of Mr. T.

After that lunch, I would meet Mr. T once a month for status
meetings in his office. I was spending more time there than was
probably necessary, when phone calls between us would have suf-
ficed. Okay, so that was my perspective as business manager. On
the personal side, I can honestly tell you I looked forward to seeing
him privately in his office, visually exploring his smoothness
while he sat behind his desk, to hearing his clear, succinct voice,
to watching him saunter around and stand closer to me, to feeling
his warmth and inhaling his clean scent. He'd use some touchy
gesture—a tap on my shoulder, a touch to my hand, an arm around
my back—whenever he was close enough to do so. I admit our attraction was on a fast track, but our meetings certainly didn't hinder
us from moving forward with the event. "Just follow his lead, Deb,"
was the only advice John could give me. "If Mr. T wants to see you,
then by golly, you better drop what you're doing and go to his office,"
he told me.

"I would do this anyway, John, for any client." I said this to
counter any favoritism I might be showing.

After a few weeks, Mr. T called me to his office at the end of the
day, only to announce we'd be leaving to carry on at Maxine's before
I even had a chance to take off my coat.

When inside, he automatically headed to the bar as if called,
sat, and whirled a finger in the air, signaling to the bartender for a
round. I remained standing, rifling through my bag, hurriedly feeling
for a pen and my BMT folder before sitting.

"I just have a few things I need to go over . . ." I ran my hands
through my loose hair, the curls having fallen out by the end of the
day. *Why didn't I pull it back to look more professional?*

"Deb, sit, please . . . you need to retire that stuff for the evening. You can't expect to enjoy your cocktail with those distractions, now, can you?" He slid out a bar seat for me.

"You never did have plans to discuss business, did you?" I asked, wiggling on the black leather seat to find its center.

"I took the liberty of ordering a cocktail for us," he said, grinning. "Cheers. To you, Deb"—he held up his glass—"and to the success of this venture we are on together." His eyes sparkled mischievously.

Startled that our after-hours meeting, or this happy hour, or whatever it was, was moving quickly, I followed his lead and held up my glass, too, tasted the chilled, deep orange beverage . . . and coughed. He patted my back.

"What? You don't like the old-fashioneds here? Jimmy makes some mighty fine ones, and Manhattans, too." Mr. T looked into his lowball glass to admire the swirling golden whiskey mixture.

"To our success . . . and I'm more of a fruit-of-the-vine gal. But this is mighty tasty." The cocktail's warmth slid easily down my throat.

"I'd like to know more about you . . . Miss Dowling." He stood and took off his suit jacket, and laid it on the stool next to him. He loosened his paisley tie and freed his neck from the constraints of his top shirt button. Not a wrinkle was to be spotted in that white shirt.

I continued with my narration like it was an oral resume: what I did, where, and when. It sounded as if I were on a job interview.

"Relax . . . please. You already have the job." He sipped his Manhattan.

"Yes . . . I . . . do." I relaxed my tense shoulders. "And what about you? You've been an ad man all your life?"

"Sure have. And I can't imagine myself doing anything different. That's pretty much all I've ever wanted to do and all I have done."

Two hours passed quickly. And so did the old-fashioneds.

"Are we . . . should we . . . I think it's time we ate, don't you?" I asked, holding onto the bar's edge while steadying myself on a swaying seat. *Oh, wait. I think* I'm *the one moving from side to side.*

"Good idea," he said, and waved a finger to summon Jimmy.

"What would you—" He paused, his face studying mine.

I closed my menu. "I'll have what you're having."

"You must trust me."

"You never go wrong, Mr. Townsend. You make excellent choices. And I will certainly drink to that." I slurped the remaining gold from my glass.

"Yes, I do, don't I?" He gave me a flirty smile, then shimmied closer. The lingering Manhattan remained on his breath. I couldn't say this coziness made me uncomfortable, even though I knew it should—this was K&M's highest-profile client, here, with me, becoming too friendly—because I was feeling more at ease with Mr. T as we shifted from discussing our careers to the personal.

"I like that you're comfortable in your own skin, Debra. Sounds like you're exactly where you want to be in your life right now."

"I am . . ." I tried to hide my smile over the unexpected happiness this evening, being with Mr. T, but I couldn't.

Our eyes lingered on each other for a while. We hadn't noticed our dinner plates, a petite filet for me, a New York strip for him, were in front of us. I could feel my face becoming more flushed. Mr. T waited for me to begin eating, then watched me take a first bite.

"Aren't you going to eat?" I asked, popping a nibble of meat into my mouth, and pointing with my fork to his untouched plate. "It's gonna get cold."

He leaned on the bar with a folded arm, his tilted head resting in his open hand while he watched me.

"Mm-hmm," he said, the corners of his mouth curling up slightly.

"Are you flirting with me?"

"Uh-huh."

After we finished a delicious dinner and I sobered, Mr. T drove me home in a black Mercedes. A half-moon could be seen through the open sunroof. A spot near my apartment building seemed to have been held open just for us. He quickly slid from the car and opened my door. I stepped closer into him when I took his arm.

"I certainly had a lovely evening." I dropped my chin, eyeing him from under a parkway streetlight.

"I like that place. And they've got some terrific jazz music. Live bands play on the weekends. My quartet is trying to get a gig there, but they already have a contract with a different group."

"You're in a band? You haven't mentioned that before."

"Well, I am now. You'll have to come sometime to hear us. That is, if you like jazz."

"I sure do. I'd love to hear you—the group—play." I clapped my hands and giggled. Being a musician suited him. It was another creative part of him I found attractive.

"We play whenever and wherever we get the chance. Mainly in small bars around the city. Nothing as fancy as Maxine's, though."

He walked me up the steps to my apartment door, where the foyer inside offered just enough light to match my key with the lock. He took my hands, held them firmly, and kissed me on the cheek.

"I'll call you tomorrow," he said, turning and walking down the stairs.

"It's Saturday. We have no meetings scheduled."

"I know." He grinned before sliding into his car and driving off.

I pulled open the wooden front door of my apartment building and took each step from the lobby deliberately, heavy in thought, up the two flights of stairs to my apartment. I shut the door behind me and didn't bother to flip on the hall light switch. In slow motion, I undressed and slipped into bed with nothing but Mr. T and an old-fashioned on my mind.

Rose

I strongly suggested to Julian that, if we were going to live together, we find a new place. I was living in a black box, on a stage with no spotlights, just mood lighting on black end tables. But what was my aversion to black, anyway? It should have been familiar and a comfort because of the very place where I stood, surrounded by it. But there was the light, always a spotlight, shining onstage. It reminded me of under the willow tree that served as our stage, aglow with the filtered light under the canopied branches. But Julian's apartment was neither a picture under the willow tree nor a lit stage.

When I was growing up, my sisters' tastes in bedroom decor varied like the weather extremes in Chicago. Linney was obsessed with bringing the outdoors in with plants and flowers, green in every shade, and yellow and blue as bright as the sun and the sky. When Char got her big-girl bed, she moved in with Linney. "You moved into *my* room, Charlotte," Linney would remind her. In other words, don't disturb a thing. Eventually, Linney's holistic living backfired. Char used Linney's stone and crystal collection to fill a terrarium planted with prickly cactus.

"You can't do that to those precious gems, Char," Linney yelled.

"Go ahead, you stick your hand in the bowl and pull those rocks out, whatever ones you need."

"And they're not rocks. They are gemstones, precious crystals, and the least you could do is to learn something from me before I leave this place."

Linney was always threatening to leave home. Told us she needed to feel more connected to Mother Nature. The farm job couldn't have come soon enough for her. I guess all my sisters have tried to feel connected to home, to a place to be, after leaving Birchwood Court, each in her own way. But to what extent, was the question. I tried on parts as if trying to find my connection to myself through acting as someone else. A distorted view, I know.

When I shared a room with Deb, her bossy ways never fooled me. Though we rarely argued, I could tell when she was acting out because of not getting her way, or when something bugged her and she needed to tell me about it. So, I listened. Not a big deal. One night, she was on her bed with papers and booklets surrounding her in a semicircle. Looked like she was writing a report of some kind.

"Did you forget to hand in a paper or something?" I said.

"Graduate school." She looked up at me, tired, and with a sigh looked down at what lay in front of her, as if it were all too much and going back to school were not a good idea. She took a break that week from her project, and then, Kinsey and Moore called the following week. So, I was used to living with someone, even when that someone might be as "out there" as Linney or as grounded as Deb.

But Julian needed to break from all the black and bring color into his living space. No, perhaps I needed it more than he did, to be reminded of my sisters in color and personality, to know I had a little bit of home with me.

We found a place in an old brick four flat in Chicago in Old Town, not far from Second City, and the coffeemaker was the only trace of black in our apartment. Though neither of us were stand-ups, we did make friends and business connections. During the first six months, we chased leads and got parts in small, short-lived productions. That was okay. I learned to never leave a curtain call without having someone to talk to about a new production in the works somewhere else.

The weekend before Julian and I were to move into the new apartment, I visited Ma. We sat at the kitchen table, something I hadn't done with her in a while because I never had much news, but this time, I did. I told her I was moving into a place in Old Town with Julian.

She put down her coffee cup. "Are you sure this is right for you?" she asked.

I paused—she had never questioned my decisions before—then I reassured her, "Yes, it is. We work well together. We're a team, doing what we love to do. Besides, he really cares for me."

I watched Ma for a follow-up response—a crack of a smile, a furrowed brow, pursed lips—while she continued to sip her coffee. Instead, she stared out to the backyard with a still face. Did she sense that it wasn't going to work out but didn't want to say? Our conversation ended, and silence dropped on us like a closing curtain.

Ma's quietness got me thinking enough to also look out to the yard, a place that had always provided direction. The willow and its backdrop appeared in the distance as I searched, as if looking for a bull's-eye, feeling a great distance from it. Maybe Ma just understood that only I could make this decision.

Thanks to our friends at Second City, Julian and I found agents, and our world as actors opened from stage to television. At first, I was moving laterally with small parts and limited dialogue and screen time. To make my downtime more useful, I started writing columns for local entertainment magazines about the theater, new productions, and the makings of local actors. It kept me connected with who's who in theater.

In the early days, Julian and I coordinated our schedules so we could meet for lunch. He was more diligent in doing this than I was. I tried to fit in writing deadlines with auditions, and in some cases risked missing the deadlines altogether. "We've got tonight," I'd always tell him with a kiss and a hug. We did have our evenings, but I was getting home late. I'd sit with Julian on the couch, sharing left-over fried rice and pot stickers in the fridge from the previous night's visit to Mae Ling's, our favorite go-to in the neighborhood. Before I knew it, I was asleep on his shoulder. Julian always had strong shoulders to lean on.

The next morning, I turned in a story on Second City alums of *Saturday Night Live*, and then I scrambled to get ready for an audition. Though it was a long shot, Julian urged me on this one, a pilot for a new drama series, a cross between *The Wonder Years* and *Roseanne*. I was to play a mother. And this was going to take some convincing myself. I had a difficult time drawing on anything within me. I didn't want to go there, that whole maternal thing. I stopped it cold.

"Hey, I've got dinner covered this Friday night. Can I count on you being home for it?" Julian yelled while standing in the kitchen in his boxers, eating a glazed donut while watching me scamper through the apartment to find my bag.

At first, I took his question as maybe sarcasm, but he'd never shown a mean spirit. That just wasn't Julian. Surely there was a point when he could no longer keep his emotions lidded. I'd been giving him good reason to be irritated with me because of my writing jobs, filling in time that otherwise would be spent together. Weren't we all like simmering pots, handling life at just below the boiling point?

"I'll make sure of it. What's for dinner?" I said with flirtation as I pulled open the front door.

"Not sayin'." He grinned sheepishly. Well, who was flirty now?

I was home by four o'clock that afternoon and was confident I had time to finish an article for *Chicago Magazine* about two local up-and-coming actors. But the editor sent it back, asking me to cut a thousand words and to redirect the focus to the starring actors in the new drama. I panicked. He thought he was asking a seasoned writer who could pull off the changes quickly. But I was no experienced writer. Experience with the theater, yes, but with writing, I was a work in progress. I spread myself and my files and notes out on the couch and began to rewrite. The hours passed quickly.

By the time Julian and I sat down for dinner, his special spaghetti dish was a stuck-together blob, the Bolognese dried. His face looked deflated like the parched mound on our plates.

I didn't get the mother part, and I was starting to wonder if I would get the girlfriend part.

Debra

I was so focused on my new job and building my reputation at K&M that meeting anyone of personal interest never crossed my mind. And then when I met Mr. T, my new client and my new boyfriend, we found a rhythm together not only in business, but also in our personal lives.

But I didn't want to tell Ma about him yet. What if it didn't work out? I thought of Rose and her guy drama, which was enough to go around for all the Dowling women. Every time you talked to her, there was a new someone.

"Bad time?" I asked Rose on the phone one Sunday morning.

"No, not at all. Haven't heard from you in a while. You alive?"

"Yes. I'm alive. Busy working. Have you gotten a good role yet?"

"No, always working it, though can't work it as good as you. What's up, anyway?"

"Dennis."

"Is it serious?"

I realized we didn't have to provide backstory when Rose and I talked about something that was on our minds. A few words, and any close sister would tell you they understood. I remembered when Linney told me she got a job working at a farm. I knew right away when she said "at" and not "on" that she was afraid everyone in the family would laugh and think she was crazy to be working on a farm.

"I think, yes, it's headed that way."

"Coming from you, it must be. Ma know?"

"No. Not yet. You're the first who knows."

Of all my sisters, I would be more likely to divulge anything personal to Rose. She always knew what kind of person I needed her to be, whether a listener, a questioner, or a cheerleader. And yet she did mind *my* giving her direction; she'd say I was telling *her* what to do. All I can say is I was the big sister, always would be, and therefore I always had good reason to give my sisters direction.

I called Ma the next day to tell her about Dennis.

"Hi, Ma, it's Deb. I want to tell you . . ." I jumped right in without asking first how she was doing, showing my excitement about my new relationship, and about sharing it with Ma.

"Is everything okay? You sound a little . . . winded," she asked.

"No, I'm fine. Just, well, I'm excited to share some news."

"Well, it can't be a new job or a new place to live, as those are still new, so it must be a man."

"Yep. I . . . we . . . work together, and, well, we just hit it off, I guess you could say."

I kept the "how did you meet?" part simple to avoid possible admonishment from admitting he was my client.

"Is he good to you? Respectful? Honest?"

I didn't hesitate. "Yes."

"Well, then, enjoy the courtship, be happy, and love unconditionally."

"Ma, courtship?" I chuckled.

"Oh, you know what I mean. Get to know each other and be best friends. And, Deb, he's your client, isn't he?"

"How did you—"

"I'm not *that* old-fashioned. It happens, Deb. But I trust that you will maintain your professionalism and business sense, and after that, I don't want to know."

We hung up, and I was comforted that I told Ma, and that she always seemed to know the right things to say. Be best friends. Be happy. And love.

Keeping my relationship with Mr. T appearing strictly business was difficult. No, it was impossible. Though our office buildings were separated by four blocks and Seneca Park, he connected each Monday morning when he had a cappuccino and two white roses delivered to my office. I think most everyone knew who they were from. "Deb, you must be having some pretty good meetings with Mr. T," John would say quietly with a grin. I never replied. I reasoned that if BMT was happy, KC was happy.

When Dennis wasn't in his office reviewing creative or finalizing storyboards, he was jamming with his band and gigging in clubs. I was his number one groupie, and witnessing his musical side was fuel to our passionate relationship. From old greats of the big bands to the smooth notes of Kenny G or Sanborn, jazz always filled the room when I was at his place. I'd watch him from the kitchen doorway while preparing dinner, see him stopping to close his eyes and sway his body to the trumpet's blended notes or bopping his head to the snap of the drums. He'd grab my waist and hold me close, and we'd blend with each other and with the music. Dinner would be a little later.

After being with Dennis for a few months, I sensed he was holding something back. When the topic of previous relationships would come up, he was . . . too vague, if not evasive.

At Union Station, this nondescript place was our usual hangout in the city. Small tables for two or three gathered few patrons, discouraging larger groups from disrupting casual business meetings, a cocktail before dinner, or a happy hour drink with a friend after work. It's a place to leave work talk behind, and quiet enough for Dennis and me to hear each other with minimal distractions.

We filled settling-in time with idle chat about . . . something inconsequential—picking up L tokens for the train, our bikes needing tune-ups, what time Ma wanted us over for dinner on Saturday—until our cocktails arrived and we could get busy on a real conversation.

I took quick sips of Chianti and shifted in my seat before pulling the plug on the stalled conversation.

"Dennis, I really do enjoy seeing you play with the band." He studied the ice cubes swirling in his bourbon and water.

"You're in a different world sometimes . . . kind of like . . . now."

More swirling. More staring.

I leaned into the table, closer to his face as if to remind him of the world in front of him.

"What *is* it? I can see something is bothering you. You can tell me."

I took his one free hand. Did he have a bad day? Maybe he lost an account. But if this were true, he'd be yacking away, irritated at himself for losing something he'd thought he had in the bag. His silence told me something was different.

Yes, I was pushing him. I wanted to get it over with. After hearing the sisterhood's guy drama over the years, I became familiar with the signs of a breakup—the disconnection, the silence. Was he breaking up with me? I tried to read him for an answer that wasn't coming quickly enough.

He slid his forearms deeper into the table and dropped his head. "I have a son, Charlie. He's five. I never married his mother." He swallowed the last of his drink and signaled for another.

A child? He has a child? The good news here was that he wasn't breaking up with me. The maybe-not-so-great news was that he had a child. It changed things. Not one male in my life, but now two. Our intimate twosome was suddenly a threesome. And what did I know about kids? I never considered having children. It wasn't included in the picture I had of myself behind a corporate desk, facing clients I was responsible for. A life of sole responsibility was what I had always wanted.

"I . . . didn't know . . . I don't know," I said, sliding back in my seat, creating space between us. I thought about what he had said, squinting at him as if the picture had become blurred.

"I'd like you to meet him sometime."

I swallowed the last of the Chianti and twirled the glass's stem, then stared into its bottom as if the right words to say or our future were visible.

"Look, I understand. I wanted to tell you soon in case, well, you know, you wanted to bail out. I'd understand, you know." He watched his index finger tapping water droplets bouncing on the faux wood table.

What I did know was that I wasn't willing to give up; that's not my nature. I reasoned I would meet the little guy and nothing more. I didn't want to admit that Dennis was a package deal, a two-pack of the same item. Open one, and I'd eventually have to open the other.

"Dennis, we've come too far for either one of us to bail out." I paused. "C'mon, look at me. I want to meet your son."

I think I said this more to convince myself. Honestly, I was torn. When I met Dennis, I met him as a client first. I knew what I had to do and how to develop our business relationship. But meeting this new little person? I didn't know. I was serious about Dennis, and because of that, had to be open to meeting his son.

I didn't know about Charlie when I had told Ma about the new someone I had met; that he could be the one. Her talk wasn't one that assumed motherhood would naturally follow. But when it came time for me to meet Charlie, I had to tell her. She'd know what to say.

"He already has a mother," I told her. "I don't want him to think she's going away and I'm the new one. Charlie's loyalty is with his real mom."

"For now, Deb, be with him. Spend the time, all three of you. Have fun. Don't overanalyze it. He just wants to be with his dad. And later, you'll see how it all works out, how your instincts kick in, and you'll wonder why you were ever reluctant to meet him."

Talking to Ma was a relief. "It all works out," she'd say. "You will see later in life how you will have come full circle."

❧ Linney ❧

Mr. Leone's offer follows me like any good shadow does. It sticks with me for the remainder of the day and into the night, knocking on the door of my emotions. I have to tell Bridget soon, yet I hold back for fear she will accept, and I will lose my home here.

I busy myself in the shop unloading a new shipment that was delivered yesterday. The area rugs I had ordered from London are nestled tightly in a crate among other floor coverings as I examine the cotton braids in earth tones of tan, green, and terra cotta. I unwrap each rug from its plastic wrap and settle one rug I particularly like on the floor. Instantly, I see the farm in the woven pattern, a pallet of color commensurate with each changing season. This will be mine, a new rug to place under the table in the office with my beginnings underfoot, grounding a former youthful uneasiness. I hold tight the roll and drag it down the hall into the office, excited that this piece of comfort and familiarity will be joining my home. I slide the table and chairs aside, then squat to push free the carpet from its roll. I hop on to its edge and nestle my naked feet in the cotton's strength, conforming to the crests and dips of the woven pattern, and then I flatten the bumps with quick steps. The hard wood flooring is now warmed, like a home should be. The rug will always remind me of how I came to be at Magnolia.

"Hi, anyone home? Linney?" I recognize the voice of Bridget's oldest, most loyal customer and hurry to the front door.

"Hi, Viv," I say, giving her petite frame a swift hug. I can always spot her in a crowded shop by the Jackie O–style suits she wears—a short jacket and matching pencil skirt—looking forever youthful. She looks her best in sky blue, a delicate contrast to her strong-black-coffee hair, worn in a half updo. "I was just stocking new items. I know how you like those yellow and blue tones in your kitchen. Well, here are new cotton rugs, place mats, and matching napkins to freshen up your look," I say, pulling out samples from an accompanying box and laying them on the table to show her. I notice how her mini shoulder bag always matches her shoes.

"You're always thinking what your customers would want, Linney," Viv says, tucking errant wisps of hair behind her ear as she dips to inspect the mats and napkins. "I've loved everything about this place ever since Bridget opened it." A smile grows larger on her face. "You've helped me to make homes of my new houses, post divorces, and you've suggested a birthday gift, even a special one-of-a-kind wedding gift. You've been through many years and milestones with me." She brings clasped hands to her heart.

The front door chimes ring. I look away from Viv to see Meredith inside the doorway.

"Hi, Meredith, c'mon over and join us. So great to see you!" I tell her.

"Heeeello, you two." Meredith is dressed in a long dirndl skirt with flat brown shoes to match, and an oversized shirt that is a direct contrast with Liv's tightly polished look. Her long limbs sway in rhythm to keep balance with her thin frame.

"I see you're unpacking a few interesting new things there, Linney," she says, bending to examine the open box.

"Restocking after a busy holiday weekend."

"From my sunroom across the street, I can see the delivery trucks unloading boxes of goodies for here. I'm always eager to see what he's brought to Magnolia," Meredith says.

"When you've been around this neighborhood as long as I have, you become a neighborhood watch." Viv winks.

We have a good laugh. Vivian and Meredith are like the aunts I wish I had—warm, down-to-earth old souls—because they remind me of best friends I also don't have. Magnolia is forever grateful for guests like these two.

Just as my pretend-aunts are on their way out the front door, Bridget appears from the back office. Her blue eyes are sleepy, dulled by shadows underneath. Her freckles are faded against a pale complexion. Each day she is in color and kindness, coming into Magnolia with a garden bouquet snipped from her garden or from behind the shop. But today, she's empty-handed and looking pale.

She's also annoyed, starting right in with what's wrong—"gutters are filled and need cleaning; hell, we could use new gutters"—and continues to make her way to the front of the shop, to a switch on the wall behind the register. She flips it and stares at the ceiling, where the fans' blades move slowly. "The fans are not circulating the air well enough, the air-conditioning units are not pumping enough cool air, and that darn ancient indent in the ceiling has never, ever been fixed right." She stamps the air with an open fist, and her breathing appears labored. I stand stiffly, watching the uncharacteristic outburst. "This is the twenty-first century; we don't need to be dropping hay down from that ceiling anymore." I wonder about her urgency. What's the hurry to get Magnolia into tip-top shape? Maybe she's had it with Magnolia's imperfections after all these years.

"Linney, we need to look at the books to see if any fixes are possible." She braces one hand on her hip while her chest rises, making her cheeks bloom pink and her forehead misty.

"Oh . . . yes, certainly . . ." My eyes lock onto her body language. She softens and takes a deep breath, calming herself, and pushes away strands of red, damp hair that cover her eyes. Bridget has never shared the books with me before.

As Bridget wanders about the place throughout the day, I keep her in sight, studying her to understand her clearer. At the end of the day, I still don't know what's bothering her.

I lock the front doors and retreat to the back office to put on a teakettle, plunking a tea bag of lemongrass and chamomile blend into each cup. I notice Bridget standing in the doorway, watching me.

"I'm ready, Bridget. Just fixing us a tray." I hurriedly fill the mugs with simmering water and place a sleeve of shortbread cookies on a serving tray.

Teatime at the day's end is an excuse to have a conversation— and a lovely one at that—about . . . well, most anything. The birds, the flowers, the sunny day, our day. It's a chance to connect to Bridget as a confidante.

My actions are not new to her. She knows that my having a tea break at this time is as essential to my well-being as plucking weeds in the backyard gardens is to Bridget's. I sit at the table to surrender into the quiet of the day's end while watching her standing at the desk, systematically pulling out files from drawers, racks, and even from under the desk, making quite a scene, as if she's a woman on a mission with a whole lot of material to cover. She loads the stack in her arms and begins to rifle through each folder in a methodical way, like a squirrel digging for nuts, then pulls out selected papers and studies them with squinted eyes.

"Here, let's take a minute and enjoy our break." I slide her mug across the table, within her reach. "C'mon, join me."

I let the cup of steamy serenity warm my hands, hoping these relaxing moments will comfort Bridget.

But she ignores my suggestion. She plods from the desk and plunks into her chair, dropping the heap in her arms on the table. I don't glance her way because I have no business peeking at what is open in front of me—Magnolia's financial details. "This place has gotten so old, and so have I," Bridget mumbles. I'm not sure she wants me to hear what she says. "Don't think there's any way to make Magnolia new again. I don't have the financial means." Bridget bows her head.

I have never heard Bridget speak in defeat. She is slumped in her seat, heavy with thoughts and emotion.

As the sun falls lower in the sky and our worktable dims, I don't answer her but rather follow her gaze out the window to the gardens. We deeply breathe in sync as a just-before-sunset twilight illuminates the sun's magic settling to sleep. Her breathing calms.

"It doesn't need to be new," I say, leaning toward her and cupping my hands over hers. "The character and charm is in its bones. And you can't make much change to an old structure without breaking it." She nods in agreement. "Anyway, you're not old, Bridget. Your red hair and engaging voice tells anyone who walks through that door that you are in charge." I look at her for a moment and smile, and I hope for one in return, but her face remains unchanged. "You are Magnolia, Bridget, and this is where I belong, right here," I say, poking the table with a pointed fingertip while blinking away tears. I slip my shoes off and let the cotton under my feet relax the day's tension.

"I started Magnolia at the age you were when I took you on," she says, smiling as if recalling a fond memory. "That's why I hired you. When you walked through that door over ten years ago, you reminded me of myself at that age. I noticed you were smart and had business know-how." She makes me think back to my job at the farm where I brought with me my experience working with Cole and the farm's visitors. "I knew Magnolia had been waiting for you all along." Her voice is familiar now, softer and more like the Bridget I know.

"It was pure destiny, Bridget. Did I ever tell you how I found this place?" I sit up taller, eager to tell a story. "Well, I was taking a walk early one spring morning, not thinking about anything in particular, just wandering. The dirt path had narrowed before ending at an orchard of magnolia trees. Each tree was showing their plumage like peacocks, busting in white and blushing pink blooms, all clustering together in hugs of connection where I couldn't see beyond them. Anyone else would have stopped when they saw the orchard and turned back, thinking it a dead end, but I continued walking through floating petals. And what a surprise I came upon on the other side!" I give the table a gentle slap. "A small, Wedgewood-blue house with white shutters. Magnolia. And the rest, as they say . . . is history." I look intently at her. "And I'm forever grateful to you for giving me a chance to work here."

Bridget's eyes tear; her words break. "Magnolia means everything to me." She drops her head and fiddles with the tails of her chambray shirt. "I restored this old coach house into a shop. I looked at it as a diamond in the rough, a gem sitting bright in wild grass and flowers." She then stares out at the wildflower beds. Her tight brows soften. She appears to find peace in the sky that has faded to a sherbet glow on the horizon. "I had a vision for this place to be like no other, for visitors to come and to connect in some way to a happy place."

We drain the teapot and sit back in our chairs. My toes further explore the braided cotton bumps, feeling their soft, breathable texture. We inhale, Bridget and I, and allow the reflection to connect our thoughts.

"This place seems to have been your life, Bridget. You've never mentioned to me if anyone is in your life, too."

"If you mean a husband and kids, no, Linney, there's no one. Never married. And I'm not sorry about it either," she says, loud and strong. "This is where I was meant to be and what I am supposed to do."

"Marriage and motherhood are foreign to me," I tell her, "something I've never thought as being in my future. I prefer to take each day and its opportunities as they come. I love my life the way it is."

I take our empty mugs to the sink, and when I return, Bridget's arms are barely holding her up as she relies on the oak chair's arms to support her.

"Bridget, are you feeling okay?" I kneel close in front of her.

"Oh, honey, I'm fine. A little tired, a little older, a little overwhelmed. But I'll manage. Things always do work out. Let's work on this tomorrow," she says, gathering all the folders and papers in no order into one stack. "I think we've had enough of Magnolia for one day."

"You go on home, Bridget. I'll close up." I stand to hug her. "Have a restful night."

We embrace, and I notice how her body, once solid and strong, is now soft. The sun has sunk below the horizon, and the back office is dark. Night has opened from twilight. I move about the place to turn on a desk lamp and another on an end table next to the couch. The room turns cozy, like home.

I wait until Bridget leaves before I linger at the table and think about Bridget's well-being. I pull my knees to my chest and wrap my arms around my legs. At first, she was urgent to talk about Magnolia's financial affairs, but she wandered into the future. Between a gaze outside and a pause in her conversation, was she thinking about what the future holds for her? With neither a husband to grow old with nor children to carry on for her, does she fear being alone, growing old and weary? Is she afraid Magnolia will become too much for her?

I think sometimes we find ourselves in places we never thought we'd be. And then we suddenly look back and wonder what happened. Perhaps we regret not having taken a different path. But where we do land, whether on the ground or in spirit, we make the best of it and are grateful. It wasn't by chance that I found a place to be on a farm and then a new home at Magnolia, but rather it was meant to be, one a life stop that led me to the other. Life is like a ladder, where we can't help but to climb each step, up, up, getting taller while we see our past selves get smaller in our rearview mirror.

You could say we have a lot on our minds—Bridget worried about her future and what will happen to Magnolia, and, well, the same for me, too.

It's time to go home. I rinse our mugs and remember I never did bring up Mr. Leone and his offer to Bridget. It just wasn't the right time.

✽✽✽ Debra ✾✾✾

We agreed to meet at the entrance to Lincoln Park Zoo in the city. The energy from a sunny, breezy afternoon and busy kids' laughter was contagious. Pacing at the zoo's entrance, I visually sifted through incoming scampering children and adult pairs, trying to single out a child who could be five years old and a mini version of Dennis. I spotted Dennis first, dressed in khaki shorts, sandals, a navy polo shirt and strapped with a backpack, looking as if he were going on a hike. No, he looked like he was in dad mode. And then there was Charlie, dressed like his father, pulling Dennis's arm to walk faster, excitedly skipping along because he knew exactly where he was.

"Well, hello, you two handsome men."

"Hi there." Dennis kissed me, and we hugged with Charlie squished in the middle.

"And this is Charlie."

Dennis stepped back, and I knelt. The five-year-old stared at me with cornflower-blue eyes, wearing leftover grape jelly on his chin and on his shirt. His button nose was perfectly centered on a round face.

"Hi, I'm Deb. And this . . . is Jax." I settled the small, stuffed brown puppy with long, floppy tan-and-white ears in Charlie's little hands. He grabbed Jax by an ear and continued staring up at me. I touched his soft copper curls and gave his shoulders an embrace. I think I gazed at him longer, wanting to know all about him, but he broke free first to look up at his dad, confused, but then eager to move along.

"C'mon, Charlie, let's go see the sea lions," Dennis said.

Content and satisfied, we melded into the crowd of families, becoming just like them.

I enjoyed that day at the zoo, especially meeting little Charlie, who couldn't have been more fun and carefree, with a personality that said he'd be a real charmer with the ladies when he got older. I'd say this apple didn't fall far from the tree.

Later in the weekend, I called Rose to tell her about my morning at the zoo and meeting Charlie.

"Ya know, it's as if I've come full circle." At the time, under the willow when we were younger, I didn't know what Ma meant by coming full circle. "But I trusted Ma's words as she never steered me or us in the wrong direction."

"I remember when you were starting out on your own, leaving home and beginning your career. Meeting someone, especially a man who had a son, was never on your radar."

"It wasn't. But don't you see? I was finding my place to be, and when I met Dennis and Charlie, those were more connections for me to discover where I'm supposed to be."

A few weekends after our zoo outing, I was enjoying the early morning sun while reading the Sunday *Tribune* on the sectional in the living room while Dennis was working in his study. On the weekends we didn't have Charlie, this was our Sunday morning routine. Next thing I knew, he was standing in front of me.

I put down my newspaper. "What? What's up? Spit it out."

He held his day planner open, turning a page back and forth and shifting from one foot to the other.

"I have a gig next Sunday afternoon. Would you mind watching Charlie? I should be back in time to take him back to his mother's."

He raked a hand through his hair, shaking his head.

"Um, whoa, wait a minute." I pushed the newspaper aside and

sat up, giving Dennis my full attention. "You've always been here when he's here. And what about Carrie? Is she okay with this?"

"His mother is fine with it. Charlie's been around you for a while now. You're not a stranger to him. You're the nice lady who gave him Jax." He winked and bent down to give me a kiss.

"What does one do with a preschooler?"

He laughed. I was serious. It was different. My sisters were once five, but Charlie was not of me. Childcare for sisters was a whole lot different than caring for my boyfriend's son.

"Not to worry. He'll have Dudley, his favorite beagle . . ."

". . . and a dog, TOO?"

"It's stuffed, not real, Deb. And he'll tell you all about him and how Jax and Dudley get along. His mother will have his toys, snacks, and his blanket for nap time packed."

"Oh, yes, nap time!" The Dowling girls never napped. To take time out was to miss something we just knew was going to happen. We didn't know what, but we'd sure be ready when it did.

He hurriedly moved around the house, gathering his backpack and stuffing into it sheet music and a notebook. "I'll see ya. I'll be in the garage, practicing."

I leaned back on the couch and got to thinking. Between the agency business, Dennis's music, and now me, I wondered if Charlie was being pushed to the end of the line.

The next day, during dinner, I wanted to tell Dennis I was concerned about Charlie's place in all our lives—that he didn't have one. At first, I thought I was making something of nothing, but then I thought I should be able to talk to my husband openly about what's on my mind.

I came to the table with a baking pan of lasagna, a salad bowl of mixed greens, sliced garlic bread, and a bottle of a mixed red, and Dennis followed, taking his usual seat, the one closest to the

kitchen. I dove in, slicing lasagna that mirrored my plan to approach the discussion—in small, calculated cuts.

"Dennis . . . you know I'm happy being with Charlie, right?
It's okay with me that he's here, spending time with you . . . and
me," I told him, handing him a full plate. "Maybe we should have
him with us more often." I put down the knife after serving myself, and wondered if I was impinging on his and Carrie's parental
arrangement. It seemed to me that Charlie should be more of a
priority over Dennis's music and work.

"Deb, you don't understand." He put down his fork and made
a fist with one hand. "When I'm not pitching new business, or
preparing for it, I'm dashing off to a gig, and then there's spending
time with you." His voice strengthened; his words became more
pronounced. "I know I need to be more in his life, but I've got
demands, Deb."

He hit the table with that fist. I recoiled. The outburst was
unlike his usual in-control self. I quietly resumed eating and
elected to not respond.

While we cleaned up in the kitchen, Dennis got a call from
Carrie. I could always tell when he spoke with her: his sentences
were clipped as if she was interrupting him. His face reddened,
and the call ended quickly.

"Everything okay?" I asked.

"We have Charlie for the weekend," he mumbled.

"Great! Oh . . . but so last minute."

"Apparently her work has taken priority." I noted his sarcasm,
if not irony.

"You mean it's *more* of a priority?"

"Well, that's Carrie. Having a son sometimes doesn't fit in with
her life." He shook his head and chuckled. "And the thing is, she
doesn't seem to mind."

"It's okay, it's all good, Dennis." I waved the air as if to clear it of ill will and gave him a reassuring squeeze. "You'll be able to spend more time with him, and I'm here, too . . . with my two favorite boys."

I was happy to be with Charlie when Dennis was out late for a client meeting or rehearsing with the band. I'd read him stories; we'd make popcorn and watch Disney movies. At times, when Carrie was unable to be with her son, Dennis would have Charlie, and me, too, more often. I saw this shift as a good thing, despite Dennis's view that it was more of a demand on him.

But a picture of Charlie's parents was becoming clearer. I was seeing Charlie as a to-do on his parents' list that had to be dealt with, moved around, as if he were an appointment that needed to be rescheduled and fit in elsewhere. I never did tell Dennis this, despite my intention to do so while cutting up lasagna in a pan.

JUNE

✷ Margaret ✷

Having Charlotte with me at the doctor's office was bittersweet. Her presence was comforting, yet I didn't want the children to know. I didn't even want Joe to know. Telling them will change everything, and I like things the way they are. We worked to get to our own places in life, and any disruption would be a real spoiler.

Besides, what a beautiful start to June it is! There are geraniums to plant, and more daisies to fill in the gaps in the flower beds. A nook out back by the shed begs for more rosebushes. Joe has his to-do list he made up in early spring, tacked to the fridge and ready to be implemented as soon as the weather permits it. We're at the starting line and have heard the gun fire.

After a morning with Charlotte at the Garden Spot in town, we pick up the season's best and return home. Charlotte unloads geraniums and Gerbera daisies and new rosebushes on the deck in the backyard, while I sit at the kitchen table, watching her. I seem to be working more slowly these days, and I admit the morning took a little out of me. I think I'd like to have an early lunch before tackling the afternoon's work. Perhaps the break will energize me.

I rummage through the fridge and pull out a package of sliced ham, Swiss cheese slices, a tomato, and a few lettuce leaves, and line them up on the counter.

"Lunch already?"

Charlotte steps through the sliding doors and stands at the other side of the kitchen counter. "We usually get started planting right away and have lunch after," she reminds me with a tipped head.

She has that surprised, confused look on her face, like when her father suddenly announced one weekend that we were all going to the Dells in Wisconsin. It was right before school had ended for the summer, and to pick up and leave for a weekend while the kids were still in school constituted a violation as far as I was concerned.

"We have time," I tell her to slow her down. "No need to be in a rush."

What I'm really telling her is I don't have the energy; I'm tired. In the earlier days, I could get all my planting done, even if it meant working until dinnertime. But now, though my spirit is willing, my body can't grant me my wish to continue.

"You go ahead, Charlotte. Place the flowers where you'd like. And tomorrow, we will plant. This way, you'll have all afternoon to do something for yourself. I'm going to rest here a moment." I have never been so grateful for a chair's seat to hold me. The clean air inhaled is an elixir for my weariness.

"It *is* a perfect day, isn't it? I think I'll go over to Gilson Park, plant a chair and my feet in the warm sand, and watch the white sails sway along the lake."

I clap my hands and cheer her on. "That's the spirit, Char. Actually, I think Linney's outdoor spirit is in you."

"But let me fix you that sandwich before I go."

I know Charlotte will enjoy the warming spring day as she sees fit. Being the youngest, she has had to find her own amusement, as she was unlikely to be included in the sister circle of entertainment. I watch her methodically build a plate: two bread slices smeared with Dijon mustard, holding ham and Swiss cheese slices, lettuce, tomato, and then gingerly nestling in a pile of potato chips. I smile in satisfaction at her taking great care of me through the comfort of food and a delightful plate presentation.

"I'll leave your lunch here on the table . . . whenever you're ready for it."

After Charlotte leaves, I take a few nibbles and realize I want to be out there, on the porch, amid the day's activities of traveling birds, popping green, and expanding flower buds. It gives me comfort to feel as if I belong. So, I step out to the porch and slide into my favorite chair. Next thing I know, Joe is shaking my shoulder.

"Margaret, you must have dozed off. It's well after the lunch hour. Your food is still sitting on the table."

I realize the afternoon has gotten away from me. I first steady myself before wandering into the kitchen to plug in a hot pot. I plunk a tea bag into my favorite mug, the pretty pink-and-white one Charlotte got me for Mother's Day last year. I push away the lunch remnants while waiting for the water to boil and look out from the window at the willow. The midafternoon sun casts a majestic spell on its reedy branches. They look as if they are suspended. It is not one of my productive days, filled with energy and accomplishment, but rather one of slowing time and recognizing the present.

I awake refreshed, remembering it is Father's Day. I dress in bubblegum-pink pedal pushers and a white sleeveless blouse and take the steps with Keds on my feet in confidence downstairs to the kitchen. I yank open the glass doors to release the house's staleness and to welcome the morning's beginnings. Joe is out in the yard, giving each growing thing, from the grass to the blooming shrubs to the birds, a drink of water. I look out the window while standing at the sink and see that the early morning's gray skies have cleared to let the sun warm the early spring chill. Flower buds grow fatter and the grass thicker. And the day is becoming a better one because of it.

I'm puttering in the kitchen when the phone rings. It's Charlotte, to tell us she'll be over soon to take us out for a late breakfast. I yell this through the open doors to Joe, who has come full circle with the garden hose, completing his watering duties throughout the yard. He stands tall and smiles in satisfaction, not only with how the gardens glisten from wetness but also with knowing that we are going out to celebrate his special day.

We don't get back to the house until noon-ish, and when we pull in, the Johnsons across the street are already celebrating, as a few cars are parked out front. I bet Ben Johnson is happy to see his three kids return home, all grown now and on their own. A child returning home is a return to a connection that is never broken. I wish the three girls could be home with Joe. It would mean so much to him.

Joe and I are settled at the kitchen table reading the morning paper when Charlotte dashes through the sliding door. "C'mon. Outside, you two," she says excitedly, waving us out with a sly grin. Joe and I do as we're told. Well, I focus on the distance and see what looks like strangers coming through the gate. "Surprise, Dad," Deb and Rose and Linney shout in unison as they file in from the driveway. Joe plants his hands on his hips and instant happiness pops on his face. And I do think there's a tear in his eye.

We hurriedly join, meeting under the willow, and greet in hugs and laughs and chatter. Linney, Joe, and I settle on the porch, and Deb and Rose hustle into the kitchen. I can hear through the screen door cabinets banging and see Rose and Deb pull out dessert plates and forks. Rose pulls a strawberry pie from a Deerfield's Bakery box. We always buy their pies on special occasions because they make them oversized. Joe likes his pie!

"How's it going with you, Deb? How's it being a mom?" Rose asks.

"Challenging. But it's working. His teenage years aren't as bad as I anticipated. Charlie is turning out to be quite a good young man. Seems like yesterday when I had first met him. We went to the zoo, and in case it didn't go well, Charlie could be distracted easily and quickly. I remember we stared at each other, not saying much. Today, he doesn't stare, and he still doesn't say much. He's a good kid. And you, Rose? Last I heard, you're ready to settle down, but not in the marrying sense." Deb cuts triangles in the pie.

"And in what sense *would* that be? In the sense I'm taking time off and writing more, right?"

"You mean you've left behind all your travels and noncommit-ment-commitments to men and to deadlines? Sounds like you're taking yourself more seriously."

I swivel in my chair to have a peek inside. Rose's arms are tightly crossed; she glares at Deb.

"Sounds like that's difficult for you to believe. I think you're jealous. Deb, why don't you stick to being your own boss, and I'll work my own life on my end, okay?" The dessert plates clank as Rose drops them on the counter. Deb halts running her finger down the side of the gooey knife.

Oh, boy. Even as grown women, Deb and her siblings haven't changed since their young-girl days. Voices rise, and my curiosity gets me to my feet and into the kitchen. I cross the threshold. Linney follows me.

"What are you all talking about? Sounds serious. I can hear you guys out here," Linney says and adds, "And, Rose, did you know you turn your stage voice on when you get irritated? Loud and clear." I know this is an innocent statement by Linney, but Rose gets huffy on that one, frowning and breathing heavily through her nose.

"Linney, we haven't heard much about your love life. Anyone special?" Deb asks, diverting the tension. She plunks scoops of ground coffee into a filter, fills the coffee maker with water, and flips the switch then fills a hot pot for tea for Linney.

"No," she says, shaking her head. "My only commitment is to Magnolia." Her head is down, her eyes more focused, I think, on her statement than her unwrapping.

Rose grabs a pint of vanilla ice cream from the freezer and a scoop from the drawer and places them on the counter. "Don't you ever think of marrying and having kids one day?" she asks Linney.

Charlotte pipes up from the doorway before Linney has a chance to answer. "I didn't realize having kids was an obligation." She joins the sister circle.

"Call me selfish, but your life changes when children enter the picture, and I like my life just the way it is," Linney says. "It's not like I'm missing out on the meaning of life because I haven't had kids." She takes a stab at the ice cream and grinds out a white ball of vanilla with the scooper.

I stay behind, just inside the sliding doors, then slowly step up to the counter, where Charlotte, Rose, and Deb are in a line with their backs to the other side. I rifle through mail tucked into my open calendar book but continue to listen in on the verbal exchanges.

"Besides," Charlotte interrupts, "people always assume you *are* a mother, and if you've never had kids, there must be a reason why not. Perhaps there's something not right with you, in which case you couldn't possibly ever understand what it's like to be a mom. What a total put-down."

"It's true. Your life does change when you're no longer a couple, but a threesome," Deb starts in. She stops doling out pie slices onto plates, and I watch her eyeing each sister. "From college on, I had a plan. I would graduate, get a job at K&M, be there for, oh, a few years. If I happened to meet someone during that time, great! But if I didn't, I always had K&M and advancement possibilities as my commitments. But the plan didn't turn out that way. Marrying wasn't on the to-do list like working my way up K&M's ladder was."

Deb pulls five mugs from the cabinet above her and squeezes between her sisters' bodies to line them up on the counter. She grabs the coffeepot and fills the mugs.

"Having a husband and a toddler in my life did change things," she says. "It's not a bad thing, you guys. I admit, I was afraid for our relationship when Dennis told me he had a child. It was one thing to handle not being alone anymore, and then another when we were no longer a couple but a threesome." She hands Rose a mug and looks at her. "I didn't want to lose what I already had, and I was willing to see where it would take me. A redirection in one's life plan does not suggest a bad thing. And it's okay, too, to like your life the way it is." I catch Deb giving Linney a wink as she plunks a teabag in a mug of hot water.

"And it certainly is okay to wonder what's ahead for you and if that future includes being a mom, too," Deb says, handing Charlotte a mug with direct eye contact. "And it's not an obligation. There's nothing wrong with you if you don't want to have children."

Deb lifts her mug to toast. "Here's to choices. And for each of us to find our own places to be."

I watch as my girls gather in a circle to raise their cups. I burst with pride as I see how they work through their lives, something I've always prayed for when sitting under the willow and watching them grow.

"When you and Dennis go out with another couple, I suppose the only topic you talk about is your kids," Charlotte says, banging the utensil drawer closed with a heavy hip.

". . . and I bet you and Dennis don't talk much about the things you used to talk about before Charlie entered the picture," Rose adds. "With kids, you lose yourself when you lose the conversations and interactions with friends that brought you together in the first place."

"No, Rose, that's not it. Sure, we talk about Charlie, but like any topic of conversation, we move on to something else. We've learned to find a balance. You have to make your lives work."

I've kept quiet long enough. My honesty is shouting to be heard.

I swing around to the other side of the counter. "In my day, you had kids whether you wanted them or not," I say, grabbing a mug and joining the circle. "It was the thing to do. But also in that day, moms stayed home with their children. You never heard of women being mothers *and* having careers. Today, it's different. Women have choices and are empowered to make those choices, and to be perfectly fine with the decisions and with no regrets. Just because you haven't physically birthed a child does not diminish the fulfilling life you are meant to lead." I direct my words to Deb. "With or without children." And then I match my daughters' soulful eyes with mine. "Your dad and I are so proud of all of you."

I shoo the girls away to be with their father on his day, and I rest at the kitchen table to watch the willow's branches flowing in tandem with the gentle breezes.

Rose

I woke up early that Sunday morning, already distracted, thoughts like buzzing flies. I sat cross-legged at the kitchen table, on a wobbly chair that resembled one from an outdated set design. With a second cup of coffee in hand, I was halfway through the *Chicago Theatre*

News when I put down the paper and welcomed a sunny day reaching through a square window next to me. The light turned on the walls to cheery buttercup.

"Well, good morning, sleepy one," I said to Julian as he sauntered into the kitchen. With mussed hair that was too long, and a beard that was too old, he looked as if he were emerging from an out-of-body experience, dressed in shorts and a T-shirt that appeared to be from last night's basketball game.

"What are you doing up so early?" he asked, planting a soulful kiss on my cheek.

I shrugged. "Don't know. Just woke up."

He sat in his seat, the one closest to the fridge, so he could show me how, while straddling the table leg, to swing with a swivel of his knees, open the door, grab a beer from the shelf, then swivel back, never banging a knee or shifting the table. Only this time, it was an orange juice carton.

"Okay. What's up?" he asked. "I know that look on your face. Kind of staring into space, eyes hiding behind the fringe of your hair. Oh, it's the TV series, isn't it? You don't think the role would be good for me. You don't even think it could make it past the pilot."

He took a swig of OJ from the carton's mouth, then closed it.

"I . . . really . . . don't know." I resumed reading the reviews of *Agnes of God* playing at the Goodman, which opened over the weekend. Letting out a deep sigh, I regretted I didn't try to get in on this one. I stopped reading and looked up at Julian.

"I'm into live productions, remember?" I pause. "You sound kind of insecure about this whole TV series thing."

"I thought we were partners." He started bouncing a knee. "We used to talk about our auditions and our roles and our goals for growing as actors . . ."

". . . we did, in the beginning," I said.

"But now, you don't seem as interested in what I do . . . in what we do."

I shifted my feet, from tucked under me to flat on the floor, and braced my forearms on the table. "It's more what *you* do, Julian, that we always talk about. It's always about television and what's next for you in it. I want to talk about new theater productions and what new article I'm writing. Lately, I feel like I'm something less-than because we're pursuing different directions. We're headed down two different paths," I told him, first staring at the newspaper, then at him.

"Where's this coming from?" He smoothed his hair away from his face.

"I . . . don't . . . know."

"I thought we agreed that we'd always be honest with one another if something was bothering us."

"Well . . . seems like it's changed."

"What we're doing, our work, has changed, but not us. We haven't changed." He tilted his head, making me wonder if he was asking or saying it as a fact. His eyebrows squished together, and he grimaced in confusion.

". . . I don't know, Julian. I just don't know anything anymore." I shook my head and laid my face in my hands. Finding our passionate places put us at odds. What had brought us together was separating us.

"Why don't we think about this and talk more tonight? We'll work it out. We've always worked together as a team." He took my hands in his. "Everything will be fine." He got up and I watched him walk down the hall and into the bathroom.

I recognized my courage in telling him this. For so long, I had taken direction from others, and now, I'd made a step toward taking my own direction. I looked out to the street, where the two parkway oaks appeared to be leaning on one another. They appeared overgrown, filling out to shade the grassy space and spreading into each other's limbs. I noticed how the two trunks looked undefinable. I couldn't decipher which tree branches belonged to what tree. I had learned early on that trees and bugs and flowers don't belong to one another or to us, but they do rely on one another. While Ma, my sisters, and I sat under the willow, we were links in a chain of connections to Mother Nature. I had come to depend on my parkway trees. They were my window to belonging.

I talked to Deb the following weekend. She said that maybe the relationship had run its course and that "it does happen, you know." She was so matter-of-fact about it as if I should have already known this. People do change, and sometimes it's not a bad thing to go your separate ways. Letting each other go can help you both to grow and find where you're truly meant to be.

After three years together, Julian and I went our separate ways. I think it was in the making for a while when my acting gigs were taking a back seat to my writing pursuits. It all happened one night when I had a piece due the next day for the *Chicago Today* newspaper. I was sitting on the couch amid messy stacks of note pages while reviewing my article. It was dinnertime. From where I was sitting, I watched Julian in the kitchen looking into a mostly empty fridge, then moving aside to open the cupboards. Soon, he was standing in front of me. I thought he was going to ask me what we should have for dinner, but he didn't. He just stood quiet, staring at me to get my attention, and when I didn't give it to him, he plopped down on the couch next to me.

"Hey, that doesn't look like prep work for your audition tomorrow," he said.

"I'm trying to finish an article for the paper tomorrow. Would you mind if I got some uninterrupted time?" I exhaled, annoyed at the disturbance and him for invading my space.

"But don't you have an audition? . . . It's a big one for you to-morrow. I want to help . . ."

I shook my head and put up my hand to stop him. "Julian, I talked to them. I'm not going. I can't do this one." I resumed making edits.

"Canceled?" Julian shifted on the couch, pushing away a few papers to inch closer. "You had a great shot at being in the cast. They know you. They've read your work in the *Theatre Times*." I could feel Julian's warm breath against my face. He was getting too pushy, di-recting me to where I didn't want to go.

"I'm not going in there just because they know me from my work at the *Times*." I put down my written pages and leaned back against the couch's arm. "Look, Julian. I have steady work now and a regular paycheck. I can't live from part to part, wondering if each will pay enough, how long it will last, or when's my next job. You're much better at handling your career. You work hard at it. I love the theater and acting. But I don't love the struggle to keep my name out there. I've got a following, here, at the paper." I held up the latest edition and shook it in his face.

I went into the kitchen and grabbed a Tab from the fridge, opened it, and took a long swig. I turned my back to him, looked out the window, and thought about what I had said. I needed to be honest about what I was feeling. If you're never honest with someone, and you don't tell them about your feelings and what you want, how can you ever expect them to know? The streetlights were aglow in muted orange, over a damp pavement. A man dressed in a business suit was walking his German shepherd in the parkway. I turned around, and took another sip and a deep breath.

"Julian, this isn't working out between us. We had so much in common when we first met. And I feel pressure from you to be that person. But I'm trying to make the writing thing work now." I could hear the pleading in my voice.

Thinking about how we were in the beginning, feeding off each other's energy in finding the parts and passion for being in theater in the city, made me start to cry. I realized I was mourning an earlier time in my life and this present time with Julian.

"Rose, I'm sorry. I didn't know you felt this way. I have never meant to make you feel pressured. I've always wanted to help. And I still do. I'm your number one fan, whether you're an actress or a writer."

I joined him on the couch.

"There's nothing to be sorry about. We met at the right place and right time. I have no regrets. I think we need to follow our own paths, wherever they are taking us." I placed my hands on his crossed leg. He stared down at his lap. "We can still be each other's number one fan."

"But . . . I don't want to let you go. I know that's selfish of me. I do want you to find where you're meant to be." He cradled my face in his warm hands and kissed me softly on the lips, lingering, before rising, walking into the bedroom, and shutting the door, without looking at me again.

The following week, while I was packing my things to move out, Julian stopped me. He looked pale and tired, a figure I didn't recognize, and contrary to when I first met him, except for the rumpled jacket.

"Sit with me," he said, putting his hand on my lower back and guiding me to the couch. I will always remember it as command central for my writing. As long as Julian and I had acting jobs, that sofa would be covered in script pages. If its cushions were ever bare, we knew we needed work.

"Here," he said.

"What's this?"

He handed me a fancy bloodred box tied with a white silk ribbon. It looked luxurious and indulgent.

"For you. I saw it in one of your favorite boutiques, the one you said one day you would buy something, just a little something from there. Well, I did, for you. It's to be with you in your new adventures."

The box looked no bigger than the size of a place mat, and no taller than a stack of four of them. It carried no weight. I released the ribbon from its tie, lifted the lid, and peeled away the tissue to find a shiny, deep red fabric. I freed it from its folds and held the tapestry up close to have a look.

My fingers caressed its silky weave as I studied the landscape in garnet, evergreen, chocolate, and a burst of tangerine sun. "Reflects glamour and beauty," Julian told me. "Like how I see you. I thought you might like this one, with the vibrant colors and the ornate design, as inspiration for all your travels."

"Travels? Where am I going?"

"All over. The writing thing will take off, and so will you. It'll be great for you, and I know you'll do well."

"You're not mad?"

"Mad? Why would I be mad? Sad, yes. Sad because we're no longer the way we were. And learning to love you is also learning to let you go." He held the tapestry as if admiring a gem's many facets. "I want you to see the shimmer in the silk and how it reflects light when you look at it from different angles. When you look at this, I hope you'll see yourself."

"It's a perfect treasure, and I'll keep it forever." I hugged it to my heart with one arm and hugged Julian with the other.

I hoped Julian saw us being together as one of many parts he would have in his life, with each one illuminating the next part to come along. Perhaps his gift to me was a symbol of our once connection to our places to be . . . with each other.

I packed the tapestry and my remaining belongings in boxes, my clothes a passenger beside me in the car as I left a life behind. I called Ma and asked if I could drop an excess load—travel notebooks, old scripts, and pictures of Julian and me—off at the house to store.

Staying with Julian until I found a new place gave us a chance for closure. Minimal conversation and closed body language between us allowed us to work through no longer being a couple, and to find ourselves individually. It was only when we started talking—like friends—that I could look ahead to moving into a small house on Juniper Road where I am today, my new place to be.

"If you need anything, anything, Rose, just call me, please," Julian said as I finished taping shut my last box in the middle of the living room. He knelt and gently laid his hands on my shoulders.

"I will. You're going to make it, Julian. You will find that role that will bring you all the rewards and happiness you've been looking for for so long."

We hugged and smiled, with understanding that we wanted what was best for each other.

Debra

A lot happened that following month. Kinsey and Moore was so happy with me that they gave me a promotion, and a managing director title, which meant I would be managing client events abroad. And Dennis was so happy with me, too, that he asked me to marry him.

I called Ma right away to let her know. "Oh, honey, I was expecting your call about this . . ." she said, interrupting me before I could tell her the details.

And then I called Rose.

"Oh, how fidgety Dennis appeared that night at Maxine's. He ordered dinner before we had finished our drinks. Dinner came, and we ate quickly, too quickly. I was getting annoyed with the rush and with him. I asked him if he was okay. 'Yep, just fine,' he said but, 'I've been thinking.' Heat sparked through my body, thinking Charlie hates me or it wasn't working out with him. Maybe Carrie hates me, or he doesn't think I'm mom material."

"Oh, get on with it, Deb," Rose urged.

"He said, 'We're stable now, aren't we? Settling in? Our schedules are working well, and Charlie is relaxed because he can depend on a routine, and he really likes you.' He told me I always have something fun to do with him. I told him it was from years of finding entertainment for my sisters when they were little. I chattered on, reliving stories of what our lives as sisters were like when we were younger, laughing at all the silly parts. I said how much I liked Charlie and that we have fun together."

"I bet he appreciated the backstory." I didn't acknowledge Rose's sarcasm. I continued.

"I noticed Dennis reaching into his suit coat pocket, rummaging around as if trying to find his keys, and thinking it was time to leave. He pulled out a closed hand, laid it on the table, and uncurled his fingers. A small blue box was sitting in his palm. I stopped talking, mid-sentence. He told me he loved me from the minute he saw me sitting at that table in Maxine's. He pulled back on the box's top, and there was perfection, a sparkling diamond. From then on, he said, he wanted to spend as many hours as he could with me. He wanted us to be together . . . forever."

"Sounds wonderful! He proposed where you had your first date. Classy and romantic."

"I clutched my chest, taken by surprise. And at first, I kept quiet, which I think scared him, but then I cried happy tears, and when he slipped the ring on my finger, took my hands in his, and kissed them, it all became real.

"You know me—I always prepare for the expected, but this unexpected left me out of my comfort zone."

"Deb, you're never really in a discomfort zone. You pull through so well in any situation. That's how you've gotten as far as you have with your career."

"I knew I was comfortable with Dennis and with Charlie, secure and safe. Yes, my words did flow in clear speech when I laughed and cried, 'I do . . . I mean I will. Let's get married.' It was all so right."

I was relieved to know that Charlie's mom was fine with Dennis's remarrying and Charlie having a stepmom in his life. The few times Carrie and I saw each other or spoke on the phone, she was pleasant and accommodating. Almost too nice, though. I wouldn't exactly say she was glad to have Charlie away from her immediate responsibility. Sometimes she did seem to need to be relieved of him.

Ma had insisted on having an engagement dinner party in her firstborn's and soon-to-be son-in-law's honor. Although I would have been fine without such a gala, indulging her would be an invitation to spend most of a day at a place where I learned how to establish my roots, at a time when neighborhoods were simply groupings of family who grew together as one, who nestled in a cul-de-sac or on a tree-lined street. Back then, I didn't think of a world beyond those points or how, if even, I fit into it because I had fit on Birchwood Court just fine. I had belonged there for the first half of my life. And I was on the road to the second half, where I was to belong somewhere and to someone, finding family and home.

I offered to help with planning the event, but this was Ma's deal, and Dennis and I just needed to show up. I think this was an opportunity for Ma to show off to the neighborhood and to her gal pals her daughter's success, and the thriving existence of her other daughters. There would be much catching up to do among people I hadn't seen in a long time. Luckily, it was an Indian summer day, and the weather continued to be beautiful for that fall evening. With a guest list of thirty, we fit comfortably under the white tent in the backyard, pitched among Ma's flower beds that were winding down their summer life cycle, and the willow and maple trees with leaves hinting at seasonal change. Later in the evening, cool breezes mixed with the music of Dennis's favorite jazz band. I must say, the evening was exquisite, down to the champagne and mini apple turnovers at the end.

When the guests dwindled, Dennis and I pulled up chairs to an empty table on the back porch, with the willow in front of us and the stars above.

"So many people, old neighbors and my parents' friends, and not enough time to catch up with them." I slipped off a silver Garolini to rub an achy foot. "And catching up with their lives—they seem to have such complicated ones."

"Most of these people are a lot older than you," he said, tipping his head back to receive a few remaining drops of champagne. "They've got their complications because they have more years on you." Dennis loosened his tie and looked up to the points of light.

"Well, I hope our life-to-be is simple, uncomplicated, and happy," I told him. He lifted my achy feet onto his lap and began to massage their arches.

"I am happy. And we'll be steering the ship, directing our own destination," he said.

I watched Ben and Barbara Johnson, our neighbors across the street, say goodbye to Ma and Dad. I remember growing up with their three boys. Benny Jr. and I are the same age. I heard he never did make it to college. He was living at home but couldn't make it here tonight. I would have loved to see him. We used to compete with one another about who'd get their college acceptance letter first and who'd have a job first after graduation. Some things don't turn out how you assume they would.

"Promise me one thing," I said, sliding my feet onto the ground and leaning close into Dennis. "If you ever think we are veering off course, losing sight of each other, that you'll be honest with me and tell me so." My pleading for his honesty was out of fear, as I couldn't shake the what-ifs. What if it didn't work out? What if, after a few years, it wasn't at all like when we were first together? I needed him to validate that we would always be moving together in the same direction.

Dennis grabbed both my hands and kissed them.

"I have your back. And you have mine. Deb, you're the strongest, most determined twenty-six-year-old woman I know, who knows herself well. And we will always be moving forward, together."

After the wedding, we couldn't wait to get out of renting a two-bed-room apartment in the city and into a single-family home in the suburbs with a backyard. One caveat Dennis emphasized was that we needed to live close enough to the city so that he could get to his jazz gigs quickly and easily. Traffic was bad enough maneuvering around city blocks, and he didn't want to have to battle the express-ways. Dennis lived for on-time scheduling, for feeling reassured as the hands ticked each moment on a clock, as time was a commodity that needed constant monitoring. My newly promoted work life revolved around scheduling events for multiple clients with simul-taneous deadlines, so we were in sync on this one.

Not exactly suburbia, but we found a tan brick house on the city's north side where old trees canopied the street, grass grew in small but adequate patches in a front yard, and there was more of a backyard than one would expect within city limits. Luckily, the house didn't need much work as the basics of roof, gutters, and paint were in excellent shape. Four steps up to a covered porch, through the screen door, and don't forget to let it slam shut, you're inside a front room that is narrow and L-shaped, leading into the dining room. The walls are colored of the earth in a sandy tan, and in a gentle sky blue. Linney would approve. A go-around to the kitchen, and you meet brightness, white, soft gray, and pebble taupe. I had an outdoor landscape with the summer scents of cut grass and flowering shrubs surrounding me. Who said this was city living? Standing in the middle of our new home reminded me of the familiarity of my girlhood home, and having the security of a soft place to fall. I couldn't have been happier.

We were only in the new house for a couple of weeks when Ma called to ask me to come over and have a look at a few keepsakes from the wedding that she had packed in a box. Since I hadn't seen Ma and Dad since the wedding, I was eager for a visit.

"Deb, you look great," she told me. "Married life agrees with you. C'mon over. Let's sit at the table."

She, too, looked good, fit and happy, as she always looks, dressed in slender-fitting tan slacks and a white sweater with navy trim.

Sitting with Ma at the kitchen table brought back memories of the time when no one would sit alone for long, as someone would always join. I think about it now, how important it is to come to the table and to be with family. You belonged, and you never felt alone.

"I got you something. It's not much, but I wanted you to have a piece of a good foundation to start your married life. And just a piece, because you will begin to fill in the rest," she said, pushing a flat box within my reach.

"Ma, I don't need anything."

I unwrapped the glossy white paper, creased inside a white box that was heavy for its size. Inside was folded linen. I held it up and caught the morning light through the weave, then laid it down to feel the textured bumps.

"It looks like . . . a tablecloth? A linen tablecloth in creamy white. It's absolutely beautiful, but I . . ."

"I picked this just for you because it is you. Linen is strong and durable. It's smooth and fluid, a bit crisp all around, just like you! After you've set up your dining table in your new home, cover the table in linen, as your new place to be, your home, where your husband and stepson will join you. There is nothing like coming to the table in security, a place where all of you belong."

"I don't know what to say. It's perfect, Ma. I love it and will proudly spread it out on my dining room table, and when I do, I will think of you, always."

It was the end of our first week in our new home, and with the furnishings between us, we managed to put a household together. I looked forward to sitting down to dinner with Dennis at the ends of our days. It was a set time that was understood between us to commit to honesty and to friendship. Our time was a commodity that needed to be gently handled, and creating a place to come together was an exercise in marital maintenance. His hours at the agency were sporadic, depending on if he was pitching new business or developing new creative for an old client. But the one thing I could count on was sitting with him at the table with no distractions.

I thought about how we spent our days, with nothing but interruptions—phone calls, voice mails, meetings. We were called upon to make decisions in an instant, and we hoped we'd made the best ones. It became a balancing act when you thought you were giving 100 percent in all directions but second-guessed at how you couldn't possibly be at full attention when you were spread thin. I got my training early. When I was young, Ma repeatedly told me, in her own delicate way, "Pay attention," when I appeared to be absorbed in something and the girls were running too amok for Ma's liking. I learned to switch my attention when the situation called for it, and to focus.

I never gave much consideration to preparing a table for a meal. I suppose it's because, as a single person, I'd find a seat in my condo anywhere, on the couch, on the floor, or to stand while eating. It was mindless, a necessary task that filled up time and often went unplanned with little consideration. Things changed after having someone in your life; it was all about planning and consideration.

It was time for us to come to the table, for me to create a special place to eat, to savor a repast together. I had Ma's linen tablecloth folded on the buffet, ready to be unveiled. Ceremoniously, I grabbed the corners of the fabric and flattened it out on the table. When I ran my hands steadily over the folds, I was reminded that the bumps and rough spots of the day would be smoothed out when coming here. Running a hand over the cloth was like magic, when what was previously there would be gone. I placed three small pots of herbs— sage, rosemary, and thyme—in a larger container made of birch wood. They were reminders of their meanings of wisdom, remembrance, courage, and strength, and the herbs offered complementary fragrances when we ate savory dishes.

Charlie started first grade, and my schedule became more flexible. I was able to work, at my discretion, from home, at the office, and at on-site events. We had Charlie every other weekend and on a weekday or two, depending on his mother's schedule. I'd pick him up midday after school, and our neighbor Ophelia, a sweet old Greek woman usually dressed in a floral housecoat with a cross at her throat, came over to watch him if I needed help.

Dennis's jazz group, the Hubbard Street Quintet, was playing small venues in the city neighborhoods. His bookings took him away some evenings, beginning Thursday night and running until Sunday night. At first, I thought if he was happy, that was all that mattered, though our time together was being sacrificed. Sure, I knew there'd be sacrifices in a marriage, but the idea of giving anything up for a greater good was something I had to get used to. If we didn't have Charlie on a Friday or Saturday night, I'd go and watch Dennis at wherever he was playing. But after a few years, I wasn't feeling so great about it. Call it jealousy; he appeared more passionate about those drums and notes than about lying next to me in bed. I let it go and decided not to see him play as often.

✥ Linney ✥

The older I got, the more wanderlust pumped through my veins. I thought about a trip the family took out West when I was in high school that started me on my way to finding a job at the farm and then on to Magnolia's doors.

Dad had business in San Diego that summer, and he thought of taking us to a surprise place nearby, somewhere in the desert. He wouldn't tell us where we were going, other than to say that each of us would find something exciting.

Clouds of dirt kicked up behind us as Dad steered the station wagon into an open landscape that was brown below the horizon and a tannish-blue blanket above it. There was not a green growing thing anywhere. We pulled up to a rustic log cabin, the visitor center, where white arrows posted on large wooden barrels marked the directions. Kids ran in circles, their laughter and screams piercing the air, and I felt it was a good sign that if everyone looked happy, then I would be, too.

The Dowling women stood in a circle outside the car, wondering where we were and what we were being called to do. Dad was the last out of the car. "C'mon, girls, we've got digging to do. Time for an excavation," he said, giggling as if he were one of the girls. He handed each of us a brochure. "Dig your own quartz and crystal," the headline read.

This was an outdoors with blistering sun and dry desert like I had never experienced. Kids unclutched their hands to show one another chunks of color in pink cotton candy, emerald, and turquoise, some with two, others with three colors clustered in their palms. What the earth held was special, kept in her composition since the day she was created. I went into the cabin to learn more about minerals, gemstones, and crystals. Large pictures and posters covered the bare walls like wallpaper. I walked out, understanding how energy from their vibrations transferred to you, and you'd feel a free flow of it throughout your body. But what bothered me was the idea of taking from it. Who were we to take from something that wasn't ours?

Sitting in the car on the ride home, I opened my hand and studied the crystals—they were alive and energetic, refracting light and color, their sharp edges contrasted with smooth finishes—and then I wrapped my fingers around them, squeezing them tight. I didn't see them as something that didn't belong to us, but rather as tools to connect our conscious thoughts with our bodies, as if to say, "Here, I've got something that will help you." I understood what Ma had told us about how everything is connected.

That morning when we pulled out of the garage, who knew that it would not be the only home I would know, but that there also was a larger, all-encompassing one? Connecting through chunks of monochromatic color from the earth meant planting deep roots and establishing home.

Unlike Deb, who preferred to spend her free time sequestered in her bedroom reading books about business and marketing, or Rose, who studied entertainment magazines and local theater guides, I spent my free time outdoors. Open spaces were magical and invisible, offering fresh air and a meeting with Mother Nature, to be with her in spirit, mind, and body.

I'm not sure if Bridget is going to be in today, so I leave my house earlier to get started at Magnolia.

As I always do first thing in the morning, I take a broom to the shop floor. Busy hands open my mind to planning the day ahead. I glance out the window and see a familiar face coming up the walkway. I set down my broom and hurry to open the door.

"Brian? Brian Kennedy? I haven't seen you since I started working here. And now, you must be . . . in college?" I smile in recognition of him. Once an inquisitive young boy with strawberry-blond hair, now he is a brown-haired, muscular young man.

"Yeah, it's me. My mom sent me here. I'm supposed to pick something up for her?"

"Yes, I do have something for her. C'mon inside."

"My mom said each time she needs a special something, she always looks here first and finds it," he says, stopping in the middle of the floor and glancing around. "I remember being here when I was little. Bridget would take us around to the side, and she'd spot butterflies in the garden, and I'd try to catch them. Just like those chipmunks, they were too quick for me to ever catch. But I tried."

I step away to the hall closet and rummage through a pile of deliveries to find his mother's box.

"All great memories that carry us through. Nothing has changed," I say, walking to him and handing him the box. "Maybe a little weedier out over there and more home accessories in here, but we're still the Magnolia from years ago that you and your mom remember. And we will stay that way as long as we can."

The phone rings.

"Sorry . . . I need to go. Good luck at school this semester." I give him a wave. "And come back and see us again soon."

I pick up the phone.

"Magnolia, this is Linney."

"Is this Miss Linney Dowling?" I don't recognize the voice that is speaking slowly.

"Yes."

"Do you know Bridget McMahon?"

"Yes, she's my employer. Who is this, please?"

I think it's Mr. Leone, again, asking if Bridget has considered his offer to buy Magnolia, but it's not. I have never heard this voice before; it sounds official, formal, and I lean up against the wall.

"Miss Dowling, this is Mr. Hughes. I've been taking care of Miss McMahon for a few weeks now, and I'm afraid I have some bad news."

"Mr. Hughes? Taking care of . . . ?" Bridget has never mentioned that she needed care. I stiffen. I'm offended that she doesn't feel close enough to confide in me about any caretaker. After all, we're supposed to be family, and family share things that happen to them.

"Miss McMahon has fallen ill and is in the hospital. She has asked me not to call you as she believes she will be home in a jiffy. But I think differently."

And I recoil in fear, my posture slipping. I find support in a chair tucked under the checkout desk.

"I'll be right over . . ."

". . . no, she doesn't want you to close Magnolia to see her. You can't close Magnolia, Miss Dowling, no matter what." His voice pleads, as if it is Bridget talking and not a stranger who knows nothing about her and Magnolia.

I will do exactly as Bridget has always done. I'll take care of Magnolia as I've been doing, until she's back on her feet.

"Okay. I'll honor her wishes. You did the right thing, Mr. Hughes, by letting me know. How is she really, though?"

"She's not well, not very well at all."

I hang up the phone. I am torn between defying her wishes, closing the shop and rushing to see her, or remaining here, restless, until I hear again from Mr. Hughes. I can only think that I am forced to tell Bridget now about Mr. Leone and his offer, as it can't wait any longer; I owe her that.

I close the shop early, as I have good reason, and dash to the hospital.

I search for her room, walking tentatively on the hospital floor's linoleum buffed to a yellowy shine, reflecting an aura of gray artificial light. A disturbing low buzz echoes from the ceiling fixtures, making anyone who walks these halls uneasy. I reach her room and knock gently. Peeking inside, her large bed fills most of the room, with one end table and a chair pocketed in a corner. Small black screens mounted on skinny poles behind her bed blink and beep in red, green, and yellow.

Her head turns to the shadow in the doorway, her eyes squinting to see who is there.

"Linney, is that you? Come closer." She waves me over.

I stand beside her bed where the gray fluorescent light mounted on the wall behind her casts a dull brightness, changing her red hair to dull copper. She doesn't look like Bridget. Her face . . . her body . . . look heavy as if she's succumbed . . . to something. This is all wrong, her, here, where she doesn't belong, not looking like herself. I shake my head and my chilled body to rid myself of the contradictory image.

"I didn't want you to close Magnolia to come see me," Bridget says in a weak voice, her once vivid blue eyes now sleepy.

"It's okay; it'll happen now and then." I lean closer and ask her softly, "What happened, Bridget? Did you fall or something?"

"Oh, I felt a little dizzy this morning when clipping flowers in the gardens. Now, did Brian pick up his mother's box?" She deflects my concerns, turning to my responsibilities at Magnolia.

"Yes, he did, but . . . please don't worry. I've got it all covered." I wave my hand to clear any anxiety she may be feeling.

"I know you do, darlin'. I depend on you; you know that, right? And so does Magnolia. You two were meant for each other."

Her words carry weight, and I have a sense of urgency to tell her about Mr. Leone and his offer, despite needing an explanation about what is going on with her.

"Bridget, I have to tell you something." I slide a chair close to her bed, sit, then glance at the clock on the wall above me. Only a few minutes have passed. Time has slowed.

"And I should have talked to you about this a few weeks ago, but with all the fixes to the shop on your mind and your concerns about the finances, I thought . . ." I slide to the edge of my seat and shift my feet to firmly plant them on the ground.

"God, Linney, spit it out."

"A man came to the shop. He liked Magnolia . . . very much," I tell her in a soft, calm voice to prevent her from getting upset. "He looked at it in concentration, walking around the grounds." I hold my words as I am afraid to tell her. "He . . . wants to buy Magnolia."

"Buy Magnolia? I don't think so." Bridget's expression perks up as she pushes herself with her strong arms to sit up. "Who is he, and why would anyone want to buy that old shop?"

"Says he's part of an investment group. They want to develop the property."

"No way. No one is touching my property and turning it into something it's not supposed to be." Her voice is defiant, her eyes alert. Pink comes to her sallow cheeks.

"I thought you should know, to at least have an option. You should think about it. After you get better, take the money and—"

"Do what? What the hell am I going to do, Linney? Retire?" Her voice is raspy and dry.

"I didn't mean to upset you. But think about it, Bridget. It might be an answer to a lot of your worries." I reach on her tray table for a small plastic cup to offer her water, bending the straw for her to take a sip. "I'll let him know I talked to you about this."

I leave the conversation there and sit with her for a short time, listening to the clock tick away the minutes.

It's just small talk after that: the gardens, the warming weather, her favorite nurse. In a few moments, she leans back and dozes. I watch her, a woman who knows so much, who has experienced life as I want to, who has made me feel I belong somewhere. We've been there for each other, with Magnolia in the middle for us to embrace. Will Bridget bounce back to her old self, bossing me and running Magnolia? Will I still have Magnolia?

I give her shoulder a light squeeze before leaving the room.

ᘒᘒ᠁ Margaret ᠁ᘓᘓ

The Fourth of July will soon be here, and I busy myself in the kitchen, filling a tray of chocolate chip cookie treats and iced teas.

"It seems the older the girls get, the more their personalities develop," I tell Joe on the back porch, walking carefully so as not to spill when setting down the tray between us. I sink into my chair, next to his. Clouds have raced in, and the winds have switched. A summer storm must be coming our way.

"And I'm not sure that's a good thing," I add, looking at him slumped in his chair. His eyes are shut, but I can tell his ears are open and tuned in, much like Jingles when she hears us crack open an egg, her favorite disturbance of all.

"You're lucky you didn't hear that conversation in the kitchen that Father's Day afternoon. Each throwing darts from all angles."

Joe cracks off a piece of cookie and pops it into his mouth. Jingles perks up from her repose next to Joe and nuzzles his knee for a piece. "It's a good thing, Margaret. They've come into their own, something you've taught them to do. Now, don't go blaming them for being who they are," he says, munching.

Joe's right. They're strong and resilient, and though they're not all happy at the same time, I like to believe they find what they're looking for when they see the willow tree.

Debra, my oldest, was always in a hurry from the get-go. As a baby, she was in a hurry to eat, in a hurry to crawl, then to walk. I'd hold her plump little hand, and we'd walk back and forth along the narrow sidewalk of step pads next to the house. When the sidewalk ended, she'd turn around and head in the other direction. Up and down we'd go, like a big person would pace. And that's exactly how she runs her life now. "Always in a hurry, as if she's late getting somewhere," Joe adds. I don't fault her. She wouldn't have gotten to where she is now unless she pushed ahead. Deb is versatile, adapting to any challenge that comes her way. She is strong, like the piece of linen I gave her before she married Dennis. She's a treasure, for sure, as the oldest and my right-hand gal, helping when her sisters were young.

And then Rose came. Not a fussy baby. She was a quiet thing who followed me with her wide eyes, watching me while I chased her sister. Just happy . . . to be. As she grew into quite the young lady, her long dark hair and slender arms were in constant motion as her fawn legs glided across a room. She was always a mover—no wonder she became the traveler of the family. "Had to see the world and to meet those who lived in it, as if she couldn't get enough of what was out there," Joe says.

When Rose moved back home after college, there was a focus in her eyes like a hawk's from above on a mouse below. Only I think she felt like the mouse that was going to be plucked by the hawk. Looking for theater work in the city was challenge enough, and so was living a long commute away from it all. "This is only for a short while, Ma, until I can find a place to get started." She got started, all right, with Julian. I don't think that was her idea of getting a place somewhere, but he was at the right place and right time, and so was she to get into the front door of a theater, and two weeks later, into an apartment with him in the city. But he wasn't able to offer Rose what she needed—a sense of belonging somewhere and not necessarily to someone, not yet anyway.

Linney grew up with a sort of earthiness I could only see as coming from Joe. She's a tree hugger for sure and has lived as close to God's earth as possible, growing her own vegetables, eating all those plants, and thriving on that narrow mat, moving her flexible body in every direction imaginable. Never much of a shoe hoarder, unlike Deb with her black pump collection, Linney is a barefoot walker, even in winter when she can get away with it, feeling the organic cotton rugs underfoot. She claims rubbing her feet on the cotton is comforting because of its softness and insulating fabric. I say it looks as if she's trying to calm anxiety by invoking the very earth God put her on. I can understand why Charlotte calls her the organic titanic, and they think I don't know. But I say cotton can wrinkle and lose its shape. How her sisters would tease her, as if her qualities were signs of weakness. But cotton can shrink, especially in high heat, and Linney has been in a heated situation or two.

Three girls, and I thought I was done, but then came Charlotte, a surprise, five years later. What a nervous little thing she was. Her nerves were like her head of hair, short and frazzled. Playing with it through middle school, running her slender fingers through a curl to wind it around her index finger, was a way to soothe her uncomfortable self. I'm sorry to say that, because of Charlotte's young age and being the last Dowling, she would be a caretaker of Joe and me when we got older. Her sisters were too occupied with finding their own places. Charlotte was resigned to having her place close to Birchwood Court and to her mother and dad. I tried to encourage her to go out and find what she is meant to be, like her sisters, but she would have none of it. Maybe that was the problem; she wasn't like her sisters. Her insecurities mounting with sibling criticism, she chose to remain close to me and her dad. Her sense of security depended on this normalcy of familiarity. This was her home, her place, despite her sisters telling her where that should be.

I hoped that our children learned what is home from where Joe and I settled. We tried to teach them that home is many things, not only the house they grew up in but also where their hearts are and their thoughts. Despite the girls comparing themselves to one another while growing up, each one would have to find her own sense of belonging.

Sometimes we set out for a path in life where our navigation can be precarious, with hairpin turns, downward slopes, and up-hill battles. I remember when Joe and I took a trip to Italy. We went to Cinque Terre, to a town called Monterosso. We set out one morning after a buffet breakfast of eggs, croissants, meats, and cheeses to hike the steep terraces. The path was narrow and full of bumps, which was unsettling to our feet. We did rest from time to time, succumbing to terraced vineyards, harbors, and coastline views like no other, before resuming. And such is life, knotted with turns, stops, starts, and views that make one excited to be alive.

July

❧ Margaret ❧

July is in the middle of a lot of things. The sun feels highest in the sky with the heat turned up, and the gardens peak in growth, with nights taking their time to dim the daylight hours. And being in the middle of what's going on with my kids figures to be their ways of finding their settling places. Deb seems to be working out some rough spots with Dennis; and Rose has moved on to a new place—I can't keep up with her schedule; from recently talking to Linney on the phone, I've learned she is very concerned about Bridget's health and the health of Magnolia; and Charlotte, well, never appears to be afflicted with any life disturbances. As for myself, I can't say I'm in the middle of anything, but just trying to find a peace I know is sure to come.

Joe catches me one afternoon, sitting on a tree stump in the shade next to the driveway.

"What the hell ya doing down there, Margaret? You're usually on your knees, not on your bum."

"I . . . don't know. I felt a little shaky is all. Must be overheated."

"Well, don't just sit there like a bump on a log. Go inside, cool off, get some water. C'mon now, let me help you inside."

He has such a way with words, doesn't he? But more times than not now, I am feeling like a bump, rough and uncomfortable.

I go inside, where the cool linoleum under my feet brings immediate relief. I take off my gardening hat, pour a glass of lemonade, and sit at the kitchen table. I admire the view from here. That's why we bought this house. The backyard, deep in landscape with moss greens and fire-engine reds and deep purples and golden yellows, is inspirational this time of year. There was always plenty of room for badminton, and though Joe grumbled when untangling a knotted net, by the time he had gotten it pitched, we lost our interest. But he left it up anyway, and sure enough, we made our way out there to start a game. And we did leave room in a back corner for a tetherball pole. Linney would be out there, slapping the ball round and round, making it swing in all angles until it was all tied up, and then it would unwind, and she would start all over. Linney's persistence and enjoyment with a simple task is shown in her work at Magnolia. I think of Rose, practicing her ballet as she pliéd through the sprinklers. "Quit your theatrics, and just run through it, Rose," Deb would yell. With maples and oaks and a lone willow offering umbrellas of shade, the trees also gave us in autumn lustrous leaf piles. It was difficult to name the colors, as they weren't one or the other but rather a mix, when the sun started to withdraw from their healthy green. When the temperatures started dropping and winter made herself known with freezing temperatures, the girls would bug Joe about when he was going to flood the backyard. He'd never announce when he was going to start the ice-skating rink, but the wood planks leaning against the shed and the garden hose coiled inside the shed's doors were good indications he was ready. And when we least expected it, we'd hear water running through pipes. We'd run to the kitchen sliding door to watch the water slowly fill inside the wood outline. "Not a skate on there until there's a good solid freeze," Dad would demand, with a pointed finger in each of our faces.

After a while, the winter-wonderland spirit would grow tired, and we couldn't wait for spring. We'd monitor the temperature, a gauge set in a squirrel's tail, leaning out from the kitchen window above the sink. At night before bed, and first thing in the morning, Linney was usually the one to report the temperature: "Peanut says it's thirty degrees. It's below freezing." She gave the squirrel this name as if it were a friend, always ready and willing to help when she needed something; in this case, the temperature outside. She told Dad with the utmost confidence because the facts don't lie; they were going to get her a skating rink. Deb couldn't have cared less about our excitement as she preferred ice-skating in the park with adults, not children.

At the first signs of winter's surrender, we anticipated the spring and flower-planting season and used the time to plan our landscaping. "Daisies," Linney would call out. And Rose would always want one more rosebush in honor of her namesake. Deb and Charlotte opted out. "Char, you help with the planting anyway. That's your contribution," Deb would say. I was worried Charlotte would feel that her planting and any other contribution defined her place in the family. "Go ahead, pick out something that makes you happy, just for you," I'd tell her at the nursery when it was just she and I. Charlotte would agonize over what to choose. And then she'd settle on a skinny, frail-looking, and unidentifiable green thing, believing she'd nurture it into something bigger and stronger.

Summer vacations, always planned and executed by Joe, were times that forced the girls' personalities to take shape. One time, Joe had to turn off, somewhere on our way to the upper peninsula of Michigan. He pulled out a map and laid it on the car's hood, then tipped his cap back on his head. With a crumpled brow and a pointed index finger, he drew a line where we needed to be. Deb was the first out of the car, nudging close to her dad, grabbing the pencil from his hand and marking with an "X" where we were. Rose stayed in the car and watched the drama play out. Linney jumped out, performing her Sun A Salutations to uncramp her limbs. "C'mon, Ma, let's get out, stretch our legs. I'll see if Dad needs help." Charlotte, always the caregiver. We'd be back on the road in no time with Joe in the driver's seat, eyes fixed on the horizon as if he was envisioning the line he drew earlier on the map.

And before we knew it, school was starting in the fall. I think Deb was prepared before we went on vacation, with her books and notebooks stacked on her desk as if ready for an important meeting. Rose wasn't much of a planner, and Linney made sure her school outfits and footwear were comfortable while providing pocket spaces to house her crystals. Charlotte never liked school, so we usually didn't discuss the preparation when she was around. It would only make her nervous.

I think about the year's cycle and how it's defined by color, temperature, and the seasons, synonymous with the things we do during those months. Each cycle is well defined and memorable. I can't tell you when we lost the rosebushes to disease or to a winter when it was too warm to keep the skating rink frozen, as it all moves forward as expected. I think it's true, whoever said it, that the older you get, the faster time goes. And here are my girls, women now, who have the memories and the connections they've made to each season.

I usually make phone calls to the girls a couple of days before the Fourth as their official birthday invitations, but this time, Deb and Rose beat me to it. Deb calls to make sure all is in order and if she needs to do anything. And Rose simply says she's looking forward to having some of her birthday cake, with all those colorful confetti sprinkles on top. And I haven't heard from Linney. So, I decide to stop by the shop to see how things are going.

And how beautiful Magnolia looks! The courtyard and entrance are an image of a French country house, with white hydrangeas, lavender, and red rose blooms creating a Monet landscape. Ceramic and clay pots of different sizes fit together like pieces of a puzzle. I'm glad I get there early before Linney's regulars stop in. I peek in the door's window and see her on the floor, crouched next to a box. She is unwrapping new candles and holders that are swaddled in brown paper. I swing open the door to the notes of the chimes, and Dottie waves a tail as busy as her nose. Her howl in greeting is interrupted by Linney's call.

"Ma, what a surprise!"

Linney, wearing sandals, a long denim skirt, and a sleeveless white linen top, looks up from a full box of discarded paper wrapping. Her long, honey hair gets tangled in the crystals hanging on a chain around her neck. She rises to her feet, and walks to the door, holding out her arms to me.

"You didn't forget about the Fourth, did you?" I ask.

"Wouldn't miss it."

Linney locks onto my face as if I have leftover breakfast on my chin.

"Ma, have you been feeling okay lately?"

"Yes, a little tired, but Charlotte comes around when she can, and . . . has Rose been talking to you? She asked me that same question."

"We just want to make sure you're doing okay."

"I'm fine. Now, I've got a birthday bash to plan, and you've got a shop to run. I'll see you in a couple of days."

I twirl and wave goodbye before shutting the door behind me.

I am forever grateful to Bridget for giving Linney her place to be, for being a role model in owning and running a business and living a best, true life. One might think I would be jealous; on the contrary. Bridget has given Linney permission to have her own identity and to be the person she wants to be, unlike the feeling I think she had at home, where Deb's demands to be more and to do more were always in Linney's head. It was difficult for the girls, especially for Linney, to find connections that had meaning. Her vegetarian ways and her organic, simple lifestyle were her way of setting herself apart from her sisters, of being unique.

I get in the car with party preparations on my mind, and I can't move. I am confused about what to do next. Foot on the gas? Steer? Turn the ignition? But there is no key in it. I shut my eyes and concentrate, breathe deeply . . . one, two, three breaths, like Linney tells Charlotte if she suddenly isn't feeling well. I need Bridget to take care of my Linney. After a respite, it all comes back, and I'm on my way home.

Before tackling that birthday cake when I get home, I shut my eyes and rest for just a few minutes and don't notice Joe walk in dressed in khaki pants and a white polo shirt. He startles me out of a slump.

"Margaret, you alright? How long you been back?"

"Not long. Now, if you'll excuse me, I've got a cake to make." Joe delays leaving the room to give me a once-over. With effort, I stand and pull an apron from the back of the chair over my head, swing the ties around my waist, and give them a good yank. I turn to the other side of the counter, grab mixing bowls from the upper cupboard, and take out measuring cups from the drawers. After a concentrated effort to focus on what I'm about to do, I begin to make their cake.

Smelling good and chocolaty, I cool the cakes out of the oven on twin racks on the counter and give each top a gentle push with an index finger to test doneness. I sit awhile on the back porch, taking in a life of trees and birds and popping flower buds as my reward where I am reminded of how interconnected we are and dependent on each other to thrive.

"Mind if I join you?" Joe says. He looks as if he's just awakened from a nap—his eyes are as clear as his complexion.

"Please do." I wave an open hand to his chair. "We need to stop every now and then and observe, Joe. Time is running fast, and I think we're missing a whole lot. And I don't want to miss anything." I look at him, and I can tell he's got something on his mind. It's how he tightens his lips and squints his eyes, as if he's bitten into a sour grape.

"Margaret, the doctor bills. They're coming in." He leans over the armrest, closer to me. "I know something is going on, and I waited for you to tell me when you thought it was the right time, but I've been watching you, and I know you're not right." Joe swings his chair around and sits in front of me until our knees touch. I drop my head.

"I know I've been putting off telling you," I say, talking to the tops of my thinning thighs, "since I found out about my uninvited brain dweller." I tap my head—well, give it a good slap is more like it, as if to tell it, "Bad, bad, you're very bad."

"It's my brain, Joe. There's a growth that shouldn't be there, and there's nothing they can do about it." I shake my head in resignation; my shoulders curl, and I feel so very small.

"But, Margaret, why didn't you tell me sooner? The doctor appointments . . . Charlotte." Joe raises his voice.

"Please don't be upset with me. I just couldn't." I begin to cry, and Joe takes my hands in his. "Telling you about it would have made it so . . . real. You'd fuss and treat me so . . . differently, keeping me reined in close, as if I'd shatter when left to going about my usual business."

"I'm so, so sorry, Margaret." Tears slip through his blinking eyes. "You've taken care of all of us. Now it's my turn to care for you. I want to make each day the best it can be." His voice is weak and trails softly.

We find each other with our eyes; his twinkly in tears, mine dry, void. I am unable to blink. He kisses me.

"It's got to be on my terms, Joe. No coddling, no keeping me from planting out in the yard or making dinner for the girls. I want to be able to do what I can, when I can, for as long as I can."

"Understood. I'm there for you whenever you need me."

He wipes his damp face and runny nose on his shirtsleeve, then grabs my shoulders in an embrace. I feel his strong arms around my weakening frame; I'm succumbing to a fight where I must concede. But I know Joe is strong, no matter the task he is up against, and I am reminded of his strength now, the same strength he showed in taking care of our girls when they were little, when I needed a break and felt as if I just couldn't.

I am resigned to my prognosis; I have accepted the inevitable. Joe and I have always been a team, operating in balance as we've shared the good and the bad. And telling Joe of this very bad has lifted my burden as I no longer have to be a team of one.

We say nothing for a moment or two, as if to refocus on the present moment and not what has yet to come.

"The willow is looking good this summer, Joe. How its wispy branches tell us which way a breeze is blowing, or if it isn't. And there's no place I'd rather be than right here with you, right now."

"And this is exactly where I'm supposed to be," Joe says.

It's the morning of our party, a time to celebrate, and I am feeling particularly energetic, relieved my illness is out in the open with

Joe. He works in the yard with such a sense of urgency to pull weeds, turn soil, and deadhead spent blossoms that I worry he won't have enough left in him to enjoy our family time. I step outside and greet brightness, a cacophony of birds, and flowers opening their sweetness. The air is still as if in waiting for us to join in.

"Margaret, you just gonna stand there, or will you eventually make yourself useful?" Joe says, sneaking up on me and giving me a squeeze and a kiss.

"Apparently, you don't see that I'm always making myself useful." I give his rear an affectionate slap with the kitchen towel.

He moves closer and hugs me in a way that is new—as if he is desperate to steal just one more embrace while he can. I wonder what Joe will do when I'm not around.

Once, when Rose was in her last year of high school, we went into the city, choosing the sunniest of days, when the city was a symphony of sounds in a rhythm that somehow all worked like any good timepiece keeping time. We visited the Art Institute on Michigan Avenue and walked north all the way to Huron, stopping for lunch off Michigan Avenue on St. Clair, then moving on to the Palmer House for late afternoon tea.

Witnessing the vibrancy of the teal lake dotted with triangles of whitecaps and sails, the architectural wonders of skyscrapers, and the smart-looking business folks swiftly weaving through the whirl of local and tourist pedestrian traffic gave me a sense of livelihood and purpose. I spent the day feeling a freedom I hadn't experienced in a long time. Actually, I didn't remember ever feeling that way before. I got home well after dinner.

"What a day you two had! You couldn't have gotten lost because Rose was with you," Joe said when I walked into the house. "Did you give any thought to dinner?"

I hadn't planned on fixing a dinner, and I also knew he wasn't going to fix anything for himself. But I knew Joe expected me to make a meal.

Will Joe be able to take care of himself after I'm gone?

⊱ Charlotte ⊰

I go to the house earlier in the morning before all the others to help prepare for the day. It's already a steamer with high humidity. Threatening dark skies are plump with rain clouds, and I am hopeful for clearing and cooler breezes by the afternoon. When I slip through the back gate, Ma is yanking on the garden hose to straighten the rubber pretzel before watering a bed of white and yellow daisy heads and popping fuchsia bee balm growing like fringe around the porch. I notice how the colors in the garden have exploded, and the flash of a smile on Ma's face at how agreeable it all looks to her. She lives in the moment.

"You're gonna drown 'em, dear. Not so much water there, okay? Move along with the watering," Dad yells from the threshold of the sliding doors. "Hello there, Char." He waves a short-sleeved arm.

Ma puts down the hose and turns off the water by the gate. Together we meander arm-in-arm into the kitchen. Sprinkles of dampness shine on her forehead. Her footing is deliberate.

"C'mon, let's sit before the others arrive," Ma tells me, getting comfortable in her chair at the table. I dally around the counter and fix us glasses of iced tea.

"You know, Ma, I always found it suspicious that all my sisters' birthdays were in the summer until I overheard you talking to Dad about how it was planned that way," I said, joining her at the table with the teas. Ma wanted our births to be in the summer so we could enjoy watching the budding lilacs, the willow tree's growth into adulthood, and the popping of rose blooms and asters and lilies. And then there's me, though not to be left out. I would enjoy my birthday celebration on my actual birthday in March.

I think Ma started this sister birthday party on the Fourth not only to bring us together, but also to relive memories. And that's what Ma is about. When my sisters and I are together, Ma unravels the memories in a way that provides a lesson to be learned. When we were young, the Fourth of July was a guaranteed eye-roller, as she'd bring out a couple of shoeboxes full of musty-scented photos of me and my sisters and previous Fourth day celebrations, then summon us to gather under the willow tree. We'd sit in a circle and watch Ma pull out carefully selected pictures, some more faded than others, pointing out the tree's growth in each photo and then likening it to our own. I think it was Ma's covert way of keeping us together somehow, without us losing the source of our connections that got us to where we are now.

"I was thinking back to when you girls were young . . ." She gazes outside, imagining our youth. "The vacations we took, the years spent nurturing the house, inside and out, making memories and connections that I hoped one day you'd still have. Do you remember when Deb got her job right out of college? Kinsey and Moore told her she had what it took, and she believed them, and that's why she got the job. She believed in herself and was determined to work there."

"I think it was the beginning of the end there. That's how she met Dennis, and she couldn't boss him around," I tell her.

Ma counters, "If it wasn't for Dennis, she wouldn't have the opportunity to be a mom."

I feel my face flush with agitation. And then I let it all out, like a popped balloon. I speak loudly, as if Ma is hard of hearing, and I sit up straighter.

"I know where you're going with this," I snap. "I'm sorry I'm turning thirty. I'm sorry I don't have a special someone in my life, let alone a boyfriend. I'm sorry my biological clock is ticking. I'm sorry I can't give you the grandkids you are hoping for, now and maybe not ever." In a single exhale, the words spring off my tongue like water from a spout.

Ma's chin drops, and her eyes widen.

"Charlotte, honey," she tells me, "you don't need to apologize . . . for any of it."

"Hey, kiddo," Dad says, sliding open the glass doors. "Oh, what a tight face. You alright?" He pulls up a chair next to mine.

I sit back in my seat and fold my arms, grab a loose curl, and wind it around my finger. Jingle looks up at me concerned. I pat his head and he lies down.

"Did you two ever think of not having kids? Did you think of getting a good job, Ma, doing something you were passionate about, and you, Dad, getting with a firm with promotional opportunities?"

"Times were different back then, Char," Dad explains. His quiet voice calms me. "We were young, and I had met your mother at work. She was the most efficient secretary in the pool—reliable and just good at it." Dad gives Ma's arm a squeeze and her eyes a smile. "My secretary got pregnant, and in those days, you left and didn't come back. Your mother filled in until I could get someone permanent. Only I didn't want someone else. I wanted your mother. Those days, secretaries dated men in their workplaces, and though everyone turned the other way, everyone knew it. But eventually, she, too, had to leave. And we got married."

"Mom, you had to leave?"

Ma gives Dad a glare, like he needs to cut himself from the narration. But it doesn't work.

"I did. Deb made me do it," Ma says.

"What? You were . . . pregnant with Deb before you got married?"

"I was crazy in love with your dad, and, well, my job didn't seem that important anymore. What your dad and I were about to have was my sole job."

"But, Dad, were you ready? I mean, a baby, marriage, a new house. So much, so fast."

"I don't know if I was ready, or if your mother was, but these things happen. I couldn't imagine not having your mother by my side or not having all you perfectly special girls in my life."

Dad gets up, pulls up his jeans, gives Ma a kiss and me a squeeze of the shoulder before leaving the kitchen.

"I'm going out to the yard and wait for the rest of you," he tells us.

Ma waits a minute in thought before continuing. "Char, you know your dad's secretary, the one who had to leave? She was the one he wanted to be with. He didn't know she was pregnant; she never told him. She was an unhappily married woman, pregnant with her first child, and I think your father thought he could make her happy. But she left the company and didn't return. He understood it was for the best. For a long time, I thought of myself as second-best. I certainly wasn't his first choice. We started dating, and I got pregnant. But I have no regrets. Sometimes life happens in unsuspected, unpredictable ways." Her voice lowers. "And you'll keep it a secret for another very long time." She stares at me for a moment. I don't know whether she still has something to say to me or is waiting for me to respond. I study the flock of wrens and sparrows gathering on the feeder in the yard. "I know keeping my illness a secret was a lot to ask of you and now this one, too. You're my best confidante." This disclosure makes me feel special as Ma told me a secret of her past. "C'mon, outside you go. Help your dad with that table and the chairs." I give Ma a hug before meeting Dad outside in the backyard.

"Where are we going with it?" I call out to Dad. His denim pant hems are water-soaked as he puts down the garden hose, and his gray shirt is already darkened with sweat stains. It's not unusual for him to look like this after being at odds with hosing down the back-yard furniture.

"Don't ask, just do," Dad replies.

"Right over there, under the willow tree," Ma yells from the porch, pointing a finger.

Dad and I take each end of the wood table and move it to a cleared spot under the willow. The table is heavy, filled with stories and memories of previous years. Dad and I grab chairs and assemble them around the table.

"C'mon out, Margaret. Is this how you want it?" Dad shouts.

I have a good look at the empty scene and then envision us kids when we used to play games near that tree, running through thin, weepy branches that brushed our arms and the tops of our heads. We'd bat them away, only for them to return, tickling us. Then Ma would clap her hands, signaling that it was time to start the circle. I'd plop down in her lap, cradled in the middle of her crossed legs, as I was the smallest who could fit. Dad would be near, futzing with the ground, stomping out bumps and filling small divots made by digging squirrels. We always came back to that circle each year, and this time was no exception.

"Everything looks fine, dear," Ma tells us as she joins us under the willow.

"I remember we used to sit on the ground with you when we were younger," I tell her, as if she needs the memory and not I.

"Yes, we did, but now that we're older, it feels more appropriate to sit in chairs at a table."

I think this is for Ma's benefit. Getting down on the ground and staying there for any amount of time is too much for her now.

"Like I said, Char, just do," Dad says, bending to pull a few weeds that have shot up around the table.

I wonder how much Dad knows, if anything, about Ma's condition. I don't ask; I just do.

✤ Margaret ✤

I'm puttering in the kitchen, grabbing paper plates, Solo cups, and plastic utensils when I see Linney hurriedly making her way through the side gate of the backyard. I can tell something is on her mind by seeing her heavy steps and bent body as if on a mission. I meet her at the kitchen sliding door.

"I need to talk to you before the others get here," she whispers, taking a big step over the open door's threshold, nearly bumping me off balance. Her flaxen hair and cotton blouse are rumpled. She yanks on a sandal to keep it from falling off.

"Of coarse, dear. C'mon, let's sit. Looks like something serious is on your mind."

We sit close at the table where I notice shadows under her eyes, where usually there's nothing but clear serenity, like a starry night.

"Apparently, I have a new friend. A Mr. Leone stopped by Magnolia, well, actually it's been a while back now, and has also called a couple times. He wants to talk to Bridget because he is interested in buying Magnolia and developing it into an apartment building with retail shops. I stopped listening to him after he said 'develop.'"

I gasp and sit taller. First, I'm afraid for Bridget and Linney, and then I'm mad. How dare he! Can't he see how successful the shop is, a fixture of the neighborhood and an integral piece of the business community? Why would anyone want to mess with that?

"And dig up and throw away all the precious wildflowers and old trees? Trees . . . oh God, the Magnolia orchard." I'm horrified at the thought of anyone coming to level the land that has given so much.

"The investors see a good thing and think they'll have an even better thing when they get through with it," Joe adds from outside on the porch, wiping Jingle's dirty, wet paws.

"And whose side are you on?" I say and give Joe a hard stare. He and Jingle come inside and stand behind me. I feel Joe's hands on my shoulders, giving them a gentle rub, while Jingle sprawls at my feet.

"C'mon, you two," Linney says. "And that's not all. I had to tell Bridget, though . . . she's in the hospital. I don't know exactly what happened, but I had to see her, and I just hated telling her. It wasn't the time or place, but then, when would it have been?"

"What? Ill? But I don't understand. That's not the Bridget we know."

My head shakes in confusion.

"Bridget said no, right? Yelled it, I bet was more like it."

"Oh, yes. But Magnolia's bones are old. Her ceiling has a gape that needs closing, her cooling system no longer cools, and she needs new gutters and a roof—new paint, too. She's looking tired and needs a face-lift. And Bridget doesn't have that kind of money. Maybe I should tell her we really don't have a choice but to take his offer." Linney's shoulders sink.

Joe adds, sitting opposite me at the table, "When she's no longer the owner, the investors will have their say, so if you were thinking you and Bridget could still be running the place, despite new ownership, you should think again. They'll probably bring in their slick, high-powered salespeople with their degrees in sales and marketing. They'll think of how much added value they're bringing, but the last laugh will be on them, when no one will walk through Magnolia's doors. Loyal customers don't want to be cheated."

"Your dad has a point. What are you going to do, dear?"

Linney stands, pushes in her chair. "I'm going to enjoy today's party and not think about it for a while." She abruptly walks outside to wave hello to Charlotte, who is making her way through the backyard. I know this will continue to trouble Linney. After all, she must be wondering what will happen to her if she no longer has Magnolia.

As if on cue, I hear Rose and Deb announcing themselves from the front hall and making their way through the house and into the kitchen.

"Girls, happy birthday to you. A picture-perfect day. Dad ordered it specially for his best girls. Let's get ourselves outside," I say, my happiness in seeing them ushering them along.

When the girls were little, we'd go out to the backyard, and I'd tell them, "We're going on an adventure. Follow me." We'd take our time, roaming deep into the back where the willow was growing into its space as each year the girls grew older. I'd talk to them about trees, how they tell us many stories because of all the ones they've heard from people sitting beneath them, canopied in safety from their leafy branches, or standing and looking up to capture the light in greeting the tallest limbs. We can hear them speak, eavesdropping on the connections to one another.

As we make our way to the picnic table under the willow, I tell them, "If you listen closely, you can hear whispers of growth in your soul. This willow is special. It's a source of renewal and a symbol of protection. One of its strongest traits is its flexibility. Look at its branches and how they can bend and twist without snapping." I grab a handful of branches and give them a soft tug. "That's why I wanted a willow near, for each of you to remember that you have a place in this world, that you are connected to every living thing, and that no matter how torn or bent you may feel, you will never break. Be nothing except what you are. Then you will be home."

I have never been happier than in these moments, sharing

them with all who sit with me. In their grown faces are their triumphs and failures.

Life's uncertainties lead me to live now, in the moment. I can't predict where we will all be in life next year at this time. But one thing is for sure: we will have our memories.

ᷓᷓᷓ Rose ᷓᷓᷓ

My sisters and I meet in the kitchen, a cheery room today. The summer sun is already high and direct, highlighting a collage of old framed family photos on a wall above the antique sideboard. When we sit at the kitchen table, we are filled with family memories.

Deb, Linney, and Charlotte grab a lemonade; I carry a tray of salad plates, a mixed-berry fruit bowl, and place settings. We march outside, where the air is of summertime, warm and bright, with birdsong accompanying us and where we hear Dad announce, "They're all here, Margaret," as we create a trail of footprints in the green carpet. We acknowledge Dad's hard work tidying the landscape, at Ma's direction, no doubt. Ma is lying on the chaise under the willow's shade. I see how she has aged, looking weary, yet content. There is silence among my sisters, and their eyes are downcast. We know it is our mother, yet we don't know who this person is—thin hands with defined fingers, limp curls worn of their bounce, bright pink cheeks faded to water-colored hues. I am afraid I will forget how I really see her, wearing an apron with pictures of strawberries and pitchers of cream or plumes of lilac heads sewn into it, while her one hand grasps a mixing bowl and the other elegantly pushes curly brown wisps of hair from her face. The picture before me is its replacement. But she's all smiles, and the gleam in her eyes hasn't faded.

I put down the tray on the picnic table. Ma comes to her feet, and we take turns hugging and kissing, and greet Dad just the same.

"C'mon, girls, join me. Let's sit under the willow," Ma announces. We let her lead, keeping the slow pace.

My sisters and I select our spots as we did when we were little ones, with the youngest and oldest on either side of Ma. This time, I recognize that Ma is always there to fill in the space between the youngest and oldest, to close the only gap we have among us. We wait patiently, turning our heads to seek a cardinal singing and buzzy bees whirling among the bee balms. Dad sits on a bench behind Ma, on the periphery, always watching out, while giving us the seats near our Ma. There is an immediate awkward silence.

"Your father took his clippers to this old willow's branches but left them long enough so we could hide underneath them," Ma says, looking to the tree's top. She then studies our faces with bright eyes, as if seeing us for the first time.

My stomach turns. I've never been this nervous about anything before, not even for an opening night, but the longer we sit here, it is as if Ma is setting the stage to talk to us about something. I glance at my sisters, from one concerned look and furrowed brow to another. Slivers of blue sky begin to break through the clouds. It's like a curtain is rising, and a show is about to start.

Ma begins, "I remember when this willow tree was slow to take shape. It hadn't filled out enough for Deb and me to sit under it to be cooled and tickled by its branches. It didn't matter. We leaned against its young trunk, touching its bark, and connecting to it in spirit. I wanted this space, where we are sitting here, to be our place of security and comfort. Over the years, I wanted to give you memories of home and what it means to be here. Now that you're all grown, I hope you'll remember when we sat here together, and believe that you will always find your place to be."

The more she talks about finding our places to be in this world now that we're grown and have settled into our lives, the sadder she looks. There is a tone of finality in her voice, as if she is talking more about herself, and not some tree whose long branches could get sucked into the lawn mower at any time, forever altering our place under its canopy.

Dad remains seated with his arms folded on his chest and a most solemn face. A stream of questions runs through my mind: *Are they divorcing? Are they selling the house? Is someone sick?*

I look at Deb; her brow wrinkles, as if she is trying to organize each of Ma's sentences to read between the lines. And just as I glance at Linney, she reaches out to touch Ma's hands, as if passing on good karma. And then I see Charlotte, looking impatient and antsy, as if wanting Ma to speed things up or to keep herself from interrupting. I do what I do best: I simply observe and watch it play out.

⁓ Debra ⁓

Starting when Charlie was nine or ten, he wanted into his dad's world. Charlie would run from the house to the garage, attracted by the beat of the drums or the trumpet's sliding notes. From the front window, I would see Charlie standing with a split body—half of it inside and the other half outside the garage's side door, hesitant to step over the threshold, uninvited, into a territory that wasn't his. But his dad and his dad's music were what he had an ear for, and my telling him not to bother his dad and to come back into the house was futile.

"Do you ever notice Charlie standing by the garage door, watching you?" I asked Dennis one night while we stood together at the kitchen sink, rinsing dinner dishes.

"Sometimes."

"Don't you ever stop and tell him to come closer, pull up a chair for him, share your music with him?"

"No. I'm usually working on a new set. I'm working, ya know?" Dennis wiped his wet hands on his jeans and went into the dining room to collect the remaining silverware and wineglasses from the table.

"He came to me after school and said his friend Jason had joined the band at school. I didn't know there was one, did you?"

"No."

He loaded the utensils and glassware into the dishwasher.

"I asked him what instrument he'd want to play if he were to join the band. He said the trumpet. He admitted he'd like to join the band, too. I asked him if he talked to you about it, and he told me no, and that you're too busy for stuff like that.

"Dennis . . . are you listening?" I stopped rinsing, then pushed hard on the faucet's handle to turn off the water. "Your son wants your attention so much that he wants to find something in common with you, so he can be with his dad. And that's through music."

"He can play whatever instrument he'd like. Just let me know what he needs, okay?"

He finished loading the dishwasher and flipped up its door then hurriedly moved along the counter, gathering sheet music and folders.

"Just let you know? I don't think so." I slapped a wet dishtowel on the counter. "Why don't *you* go talk to him and find out?"

I didn't like what was happening among the three of us. It was like we had scattered to our own corners, Dennis into the garage, Charlie into a guest bedroom that was no longer for guests but for him, and me to the table, never meeting anywhere in the middle. The dining room table had been our middle, a safety zone, a secure place to drop harbored animosities or insecurities. I must have been the only one who remembered this.

"Yeah, okay, I will. Just as soon as I can." His words trailed him as he walked out the door to the garage.

This was the start of an uneasiness I couldn't put out of my mind, and that also begged for Dennis's attention.

One afternoon, I was seated at the dining room table, doing K&M work. "I'm reminding you it's next Sunday when Charlie leaves for camp. He must be there by noon," I said quickly as Dennis passed me through the room to the kitchen.

"I can't take him on Sunday. I've got to be at City Tavern," Dennis yelled while opening, then banging shut cabinets and drawers.

I walked to the doorway. "He can get there anytime as long as it's before noon. You'll have plenty of time to get to your event."

"It's cutting it close . . ." Dennis stuffed a granola bar, a wrapped bagel and peanut butter, and a bottle of water in his bag, along with binders of sheet music and storyboards from work.

"Dennis, can we talk? Sit down, please. Here, at the table, remember?" I said, resuming my seat.

"But I—"

"Now. Please."

I sat first. Dennis made his way to the table, then stopped before sitting. He ran his hands through his hair, grasped the bag's straps from his shoulder and tossed it against the wall.

"So, what's up?" Dennis said, elbows on the table and leaning in, looking at me as if I wanted to ask him a quick something—can we go to the beach this afternoon? How about ice cream after dinner?

"You're disconnected. You're not here as often. And you appear preoccupied, like you're somewhere else," I blurted. I grazed the linen cloth with my fingers as if trying to wipe last night's crumbs off the table.

He leaned back and folded his arms on his chest. His jaw tightened.

"Have you noticed how Charlie seems to be giving up? When he's here, he's withdrawn. You two don't go to the Skokie Lagoons anymore and kayak. You used to go in the fall."

"C'mon, he's a teenager." He chuckled. "He doesn't want to be with his old man anymore."

I didn't like Dennis's jovial comment, as if I were the silly one who failed to see his age as an excuse for Charlie's out-of-character behavior.

"Is that your excuse, or have you given him a chance to tell you by asking him to do something together?"

He drummed his fingers on the table as if tapping keys on a piano.

"Talk to Carrie," I directed him. "You two need to work this out. Charlie needs you both, now more than ever. He's trying to discover the person he's meant to be, and he has to know his dad is there."

"I'll see what I can do." And with that empty, emotionless declaration, he grabbed his bag, slung it over his shoulder, and left the room.

My hand continued to move along the linen's textured weave. I noticed its tight fibers woven after their good spinning. Perhaps I was trying to wake the settled threads, calling upon the cloth's healing properties. I hoped this natural insulator would keep disharmony away from us, and from the table.

A few months later, Charlie's school principal called. She wanted to meet with his parents as soon as possible. I called Dennis right away and didn't care that he was in rehearsal for a big event at The Drake hotel downtown. I needed him to know that the school was sounding an alarm about his child.

"Miss Cantrell called. She tried calling Carrie at work, but I guess she's at a business conference, and she tried to get you but couldn't reach you either. That left me. She needs to see Charlie's parents as soon as possible," I told him.

"What's up? Did she say why?"

"No, she didn't. Just the fact that she needs to see his parents should say it all, don't you think?" I put a hand on my hip and cocked my head.

"I'm not sure what to do. I can't leave here." In the background, I could hear a muffled voice, clanging glasses, and a woman's laughter.

"Oh, for God's sake, Dennis, figure it out. Call his principal, call his mother, DO SOMETHING."

I slammed down the phone.

I let Charlie down. He must have been thinking how unimportant he was, if neither of his parents were coming to get him. I felt I was Charlie's only remaining rescuer.

Anger and resentment percolated. I was the default parent, the good gal: don't worry, Deb will handle it. I lost patience because Dennis didn't jump on the principal's request. Instead, Dennis did what he thought was more important.

I read Dennis and his behavior just fine. Charlie no longer appeared as a priority to him, not like he used to be.

⚶⚶⚶ Rose ⚶⚶⚶

After moving forward and settling in my new place, I didn't look back to consider if I was missing out on auditions I believed I could clinch. I gave myself a pat on the back for developing the thick skin and perseverance necessary to becoming an actor, to get my name out on the theater streets of Chicago. And now I was making a name for myself in a different way, as a writer, creating a new audience who would read my words in print. I put onto the page as much personality, drama, and character as I did onstage.

I took a year to be a tourist in my own state and surrounding states. Travels to Wisconsin, Indiana, Michigan, and downstate Illinois kept my freelance reporting well informed with seasonal news, attractions, and my commentaries. Phone calls and letters from readers were encouragement. However, my ability to promptly reply was slipping, and I had this funny feeling that I should put this task ahead of anything else. As I fingered through my unopened mail stack from four days ago, I noticed a larger envelope with *Abroad* magazine for a return address. At first, I thought it a solicitation for a subscription, but I was curious, as I had long admired this magazine's work and hoped someday I could contribute to it. I sliced open the envelope and read the cover letter. "We recently read your work in *Chicago Today* and *Chicago Magazine*, and we'd be interested in you joining our team as a staff writer," they said. "We need someone who can commit to traveling for weeks at a time, away from their family and spouses," they told me. I called them right away and shouted, "Yes, I can do that!" into the phone. I was ready to leave the local writing scene to join a top-rated, well-circulated travel magazine.

In a year, I became head of the Midwest region, based in Chicago, traveling with a couple of writers from overseas locations. I didn't write about what to do when you're in Beijing, Amsterdam, or Munich, for example, but about my impressions of its people. No heavy stuff about politics and economics in this magazine. I immersed myself in Chinese, Dutch, and German culture, and living with a host family for a month at a time gave me insight. I couldn't wait to share my experiences in my article. I logged thousands of miles in three countries on two continents my first year.

I'd be lying if I told you I never got involved with anyone while I traveled to these magical places. I couldn't help but fall in love with the suspense of discovery in the unfamiliar and with the people who shared their familiar with me. It was a fantasy, living in another country and pretending to be one of them. I was an actor in a setting to be played out in daily scenes where I wasn't myself, but someone else who didn't need to play by any responsible rules, who could have fun and flirt and entice. My conviction of instant self-gratification and happiness came with not being committed to anyone or to any one place for too long. After all, Julian and I didn't last long. I realized that my romances were self-centered, and mine with him was no exception. As in my acting jobs, I knowingly declared relationships short-term as my self-discoveries and vagabond-like nature never settled. Keeping my relationships short-term had always been and continued to be my conviction.

Abroad's tenth anniversary double issue took me to Ireland, where I wrote an extensive piece. I lingered in mind and body, mesmerized by the landscape of sprawling emerald running parallel with craggy, deep blue cliffs, and sandy beaches of the enchanted Dingle Peninsula. When I had only a week remaining of a month-long visit, I stopped at Mulcahy Pottery to feed another artistic side. And there he was, a man who tested my conviction.

"Well, hello. Let me know if I can help you," he said in a gentle brogue, talking over door chimes. It was an open space, tidily arranged, with rows of long tables in beechwood and halogen lights hanging from shiny steel wires above them. An ashen gray wood floor and white walls made the showroom look modern rustic.

I noticed his height; he was not as tall as I would have expected from such a robust voice. My gaze went from a stack of blue-green dinner plates on a bench in front of me to his knees behind it, imprinted in worn denim, then to a beefy waist and loose-fitting shirt, stopping at a boyish face with sea-blue eyes.

"Yes . . . I will, thanks."

The floor squeaked as I walked toward him. We held our gazes, anticipating further conversation. He moved around the showroom as if we were dancing in the aisles, tangoing up and down among the displays and making sharp turns.

"I think I'm ready," I said. "I'd like that tea place setting, for six, and four of those mugs." I pointed to a table of black and tan pottery.

"Right away. Anything else?" he asked.

"Yes, may I show you?" I gestured with a wave of my hand and a "come this way" look in my eye.

I could feel him at my heels all the way to the corner, where the flowerpots were boldly displayed under warm lighting on horizontal shelves.

"Those. Top shelf, the ones on each of the ends."

"Excellent choice," he said, grabbing the gray candlestick lamps.

"That should do it . . . for now." I smiled.

He blushed, I think, and cast his glance to the floor.

"Follow me." He waved with a pointed finger to the front of shop.

"Certainly."

Trailing behind, I noticed his happy gait: he was lively on his toes as he bounced from one foot to the other, his sandy-haired curls bouncing, too. I tried to keep up, wanting to tell him I wasn't in a hurry.

"Shall I ship these to America?"

"Yes, please."

He handed me his business card. "If you need anything more or have any questions, please call."

I glanced at the card. Then at him.

"Michael Mulcahy," I said, slowly pronouncing his first, then last name. "Thanks for your help. You've been very attentive."

I thought a moment before speaking again, looking at his card and then up at him while he busily began wrapping each plate.

"Um, Mr. Mulcahy, I'm a travel writer for *Abroad* magazine, and I would love to acquaint myself with you and Mulcahy Pottery. The daylight hours are begging to be spent with a pint. What do you say, would you like to join me for one over some conversation?"

He stopped wrapping each piece in brown paper as if to ponder the question. Then he grinned, turning on a set of dimples and arching one eyebrow upward as if pleasantly surprised. Just when he thought a transaction was completed, it wasn't.

"Well, I . . . suppose . . ." He scratched his head. "I'd be stopping for one anyway on my way home."

He quickly finished packing the pottery in boxes and setting a shipping label aside.

"I'll just be a moment." He struck a faint bow. *He's so polite.*

While I browsed, waiting for him, he swiftly closed up, locking doors and stowing logbooks and folders into a cabinet below the desk. He was efficient, all right, working up darker pink in his cheeks and accelerated breathing.

"Clancy's Pub is up the street, 'round the bend. Let's get on with it. I'd love to hear more about America." He cheerily followed me out the front door after turning the double locks on them to close. The air was damp, with a chill that was invigorating.

Four doors downhill on cobblestones, he opened a small, weathered green door. Inside was a dark, snug pub with only a half dozen tables for four and about the same number of seats at the bar. Humidity fogged four small square windows. With a pint in each hand, Michael needed only two steps to get from bar to table.

"You say you work for a magazine?" He slid out a chair for me then shimmied into his chair, fitting snug between it and the gentleman seated behind him.

Michael quickly took exactly three swallows of Guinness, then, with his tongue, traced his brown foamy lips.

"I do. I travel and write articles about the places I visit and especially the people I meet. This is my first time to Ireland, and I'm delighted with the people here. Very special people, indeed." I took a more conservative sip.

I would be lying if I said I wasn't taking advantage of the evening's golden glow and the intimate setting to act as if I belonged. It felt familiar, as if I always knew this place, had been gone for a while, but now was back. How uncomplicated and forgiving it was here. And Michael seemed to be that way, too.

We ate steaming Irish stew from rustic bowls cupped in our hands and started another round of beer that Mr. Clancy produced from a hidden dumbwaiter, lit only by a dim light.

"I have only a week remaining here to finish up," I whispered, bowing my head regretfully.

"Then we'll have to make the best of it, won't we?" His eyes were eager and comforting. My smaller hands warmed when he took them into his generous palms.

We talked about our childhoods, where we grew up, and how we learned the value of home. We were catching up with one another as if we were old friends who hadn't seen each other in years.

It was well after midnight when Mr. Clancy came from around the bar, grabbed our empty pint glasses, and whispered something into Michael's ear.

"Best be getting on now," Michael said. I caught Mr. Clancy giving a wink to Michael as if in approval of his new lady-friend.

Outside, we folded into the quiet and the dark of night's sleep, strolling along narrow bumpy streets, shiny from a drizzly fog, for what felt like miles.

That night lasted into the dawning of a new day.

During my last week in Ireland, I toured the town of Tralee while Michael kept the shop open in the mornings. My eyes bounced from gaily painted shop storefronts to obscure pub entryways. I furiously made notes for what would be an outline of my piece for *Abroad*, talking to shopkeepers and their patrons; I didn't want to skip a beat of my experience. When not doing what we did separately, we met for lunch at Clancy's together, then took a drive to the countryside. Through rain, then sun, we held steady through high winds while winding up hills and hugging curves, through undisturbed vistas of brilliant green in contrast to the dull gunmetal gray of craggy rock. I oohed and aahed when overlooking dramatic drops from the road to yet another vista of ancient storytelling.

Michael pulled the Mini into a turnout. Our heads followed the movement of the angry surf and angles of the black cliffs.

"I have to go back . . . as much as I'd like to stay . . ."

"Then stay. Do whatever it is you need to do here. We can work it out. I've got space in the back, next to my studio. I can make it a writer's room, your room. It would be quiet there, with windows that look out to the pastures and wildflowers. We can create separately and then together. Please. Stay." He took my hand and held it tight.

He had a plan. The only plan I had was to finish the piece about the locals and small businesses in Ireland.

"I have to go back, Michael. I've been in Ireland for a month, and I need to finish this piece at the office. I'm sorry I met you at the end and not at the beginning of my stay."

I hated telling him this. I felt as if I were saying I needed to end this story, us, here, as we never really could be together.

After our deep sighs, he turned the car around, and we headed back to where we had started.

Back in Chicago, I admitted this was a difficult piece to write. I paged through my copious notes, some in sentences, others in just words that on paper made no sense but in my mind were clear memories. As much as I tried to distance myself from it, my voice read too personal with references to filtered light, flirtation, and romance "nestled in sweeping vistas." Writing about the Emerald Isle's lush greenery, endless hills, and well-known attractions for tourists was one thing, but I needed to remain objective with an overall look inside, to the people who thrived in Dublin, and to those who preferred the coastal enclaves. I didn't think I would have angled this piece in this way if I hadn't met Michael. Getting to know him was getting to know Ireland, its farming and Gaelic, singing along to Molly Malone, having a look at the Book of Kells. My editor said it was the best piece I had produced for the magazine. With Michael in my heart, the greens of Ireland's earth were more vibrant, and the sky vaster; it was what delighted me, and I transferred the emotion to the page. I hadn't felt like that since my beginnings when walking onstage in the theater to act.

After I completed my piece, I decided to return to Ireland.

Linney

The following week is Magnolia's open house for its summer sale. It is a tradition, like a block party, where neighborhood visitors come and help set up tables and bring with them homemade cookies, pies, and other sweet treats. We have a popcorn machine and cotton candy for the kids, a balloon-maker, and a magician, not just for little ones but for big kids, too. It's a day of celebration of summer's color, warm temperatures, and starry nights. It's also a day when we clear the shop; we sell out most of our inventory, providing space for fall merchandise.

Before the early evening falls to darkness, I acknowledge everyone who means so much to Magnolia and who has always supported the shop and Bridget.

"If I could have your attention, please," I shout, standing on a wooden chair near the firepit. Glowing lanterns surround the gathering in deep ember. Fireflies blink among a crowd of thirty loyal patrons who hush their voices and give me their attention.

"I want to thank you all so very much for being here. Bridget wishes she could be here, but unfortunately, she's not feeling well. She'll be happy to know that we've had a winning day, thanks to all of you. Successful, because we've connected with old friends, and made new ones, too. As you may see, we need some repairs for Magnolia's roof, and, well, other upgrades, too. Your support today will help toward those expenses. This place that Bridget started over thirty years ago was created with all of you in mind. You are a part of Magnolia as much as are Bridget and I."

A round of applause follows. I step off the chair and mingle with the guests. They linger until twilight, when the stars turn on their magic, and the guests saunter home.

I methodically start cleaning, moving tables and folding chairs inside, collecting spent napkins, plates, and cups, and stuffing them into a garbage bag. I do this unhurried, thinking of Bridget, and suddenly feel alone despite having spent the afternoon with our family, really. I slow time and pause in the courtyard outside Magnolia's front doors, like Bridget does before closing. She always said she could see Magnolia's insides and outsides from standing in one spot.

I am suddenly reminded to get back to business and ready a sales and inventory report. Sitting at Bridget's desk is a comfort knowing that her spirit is with us, and that Magnolia had a good day.

When I finish, I leave the papers on the office desk and turn the lights out on Magnolia to head for home.

Mr. Hughes calls me that night upon a request from Bridget, to let me know she is home from the hospital. "I'll be here for her, Miss Linney, to offer full-time care," he tells me.

"I don't understand. Full-time care?" I ask him. He avoids answering, telling me to have a nice evening and saying we'll talk more later.

Enough of finding out how Bridget is doing through Mr. Hughes. I call Bridget in the morning myself. I want to hear her voice. I want *her* to tell me everything will be alright, but it is *I* who needs to assure her. When she asks if the shop is doing okay and if the fans are working and the roof not leaking, I tell her not to worry and that all is well. I never do bring up Mr. Leone or ask her if she has spoken with him since she's been home. I figure telling her once is sufficient. She never did need reminders to do anything before, and this time is no exception.

One afternoon, later in the week, I stroll through Magnolia's inspiring grounds, refreshed from the sweet smells of wild grass and black-eyed Susans. I stop to follow a monarch's travels and catch a glimpse of paired bright yellow finches. With Dottie at my side, we take in Magnolia and are reminded of what a special place it is and has been. With a fresh vision and a desire to never let it go, I pull an empty canvas from a work corner in the back office and start to paint in watercolors a picture of Magnolia and the gardens, with the serpentine flagstone sidewalk leading to the front door. I turn the painting into a get-well card and ask all our loyal guests, her friends, to sign it. After accumulating signatures, I call Mr. Hughes to ask him when a good time is to drop it off.

"How thoughtful of you, Linney, but unfortunately, she doesn't want to see anyone. I would be happy to stop by the shop tomorrow to pick it up and give it to her."

Doesn't want to see anyone?

"I'm sorry to hear that. You would tell me, Mr. Hughes, if she isn't doing well, right?" I plead.

"She's enjoying her days and coming along nicely, up and walking in her gardens, a sure sign that she's tending to what matters to her. I can come around tomorrow morning to pick up the card. Would that be alright with you?"

After I agree and hang up, I sit awhile at the farmhouse table, feet digging deep into the cotton, where I search for resilience and strength. I put the poster-sized card in between two pieces of cardboard, wrap the board in brown paper, and draw a big bow in green, blue, and pink on one side. I lay it on the office desk for Mr. Hughes to pick up in the morning.

The next day's dawn awakens me and Dottie early. After a walk in the gardens with my best beagle, and moments of meditation and asanas, it's time to open Magnolia. As if on cue, strong scents of lemongrass and verbena are released with the opening of the front door. The humidity this July draws out lingering sweet fragrances, floating from inside Magnolia to the outside. I sit at the desk in the back room to look over the report one last time, before Mr. Hughes picks it and Bridget's get-well card up later this morning.

The gardens are at their peak of fullness and thick with color as the summer is well into her first month. I am so involved in thoughts of Mr. Leone's offer while sweeping the shop's floor that I don't notice Rose walking up the sidewalk. Her long black hair matches her all-black attire, from her shorts to her tank top to her sandals. By the looks of her, I wonder if she is preparing for a new role.

"You know, you can get a high school kid to do that kind of work for you," Rose says.

"I enjoy the work. And if I remember correctly, sweeping floors was one of your assigned chores when we were kids, yet I was the better sweeper," I tell her proudly. "Hello, by the way. What brings you here?"

"Visiting my sister, that's what I'm doing. I knew you'd be here this early, fixing and rearranging the goods."

"What's up?"

It's not a normal thing for Rose to visit me here. Her travels take her out of the country, and the last thing Rose wants to do is to travel more. "C'mon back, let's sit and have some tea."

"No coffee, huh?" Rose asks with a grin, as we make our way to the back office.

She settles at the table and watches me plug in a kettle on a counter next to a small sink. I pull two mugs and a couple of tea bags from a cupboard above.

"Funny, Rose. You know we don't drink coffee here," I remind her.

I plop a bag into each mug. While waiting for the button on the kettle to turn green, I join Rose at the table, kicking off my sandals and rooting my feet into the rug.

"So, where's the display of your stones and those crystal things? Don't you keep them out to remind you of what they do?" With a smirk on her face, she tilts her head while sprawled in a chair, limbs stretched out and hands folded on her belly.

"They lurk in hidden spaces, Rose, where the positive energy can strike any minute." I jump and wildly shake my open hands in her face to scare her. She rolls her eyes and does not flinch. "You didn't come here to check up on my stones and crystals. What's up?"

I rescue the boiling kettle and fill our mugs, then settle our steeping teas on the table.

"Have you talked to Ma recently?" Rose shifts and leans over the table. "When I talk to her on the phone, she sounds so tired. Her voice is kind of weak."

"No, I haven't. Did you call Charlotte? She sees Ma three days a week . . . not sure if you knew that," I say quietly. I take a sip of tea.

"I did know that and I'm not that unplugged. I'll call Charlotte and talk to her. Charlotte is able to see more of Ma than any of us." This, I reason, is to temper my guilt about not visiting Ma more often.

Rose surveys the other end of the room as if performing an inspection. I watch her eyes travel from a seating area of two stuffed chairs in evergreen and a handcrafted wood table between them, to pine shelving holding books, plants, and knickknacks, and stopping at pictures of landscapes on sand-colored walls.

"How about you, Linney? How are you doing? You seem to spend every waking moment in this place, tucked away, with quite a short commute home."

"I don't need to get out much. Everything I need is here."

"I can tell something is bothering you, and I don't think it's me being here."

I put down my mug. My face tightens with concern.

"A guy came here about a month ago. An investor who wants to buy Magnolia and develop it into something . . . the 'something' is not meant to be. I told Bridget about him and his offer when she was in the hospital . . . she's home now, by the way. She's had a lot on her mind about the shop and how much it's going to cost to repair all that needs fixing. She shared the books with me, something she's always kept private." I sip then stare at the bird feeder in the window. "I haven't seen her. Mr. Hughes, her caregiver, says she doesn't want to see anyone but tells me she's up and moving around."

"What are you going to do?"

"Not sure. If she does sell, I'm not sure where I would go or what I would do." I think a moment while staring outside at the prairie dotted with sunflowers, then look at her intently. "Yes, Rose, this shop is my life. I've made wonderful friendships. This is where I belong."

I feel the rug's braids under my bare feet, reminding me of where I am rooted and how the nature of our lives is circular. We start tightly knit, then go our separate ways to find who we are and to experience ourselves, and slowly, we start to return, with our wisdom leading to acceptance of each other.

The ringing phone on Bridget's desk startles me, as I am absorbed in my solitary routine of checking the closet's inventory and empty-ing it of boxes of new deliveries.

"Magnolia, this is Linney," I answer.

"Miss Dowling, this is Mr. Leone."

Not again.

"Yes?"

"I want to let you know I haven't heard from Magnolia's owner or from you about my offer. I'm eager to come to a settlement quickly, as my investors need a decision, one way or the other. I think we're in agreement that I've made an attractive offer, and I hope you communicated that to Magnolia's owner. Or maybe you didn't?" His voice is stronger and more efficient than the first time I met him.

"Mr. Leone, I did speak with the owner; however, she has been under the weather and not able to make such serious business deci-sions. I'm sure you can understand."

"Yes, I can. And I'm sorry to hear she is ill."

"Either she or I will get back to you when convenient."

"Fair enough. I'll speak with you soon . . . I hope."

Being reminded of his offer makes me want to cry. Here is the person who could destroy all that Bridget has made for herself and turn me away from my place to be. And then I get mad, about everything: Bridget's illness, the shop needing repairs, Mr. Leone's persistence, my home being in jeopardy. But when Bridget sees all the get-well wishes from those who love her and my report of the numbers from the summer sale, she'll bounce back and be ready to tell Mr. Leone herself just where he can go with his offer to buy Magnolia.

August

Debra

For a while, Dennis has either been away for work or for a gig, and I am back at my old, single ways of eating solo, standing up in the kitchen or sitting on an ottoman pulled up to watch the news on television. And now, after a long week, I'm glad we can come to the table. I am looking forward to having a well-prepared meal; I'm going all out in making pasta Bolognese from scratch, garlic toast, and a salad. I search for a bottle of red in the wine rack and find one that we have been keeping only for "special occasions." I think this is a special occasion, as I haven't seen my husband in over a week, let alone talked to him in more than a couple of words instead of whole paragraphs. The alone time has given me an opportunity to think about where we are together, or not. I'm ready to get real, and to be honest and talk about what's been on my mind.

"Feels like you've been gone longer than a week. I hate making dinner just for me. So glad you're back and we can sit and have a nice dinner . . . and talk, too." I shift dinner plates, silverware, and wineglasses to fit well together in front of us at the table. Dennis wiggles in his seat to get comfortable, then hurriedly dives into his salad, plucking away at lettuce leaves.

"Uh-huh. It was a busy week," he utters with a full mouth.

"Were you able to get done everything that you needed to?"

"Yep, that's about right."

I swallow a little of the red wine.

"How's work going? Have you been busy because of new pitches?"

"Yeah, working on a couple right now. Packaged goods—not too exciting, though."

So much for engaging conversation. He hangs over his plate, swiping a piece of bread through a puddle of sauce pooled on his plate, and then popping it into his mouth. I continue to work through my salad.

"So . . . what did Miss Cantrell say? You DID meet with her, right?" I look directly at him, but his attention remains on his plate.

While waiting for his response, I note the settings on the linen tablecloth, the intimacy of pairs—plates, wineglasses, dishes, candles, us. I have missed this. I am missing home.

"I did. Seems Charlie is getting a little physical with a few of the boys, probably because they look at him the wrong way." Dennis laughs with a mouthful, trying to make light of an obviously serious situation.

"Really? You can't possibly think that's the reason. Did you even ask him what got him so angry?" I fight to keep my voice calm, but I'm losing the battle.

"He didn't want to talk about it."

I drain the wine in my glass.

"Of course he didn't want to talk about it. He gave you the easy way out. But you must have talked about something besides school."

I sit straighter and stab the air with an open hand to punctuate my sentences.

"No, not really. He wanted to go home."

"Dennis, I'm gonna be honest here."

I put down my fork and fold my hands in front of me on the table as I usually do when starting off a business meeting. Only this is not business, but personal.

"I don't know what's going on. You don't include me in what's new at work, new pitched business, lost clients, your gigs, who you're playing for . . . and please don't tell me that I don't ask. I shouldn't have to ask. I would hope you still want to share your life with me." I search his face, but he is lost on my need for his attention. "Don't you?"

I'm ready for any answer. I want the truth.

"We're at the table here, Dennis. Remember when we first came to this table? We were open books with each other, narrating our days and our thoughts as we turned the pages and learned more of us together. What happened to that?"

"I don't know, Deb. It's different now." He cleans the last bits of sauce from his plate. "There's a lot going on. Charlie is finding his independence, and Carrie's business has taken off, so he's with us more often. And I'm working new creative all the time, yet I need to be out on my own, making music, too. Don't worry so much. We'll talk more tonight, okay?"

Dennis wads up his napkin, scoops up his plate and wineglass, goes into the kitchen, and drops it all into the sink. I'm left alone, just as I have felt when I've sat here lately. He never did answer my question. He, Carrie, and Charlie appear not to be sharing their lives, so maybe he's not interested in sharing his life with me anymore.

Or maybe it's a midlife crisis. Either way, I am defeated. I can't do this anymore. I've been fighting for Dennis, for my marriage, and for Charlie, but a one-lane road isn't allowing for two-way traffic.

The night's darkness distracts me. Ma used to tell us to look to the backyard if we ever needed answers about something we might be confused about, or just didn't know what to think. I think of our marriage and question if we are moving in opposite directions. Am I really thinking of ending it? I always thought you had to earn your way out of a marriage. The soft excuses he brought up at dinner don't end a lifetime commitment; they don't hold up. And walking away while throwing up my hands in defeat would be a soft, easy exit. Getting out is not meant to be easy. And just because it's been difficult with Dennis lately, I quickly reason, that doesn't mean I've earned my way out. "Look for details in colors and shapes and movement. Notice how everything takes time to get to where it needs to be, for a bud to become a flower, for a caterpillar to become a butterfly. You may not have your answers as quickly as you'd like, but you'll get them, all in due time," Ma would say. My answers are covered in darkness; I just can't see them.

"Deb, ya there? Hello?" Crystal asks. She is my assistant, my confidante, drinking buddy, pizza-sharing terrific friend. We met in the ladies' room on my first day at K&M, when she rescued me from a wardrobe malfunction: a flagrant run in my hose.

"You're calling to go to lunch, right?" she says.

"Yes," I mumble into the phone, calling her at her desk on the other side of the floor.

"Now?"

"Yes."

Haggardy's isn't much of a life-giving place, but a dismal corner local establishment. White-collar workers sit hunched and talk quietly, appearing unsure of themselves. The pub is among a line of similar bars and eateries in an intersection marked by apartment buildings filled with singles, young and old. A Haggardy regular could slip inside and hash it out with Brad, who wears a white apron that fits taut around his middle-aged middle, and who never hesitates to tell any drinker he's had a few too many. Well-used stools line up along the shellacked dark wood bar, where many elbows rest and fists pound for another. Crystal and I have been known to hit the bar rail here on a Friday night when Dennis was out playing somewhere with the quintet.

"Sooo," she begins. "Charlie?"

"No. Dennis." We sit at a round table, tightly fit into a corner where, apparently, they ran out of overhead lighting—a spot usually taken by a pair who want to go unseen. "I wonder if I've been wrong to think the happily ever after is indeed ever after. He's changed. He's stopped being connected to Charlie, and in a sense, to me. I feel like a roommate more than his wife, lover, and best friend."

"What are you going to do—that is, if there's something that needs to be done?"

"I love him, Crys. My heart still skips a beat when he walks into a room, and that's not because he's angered me in one way or another. I tried to sit and talk to him at the table the other night, but he wasn't very conversational."

I recite my troubles and halt when I catch a glimpse of myself in the smudged mirror on the wall behind Brad. My image looks out of focus. Kind of like how I feel.

"I'll have the chicken sandwich, mayo, lettuce, tomato, and gimme some slaw with that on the side, and I'll have a Chardonnay, only your best," I order as I take off my jacket.

"Ditto," Crystal says shyly, batting her false black eyelashes at the waiter. He has a moment with her. It's her hazel eyes, enhanced with "dusty seas" blue eye shadow that looks more like polluted seas, that make him stare.

"I never get the whole 'connection' thing with people in the way they talk about. Sure, I connect to a lot of people," she says with a wink and a hearty snort.

I bust a laugh. "I know you do . . . have done. And I'm not talking in *that* way. I mean plugging into each other's lives, becoming a part of it, feeling as if you belong with one another."

Brad returns quickly, balancing a pair of luncheon plates on the crook of a bent arm.

"Well, you can count on me to connect with you, Deb. We've known each other since our first days at K&M. We belong, like, ya know, mayo, lettuce, and tomato on a chicken sandwich," she says, holding up half a sandwich. "Everything can't be perfect all the time, Deb. You're going to have some growing pains in a marriage. And not all pains are red flags that mean you need to run at the very feeling of discomfort."

"I'm glad we became friends, Crystal. It's comforting to know you can talk openly to a woman friend about work and personal stressors . . . and not be judged."

"I'd never judge you, Deb. You're an awesome businesswoman, wife, and mother."

"I'm used to being able to multitask well. And right now, one of my tasks as wife is not going so well."

"You're analyzing things too much. Take your time. There's no rush to come to any conclusion."

Thoughts in my head whirl as I stir the coleslaw in the tiny plastic cup.

"So, what's up for you next? Any business travels?" she asks.

"As a matter of fact, I'm going to San Francisco."

"Well, there you have it." She slaps one hand on the table then lifts the other with an empty wineglass, signaling to Brad she'll have another. "It'll be an opportunity to take some time away from thoughts and home."

"When I return, maybe a few of those bumps I'm feeling will have smoothed out."

The timing to get away couldn't be any better. On the day before I leave, I sit at the dining room table and go through my to-do list. I call Carrie and tell her I will be out of town should she need me when Dennis is unreachable. After I hang up, I realize what I said—if Dennis isn't available for his son. I am struck with a feeling of being responsible for Charlie. But I remind myself it's not about me. Or is it?

Thursday morning, and we are well into check-in at the Stanford Court on Nob Hill. Stationed adjacent to the hotel lobby, I expect about eighty people from Compass Marketing Group. Their head office is in the Bay Area, and apparently Chicago wants a change of scenery. I focus on having a successful experience, assuring CMG will be well taken care of by K&M, and remember that I took on this client after the previous account manager was fired for a conflict of interest; he got caught loving a board member just a little too much.

Though this isn't a good personal time for me and Dennis, I recognize my resilience in adversity, and I have a renewed outlook. I believe things will work out. Through the hotel lobby's window, a smile in the foamy clouds looks down at me.

The lines grow longer here in the west corner, where designated tables are dressed in black linen with CMG's logo splashed in gold on the front panel. I'm standing next to one while shuffling papers, crossing off names, and handing out file folders of more important papers, when I hear a woman's voice carry over the bustle of a condensed group of people. I need to put a face with the familiar voice, and when I look up, I see it is Tracey, long-lost number four of the college sisterhood foursome. I scoot to her to say hello.

"Tracey? My God, you're still with CMG?"

She steps back from my attempted embrace, putting distance between us.

"Oh, Deb, so good to see you. I . . . you . . . you're in the San Francisco office of CMG?"

"No, I'm running the conference. I'm an account director for Kinsey and Moore. I planned this event."

"Oh . . . I . . ." Tracey looks around the room as if searching for someone. Her red ringlets and large gold hoop earrings get caught up in the straps of her tote bag that slip from her shoulders. She nervously adjusts them.

"Can you make lunch today?" I ask her, reaching out to help her grab her sliding tote.

"Um, sure, that'll be good. Not sure when, though." She pays more attention to sorting file folders and loose papers popping out from that tote bag than she does to me.

"Great! I'll find you on the register and call you. It was great to run into you, and I'm looking forward to catching up. I got to run."

Given we haven't seen each other for months, Tracey was a woman of few words, flustered and surprised, like I caught her stealing a cookie from the jar. I reason her surprise and the awkward moment was because we are out of context, in a different place.

The first day of any event feels long, but when everyone is checked in and well on their way, the schedule plays out quickly. I never do see Tracey at any of the meetings this morning to ask her about lunch, but I am certain she will be at the cocktail party tonight, as liquor and live music will be involved.

I gladly go to my room after the party and fall into a chair, bending over to slip off my Garolinis. They've never failed me before, as they've become my good-luck pumps; they make my feet happy and my face smile. I realize I forgot about Tracey, but, then again, I don't remember seeing her. I look at the time and calculate what time it is in Chicago. Dennis would be at the Brass Note tonight, and I wonder if he is thinking of me as I am thinking of him. I didn't leave him with a particularly warm embrace, though I could have at least tried, reached out, let him know that I would miss him.

I want to hear his voice, talk to him for a few minutes. I call, but he doesn't answer. Then I call Tammy, the wife of one of Dennis's band members.

"Hey, Tam, it's Deb. How's it going over there? I know it's a couple hours later, and I hope the boys are delivering it tonight in front of a warm crowd."

"Deb, Dennis isn't playing tonight. Something about having to be with Charlie because you were out of town."

"Is something wrong with Charlie? Did he say?"

"No, he didn't say anything more."

"Thanks, Tammy. I'll be sure to drop in next time they're play-ing."

What was so wrong with Charlie that Dennis had to stay home?

I hang up and quickly call Dennis, and when he doesn't answer, I leave an urgent message for him to call me. I think of the what-ifs. What if Charlie was in an accident? What if he was so sick that he had to go to the hospital? In the meantime, I work on tomorrow's agenda, or mindlessly reshuffle papers is more like it. I call Dennis about an hour later. Still no answer. It is getting late, and I have an early morning setup. I try to sleep but my thoughts keep me awake, how Dennis and I used to stay connected with daily phone calls when either one of us was out of town. And now he doesn't even return my calls.

The next two days are a blur. The hours escape me, and I never do hear from him. I call him again before getting on a chartered bus to Napa. Again, no answer. But Carrie returns my call from a message I left her earlier.

"Deb, Charlie's fine. Not to worry. He's with me while Dennis is out of town. Hope all is well with you."

I stare at the receiver as if I can't believe what I'm hearing. Dennis? Out of town? He never told me he was going out of town. Not answering his phone? Not returning my calls? I shake the questions from my mind and refocus; can't let my unanswered questions steal my concentration from my job. It will be a long day of wine tours and tastings, a lengthy bus ride, and hoping for tomorrow's closing day to arrive quickly so I can return home.

We are an excited group of twenty arriving at Domaine Carneros winery, a French-inspired chateau. The formal gardens and stunning vistas require us to stop and stare at the panoramic view while enjoying sparkling wine. While the others find seats on the patio, I sit at a quiet corner bistro table inside where it is cool and quiet. As I flip pages of the itinerary to check the day's remaining agenda, I remember to look for Tracey's name on the attendance sheet. I run my finger down the list, but I don't see her name. Surely, she will be at the breakfast on Sunday, our final meeting to close the event.

While on the bus on our way back to the hotel, my thoughts return to home. Why hasn't Dennis called me? Why is he unreachable?

It is the last day of the event. During the morning's breakfast meeting, I take a quick scan of each table in the room during the final speaker's closing remarks. But I don't see Tracey. I slip out to the front desk.

"Has a Tracey McMahon checked out?" I ask the concierge. He is busily juggling blinking phone lines and flipping pages of scribbled notes.

"Let me check." He pulls a sheet from a stack and runs a short finger down the long rows of typed names. "Um, I'm sorry, but her name isn't here." He doesn't look up but answers a ringing phone.

"Ohh . . . okay."

I sigh. She was here to check in—maybe she never did? But why? I reason she had to fly back to Chicago, maybe because of illness or she needed to return to her office. I return to the meeting and take a lone seat by the door, distracted by the unexplained, until the meeting has ended.

I hurry to my room and pack quickly to catch an earlier flight home. During the hours-long flight, I think about how I will approach a conversation that needs to happen with Dennis. We must get away, just the two of us, to a place that once brought us happiness, to where we were at home with each other, familiar, secure. I miss home with my husband.

Rose

I arrived in Ireland late in the evening and talking to Michael was the only thing on my mind. I traced with my finger the indented marks in the sticky wood table at Clancy's Pub, stalling for time because I didn't know how to tell him the real reason I came back —to break it off with him. If I could write it in invisible ink among the scratches, I'd have a clearer picture and a start to the conver-sation.

"I want you to stay this time," Michael said, taking my hands in his and leaning farther over the table. "I've crafted a writing space, just for you, in that empty nook you told me I should do something with. I know you'll like it, with your favorite view outside of the sheep grazing in the grassy open, and whatever a writer could want inside. I would be near, pottering in my workshop while you could be writing at your desk. We'd have our lives separate, and then to-gether." His voice quieted. "I love you, Rose."

"Michael, this sounds . . . perfect. I could leave Chicago, my job, my sisters, and be at a new home here . . . no more long distance. But . . . I don't know . . ." I evaded his stare.

Problem was, I did know. It wouldn't work because I didn't want to make it work. I shook my head to hold strong and not succumb to the possibility that maybe it could work out.

"Michael, I've thought about what this would mean, moving away from my home and family to be with you . . . and I can't do it . . . I have my job."

"Then I'll move to America." He slapped the table as if that was the answer and all was settled. "I can find space for a workshop. I'm sure there are many opportunities for an Irishman and his pottery in Chicago. You would have your job, and we could be together. We can make this . . ."

". . . but your home is here. It's in your blood, your DNA. Ire-land is in your heart. You work the land into your pottery, and to leave here would be to leave your work and your shop."

My eyes shifted from his to the etchings in the table. I wondered what stories of long past were embedded in the markings. Declara-tions of love or bitter breakups? Unrequited love or reunions?

"Rose, why *did* you come back? You seem confused, telling me as if you need convincing that you have a job and a family you can't leave, yet you come back to see me?"

I contemplated my response. I wanted to tell him that it was over, that I wasn't moving to Ireland, but I just couldn't say the words.

"C'mon, let's get out of here and take a walk." He stood, then extended an open hand.

I held it tight while we treaded a lush, green field, following the streetlights to Mulberry Street knit tightly with dark pubs and colored storefronts, and a bumpy cobblestone street to show you the way. Now would be a good time to tell him that I had to break it off for good. But the hours ran away from us as we lingered to catch a glimpse of the evening's stars glistening against an ebony sky, with nothing but murmurs of occasional conversation about the locals and our work.

I couldn't tell you what we did during those few days that followed. We neither talked about the past nor the future, but lived in the present we shared, dawdling. Avoidance was easy. Confrontation was difficult. The stance I had taken when I left home was weakening.

We woke up midday and started not with lunch, but with a usual morning routine of hot coffee, bacon, fried eggs, and soda bread to share at a small square wood table, nestled in the corner of a quaint pale yellow-and-white kitchen.

Our knees touched underneath the table and green pottery plates tapped each other atop it. I separated lacy curtains to peer out the window where fog was settling like a wet blanket. Neither a hummingbird nor a butterfly could be found.

"This is my last day here. And we haven't talked about us all week," I said, sipping a steaming cup of coffee. But, I reasoned, I had a day. I had time.

"Don't you see? It can all work here. We've proven it to each other these past few days." His voice was eager and searching.

I pushed my plate aside. I thought him very convincing.

"Oh, my Rose . . . we've got the day. Let's make it a good one."

We cleared the breakfast remnants and readied for an afternoon that had promise with clearing skies.

It felt like there were more minutes to the day than bits of conversation. Streetlamps dimly lit the narrow alley, summoning forth a sunset. We stopped under a lone darkened lamp.

"I . . . I'm sorry . . . this has all gotten so complicated," he said, shaking his head. "We've managed to find ourselves unhappy now, haven't we?" I stiffened when he pulled me closer. He took a step back and replaced the cold of my hands with the warmth of his coat pockets. "But it's not about my understanding, but about your happiness. I can't bear for you to be unhappy. You have to do what you must, Rose. You have to find your own Ireland in your heart."

Perhaps I was waiting for him first, to tell me this, before I was the one forced to break away. By him letting me go, I could be free of guilt, and my conscience would be forever cleared.

While thirty thousand feet in the air, heading home, I thought about my goodbye at the airport. It wasn't much of one because I ran. I looked the other way without saying much of anything but just a goodbye.

I felt suspended in cloud formations of soft white and dreamy blue as the plane parted their images. Saying I loved him would be making a commitment, and I didn't want one, not to him or to anyone.

I called Marcie the following week.

"Let me see if I get this. You go to Ireland to see him, to break up with him in person, but you really don't talk much because you're confused, because he's trying hard to get you to stay. So, because of your inability to break up in person, you break up with him on the telephone, which you never wanted to do in the first place? Talk about being noncommittal, Rose."

"Yeah, well, I guess I did. I called him to let him know I got home okay, and, well, the conversation shifted beyond how we were doing. I told him I wasn't coming back, ever. And that's the reality."

"You were going to break it off when you went out there, and then you chickened out. You two flirted and had fun, picking up where you left off, without thinking about what was next. You avoided the what's-next part, Rose."

"And what *is* next for me?"

"How about that book I suggested you write? Put all that writing you did for the magazine to good use in a different way. Write a book about your experiences, kind of like a memoir. You've been to places and met people most of us see only in pictures in travel magazines. Hell, you ARE the travel magazine. How about revealing the professional Rose and the personal Rose, and talk about how men and women around the world really live, together? Only change your name and those of your boyfriends to avoid libel, slander, and any possible litigation," Marcie said with a chuckle.

"I'm not sure I've got a whole book's worth of something to say."

"I bet you do. It'll be a commitment, Rose. You'll have to commit to staying here, at home, to going back in time, to bringing up memories you don't want to. It'll be different writing for you. You'd be writing with a purpose this time, not about how you found the best-looking Parisian men in Saint-Germain-des-Prés among the best creperies."

"What's my purpose, Marcie? Do people even know their purposes? Is that something that keeps people up at night, wondering if they'll ever know what they're supposed to be doing in life?"

Marcie's purpose was to be a wife and mom. Was my purpose to show that women don't have to apologize for their choice to not be like her? Was it to help empower women, to tell them that they truly have choices, personally and professionally?

I remembered when I sat with Marcie at the block party. I didn't understand the life that was in front of me. Moms and dads chased their kids; adults were unable to have an uninterrupted conversation of their own. Moms nurtured fallen kids; dads handled crises of broken bikes, sparring twelve-year-olds, and barbecue grills that wouldn't light. How did husbands and wives, moms and dads know what to do, being dependent on one another and their kids dependent on them? Their identities were defined, and they knew their places to be; they were committed. Was that their purpose? Family? That wasn't for me. The only commitment I'd ever known was to acting, and being someone else.

That night, I wrote in my journal about my experiences writing for the magazine. I spilled my actions onto paper, running pencil tips dull and filling white space quickly, recalling the places I'd been, my assignments, and the people I'd met. From the looks of my crammed timeline, I had moved from one place to another, from one man to another. The theater made me comfortable because I knew who I was supposed to be with and where I was supposed to be. But the show would end, and the actors would leave. I, too, had to move on. I saw myself as a drifter, moving from one place to another without sticking around.

And that was the professional me. And maybe that was the personal me, too, back when I met Julian, a rescuer of me and my wandering tendencies. Julian had made the uncomfortable comfortable. But I had made it not work by declaring that my interests had changed. Our common goals of acting kept us together in the short term, as pillars that held each other up; we worked together to get to the same places. I never did think of him, us, in the long term. The show was going to end. The professional me and the personal me worked the same threads in the same cloth. But there were always new threads to be woven into the pattern, to work together, in balance, to become a new, stronger piece of cloth.

Writing a first draft of a book was a triumph over my addiction to noncommitment. It was an act of sticking with the uncomfortable to get to a rewarding place after putting in the hard work. I put the manuscript into a drawer, not because I wanted to hide revealed secrets, but because I wasn't ready to read about a life far removed from the life depicted on that day of the block party. It was as if stitches sewn into the fabric of my life had split, revealing frayed edges that disconnected the big picture.

With the manuscript in incubation, I got my house in order. This time, I had no excuse not to throw out the dead ferns that turned my white windowsills to brown dust, clean out my closet of clothes I had since college, and toss expired Planters Cheez Ball tins and Doritos bags. And I really needed to do something with my out-dated bathroom. Being a homebody felt good. I couldn't remember when I had last felt good about something I had stuck with until the end.

I thought about the silk tapestry that Julian had given me when we broke up. Its silky natural fibers were breathable, like a second skin, and shone in reflective light. Its picture, with bold and brilliant colors, defined stitched edges that fit into place. I thought of my own travels, my own bits and pieces of life that were moving and jostling to find their places to be.

"How've you been, Ma? I know I haven't seen you or Dad much lately," I say, joining Ma and Dad outside on the porch for a visit. We hug and exchange pecks on the cheeks.

"I'm fine, just fine," Ma says. She's hunkered in her lounge chair, warmed with an emerald green and navy cardigan over a crisp white blouse despite a hot breeze, typical for late August.

I see her face lacks the tan of summer she normally has and notice how her eyes wander. I never considered my mother to be a senior citizen, or even old. What child thinks *that* of their parent? But I can't deny that she has aged, her body covered despite the temperate air.

Sitting awhile with Ma brings memories, vivid as if I am an out-sider recalling the past small joys of a summer day, when Ma read stories around the willow tree. The rose blossoms' sweet perfume and the soft buzz of bees enlivened her narration.

"You didn't come here to talk about when you and your sisters were younger. What's on your mind? And don't tell me there's noth-ing, because you've got those brows dancing and furrowing, like when I used to take you to auditions."

"I miss the theater." I sigh and slide deep into the glider. Its back-and-forth rhythm soothes me.

Not sure exactly what it is that I miss. Maybe it's the becoming someone else part, uttering another's words, moving my body in ways that weren't mine but were possessed by another. Being a part of live action in a setting that was new and undiscovered was an elixir for my chameleon being. Or maybe it's home. I miss home there.

"I never did understand why you stopped. You're such a natural, Rose. Your passion for it came out in the confident way you per-formed."

"I guess it became difficult to find jobs. And writing articles was easier. I got phone calls from editors at other publications and not calls from directors for new projects."

"It's not like acting is gone forever. It'll always be there, waiting for you. It'll happen for you when you're at the right time and right place. I just know it," Ma says.

I watch her eyes slowly close for sleep, and then I watch her for just a few more minutes.

This morning, I wake antsy; I don't know what to do with myself, as I have no lines to learn and no article to write. Knowing what I should do—work on my manuscript—and what I want to do—go outside—I choose the latter.

The day is too inviting not to answer her request. The sun, high in the sky, pairs with the music of birdsong. I walk up Lincoln Avenue, where a couple of small theaters, bars, and restaurants keep the locals meeting up. I know an old habit is following me: wide eyes open should there be a call for casting announced on a posted flyer. And sure enough, on my way to the coffee shop, I spot it. A theater that, until recently, has been boarded up, but now appears open. "The Green Lantern proudly announces its reopening with *Jake's Women*, by Neil Simon," reads the poster stuck on the window. Maybe there's a part for me? I stop and peer through the smudged window, my eyes looking inside deep to a stage and chairs scattered around the floor. A bar lines one wall, short but effective. I laugh that maybe it's one of those "it was meant to be" moments.

A soft knock on the window gives voice to my self-assurance as an experienced actor, seeking to secure a place in this neighborhood production. A lithe body I watch in motion stops, and the man stares at me, then scowls. I wave enthusiastically and give him a broad grin to counter the annoying interruption.

"Can I help you?" he says, holding the door open. He appears taller as he is standing on a step. Threads of silver run through a shaggy black head. He looks down at me.

"No. But I can help *you*. I'm Rose Dowling. And you're . . ."

"Director." He pushes up the rolled sleeves of a wrinkled white button-down shirt.

Again, the one-word conversation. Reminds me of a piece-of-work director I once met, after passing a tall guy wearing a rumpled jacket in a doorway of one downtown theater.

"Does this director have a name?"

"Ryan."

"Okay, Ryan. There's a part for me in your next production." I smile and wink.

"Oh, there is, is there?" A side of his mouth curls, and a dimple pops. "Come in and tell me which part." He opens the door wider for me to pass.

I hope moving chairs in the small, forty-seat room will stir the warm air, but it doesn't. I forgot how close everything feels, from the air to the props, to the audience.

"Please, have a seat." He slides a pair of metal folding chairs across the scuffed wood floor then offers one to me. "Have you worked recently?"

"No, I haven't, but I've worked theater and cabaret shows downtown for a number of years, until I needed to make money not as a waitress but as a freelance writer."

I sit gently, smooth my wayward hair, and straighten my jacket.

"By the way, thanks for giving me some time for this audition."

"Who says this is an audition?" He tilts his head to one side.

"I do. Might as well, as long as I'm here and you have time. Right?"

A short, stocky man stands slightly behind Ryan and clears his throat. He bends and talks quietly into his ear. "We're ready for you now."

Ryan doesn't respond but reclines with a wrinkled brow and a slightly dropped jaw, unaware of the interruption to our conversation.

"Looks like the gentleman there needs your attention." I point to the intruder.

"Um, sorry, Pete. Go on with act two, and I'll be right there."

He waves Pete away.

"Miss . . . I'm sorry, I forgot . . ."

"Rose . . . The theater is mysterious, isn't it?" I nod my head, hoping he will join me in agreement. "An audience never knows what's going to happen when the characters start talking. We're all trying to figure out our characters and what's going on with them." He crosses his legs and looks over his shoulder at a couple who are loudly running their lines.

I shift forward in my seat, elbows on my knees, and tell him intently, "I like to read people."

He stares at me. "You say you started at Alley's Door? Do you know Julian Springer, by any chance?"

I pull back and grab a water bottle from my bag. I take a slug, swallowing hard before answering, "I do. We were in a group called White Noise and played at the Door for a while. You know him?" I redirect the conversation from me to him.

"We were roommates for a while. I remember him talking about a girlfriend he couldn't get over. She was the most beautiful thing he'd ever seen. Her flirty ways and sense of adventure got him good." He nods his head. I chug more water.

I don't want to tell him I think that girl is me. Julian always commented on how flirty I was.

"Do you know . . . where . . . what he's doing now?"

"Don't know. I left for Seattle after a couple of years, and he had gotten a new agent."

Sometimes staying with someone can be a hindrance to them rather than a help. I don't think either Julian or I would have had the opportunities we had should we have stayed together. Being with Julian was a connection, like a bridge for me to get from one place to the other. Hearing of this connection tells me that bridges never break.

Julian didn't deserve me; he deserved an agent. I couldn't help him to move forward in his career like an agent could. I think of how my leaving was the best thing for him . . . and for me.

"So, how about it, Ryan? Am I in?" I put my hands together in hopeful anticipation.

"You got in the door to talk with me, so the last part should be a piece of cake for you." He stands to end our chat, then tells me to stop by tomorrow at nine.

I return the next day as directed. Once inside, I promptly offer him my resume; he gives me the script for *Jake's Women.* While he skims my bio, stopping to glance at me, I take my time paging through the script.

"I think we need to go next door for coffee," he interrupts.

We find a tight corner at Grinds coffee shop where ceiling fans do little to stir stuffy air. I take off my jacket and push up my sleeves. He's focused on unfolding a rolled tube of papers clutched in his hand and flattening them on the table in front of him. Ryan starts right in with the questions.

"I see your theater experience isn't quite as long as your writing career. Which is it, Miss Rose?" I try to listen carefully to his words, not because I'm focused, but because the noise from other pockets of conversation competes with ours.

"If you're doubting my seriousness and commitment to this production, don't. I remained committed to each job I had while working on my writing projects. I'm sure you've worked a couple of jobs at a time. Most actors have."

"I certainly have. Too many to recount. I like watching people, studying them, really, so I guess you could say . . ." He flips his wrist to look at his watch.

"Oh, geez, I gotta go. They're waiting for me." He stands and grabs his coffee. "Sorry for the abbreviated meeting. I'm going to have you come back tomorrow and read with the cast. I want to see the chemistry among you."

"I'd be happy to do a read-through with some of my new friends." I grin to break up his serious demeanor. "And, hey." I hold up my paper cup. "Thanks for the coffee."

"You're welcome."

He pivots to face me and points a finger at me. "Dinner?"

"Are you asking me out?"

"Yes. I want to talk to you about your new friend Sheila."

"Ahh, yes, Sheila. A telling character as Jake's girlfriend in a play about the women in his life, wouldn't you say?"

⤜ Linney ⤛

I am so preoccupied all day with thoughts of Bridget's health that I don't realize the financial report and get-well card remain on the office desk. I will call Mr. Hughes tomorrow.

Late summer days dwindle, and I like to stretch out the hours by working in the backyard gardens before closing the shop, rear-ranging flowerpots and shifting stands to meet the evolving light. Satisfied with the refresh, I leave for home. My arrival there is well timed with the sun's descension as I slide a basket through my arm and poke around the vegetable garden. There is enough light for me to see ripened bounty ready for harvest—a few tomatoes, a handful of basil, a couple of zucchinis, and a red pepper, too.

I put nature's yield in the kitchen sink for a rinse and try to come up with something to make with it for dinner when the phone rings.

"Miss Dowling? Mr. Hughes here. I'm afraid . . . I have some . . . bad news. I'm so sorry, so very sorry to have to tell you . . ." I strain to hear his voice; it is soft and trails.

"Mr. Hughes? What is it? Why are you calling me at home?"

"It's Miss McMahon. She went into the hospital early this morning, and, well, she passed this afternoon."

"What do you mean? Died? Bridget died? But she can't." I am defiant. "She has Magnolia, and I've got a financial report and a get-well card waiting for her. Mr. Hughes, this can't be," I say loudly, shaking my head, on the verge of crying.

"I am so very sorry, Miss Linney. I will talk more with you to-morrow."

I hang up the phone in slow motion. Where am I to go? What do I do now?

I wander outside in disbelief and sit in a wicker chair. The hours tick until shade darkens and twilight blooms. There's nothing but the light of a half-moon to see by. Bridget is gone? I think of how it happened fast, too fast, that she had been sick for a while and never told me until . . . she was close to the end. I'm ashamed when I remember the last time I saw her, in the hospital, and I had to tell her about a stranger who wants to buy Magnolia. In my insensitivity, I was blind to her tragic knowledge that her life was coming to an end, and possibly Magnolia's was, too. The ending of her, the ending of Magnolia. That's all I can think of.

Dottie's howl at a glowing full moon doesn't distract me from the memories of sitting with my sisters and Ma and Dad under the willow while listening to Ma. She directed our attention with a pointed finger that made its way around the yard as if all the answers could be found among those points. I ask God for answers, for why Bridget was taken from me, from Magnolia, but I only find more questions.

The days are getting shorter and the darkness getting longer.

Murky skies mute dawn the next morning when I reach Magnolia. I notice I forgot to put Magnolia's front lights on the night before. It's dark. Magnolia is in mourning. I stand in her doorway, hesitant to step inside, and instead I look out to a bounty of colorful flowerbeds that are now dull. Life, once defined in color, is blurred. I feel how Magnolia looks, slowed and lifeless. I step inside and prepare a sign to hang on the front door: DUE TO THE SUDDEN PASSING OF OUR BELOVED SHOP OWNER AND FRIEND, WE WILL BE CLOSED THIS WEEK. I can't think of walking through Magnolia's doors, knowing Bridget isn't on her way. Time has stood still.

During the week, Dottie and I take walks to fill the empty spaces of the day that ordinarily would have been spent with Bridget, talking about orders and shipments and rearranging displays. What is going to happen to Magnolia?

On Saturday, I open Magnolia's doors. Spiderwebs across wall corners and among table legs tell me it has been a long week. The air is dank, musty, and settled when usually it smells of lavender and floral, of life. Magnolia doesn't look right. The ceiling's indentation looks bigger; the air feels stagnant. Tables are bare, shelving items scattered. The lack of order is disorienting. I don't recognize the place.

"Linney, are you there?" Door chimes announce a visitor.

"Hi, Viv."

"Oh, Linney, I read it in the papers. I can't believe it. Bridget is gone?" she says, sniffling as we embrace. She rummages in her purse for a tissue. Her husband, Todd, a tall, muscular man with a sharp receding hairline, stands quietly behind her.

Soon the shop is filled with Bridget's guests and friends. So many come together to remember her.

"You've all been her family, and I'll include myself in that, too," I tell them. "Thank you all for being here, for me and for Magnolia."

I cry for Bridget and for me. Happy tears are for Magnolia, too. Bridget has shown me her love for this place, and through her, I've learned the meaning of having my own sense of place.

After everyone leaves, I stand in the middle of the shop's floor and look among the display tables of place settings, bookcases of home accessories, local artwork on the walls, and the small French windows. I am stuck and can't think of a thing to do but to lock up Magnolia and leave it at peace, to mourn one last time for our loss. I shut the doors and hear, for the first time, an echo. Magnolia will always resonate within me.

I think Bridget wouldn't have minded me closing early as it was her favorite time of day when the hours and the landscape surrender to the afternoon's tranquility.

The next morning, those first steps to the shop are difficult as they are heavy with grief, sadness, and fear, rolled up into something I can't lighten. It's just me now, sitting and pondering at the farmhouse table, noting the heaviness and emptiness in the room. I slip off my sandals and rub my feet on the rug, feeling the cotton's strength and versatility and wishing for it to travel through my body, like home feels, warm and comfortable.

Today is a copy of yesterday. Few visit the shop; the phone doesn't even ring. I sit more than I should, watching the dust float amid the sun's streaming rays, then putter about the shop, fixing this and rearranging that, checking the inventory closet to make sure there is nothing boxed that hasn't been opened and put out. By four o'clock, I start to close Magnolia. I slip on my sandals then lock the file drawers in Bridget's desk, where I'm reminded that the financial report about Magnolia is sitting in the middle of it, along with her get-well card. I can't bring myself to touch it, let alone move it. Doing so would be disrespectful. I don't want to be impolite in handling something that isn't mine.

The opening of the front door jingles the chimes.

"Ms. Dowling?"

I freeze, thinking it is Mr. Leone's voice I hear, but I then recognize the softness in the tone.

"Yes?"

I hurry to the front to meet the voice. It belongs to an elderly man wearing horn-rimmed glasses, looking spry and well dressed in tan slacks and an olive-green shirt. His navy jacket is comfortably tailored. He's someone I've never met before. And then I realize it's Mr. Hughes. My body tenses at the sight of him, as I remember he never did tell me how bad Bridget was so I could see her one more time before she died.

I lean against the doorway for support should I need it, fearful of what he might say.

"Come in."

We stand just inside the doorway. I hold back tears as Mr. Hughes holds out his hands for mine, lessening the grief. We hug, and I succumb to my emotions as he holds me up, just as Bridget would have done.

"It was cancer," he explains in my ear; his voice is gentle.

"Please, this way," I tell him. He follows me to the back office.

He waits for me to sit before he does. "She hid it for such a long time, from what I understand. When I started taking care of her this summer, the cancer was . . ." I hold up my hand for him to stop talking.

". . . I can only think of how much pain she was in. And she never told me."

I bow my head. The tears drop to my lap.

He doesn't need to explain further. It doesn't matter. I hurt because of guilt that I didn't do anything to comfort her.

He moves to the end of his seat, closer to the table.

"I was going to wait until next week to give you this, but the attorney said I needed to advise you as soon as possible."

He pushes a manila envelope across the table within my reach. I stare at it before pulling out a stapled pack of white sheets of paper with several typed paragraphs.

"What is all this?" I thumb through the pages. "Looks like lawyer-speak, which I'm too tired and distracted to decipher."

Mr. Hughes walks around the table to stand beside me. He gently places his hands on my shoulders, and I reach to touch his hands with mine. "Magnolia is yours, Linney. Bridget has given you Magnolia as sole owner and operator."

After Mr. Hughes leaves, I sink into the comfort of Bridget's desk chair and search for wisdom and strength in the backyard. I keep an ear to the front of the shop, listening for Bridget's footsteps, and the echoing of her saying, "Hello," drawn out as if calling all to attention to come alive now that Magnolia's matriarch had arrived. But there is quiet.

Night has fallen. I close the shop, flipping the painted "Open" sign on the front door to "Closed," and begin my walk home. During the many walks I've taken to and from Magnolia, my sense of place couldn't be more apparent now. My steps are slower, compensating for a heavy load I feel I'm carrying. How will I do it? How will I ever manage this place on my own? Being alone allows your fears to take over, as if a demon has struck. I think I should be doing something as "there is always work to be done with a place one is responsible for. So, keep busy, find a path to making something, anything, better, even if it is such a small thing," Bridget would always tell me.

I now understand why Bridget was so insistent on sharing the books with me. She wanted me to know about Magnolia's finances. Do I have what it takes to keep Magnolia running? I had the best teacher, who set an example, and I know she wouldn't have left the shop to me if she didn't think I, too, could be successful with it.

I thought I was in tune with myself, my body in sync with my thoughts, but when grief strikes, it's as if you don't know yourself anymore. You're no longer predictable. Grief has a funny way of making itself known. It can feel as heavy as a pile of bricks, cold and raw as any ice storm, deep as any Grand Canyon. Someone once said, "Grief can be the garden of compassion. If you keep your heart open, your pain can become your greatest ally in your life's search for love and wisdom." I say it over and over to try to lighten my load of bricks, to warm any storm, and to make shallower any canyon.

I've been going to Magnolia earlier each morning, only because I can't sleep. Dottie is ready when I am, waiting patiently until I hitch up her leash. I stretch the time between my little house and the shop, walking the narrow trail that now is overgrown by tall grass, mustard weeds, and Queen Anne's lace. The smell of thistle and black-eyed Susans flowers from the coolness of the dawn's morning wakened from night. The trees in the distance look as if they've paused their growth, anticipating a change of season. Calm thoughts and a meditation in gratitude make my grief more bearable.

Monarch butterflies dance through purple flowers of butterfly bushes under the office window. Bridget is with me. Dottie's nose finds the flutterers and delicately tracks their moves. When I walk through the back door, a cool breeze worries me as the chill is ominous. I search the front of the shop but am only caught by a sun rising and splashing light on the floor and shelving. The front desk and register are undisturbed. Throw rugs remain where I dropped them yesterday. The front door is locked. Dottie comes skipping from the back and howling as if a full moon is outside instead of a rising sun. This is an unusual start to an otherwise usual day.

I sit at Bridget's desk and pull out the books and registers. A pair of red finches catches my attention on the bird feeder outside. Occasionally, a bird would get bumped off its spot, but try and try again, and it would be sure to find its place.

I call on the grace of all connections that surround me to never lose my place to be.

ꙮ Debra ꙮ

When I walk in late at night, the house is quiet, seemingly unoccupied. In fact, it looks as clean and tidy as I left it. I hear water running and I trudge upstairs to our bedroom, dragging my carry-on. Dennis is in the shower, and I hurriedly undress and sneak in to join him. The hot steam is inviting, and I wrap my arms from behind around his thick middle, pressing tightly against him, wanting him. He turns, startled, as if I am an intruder.

"Did you miss me?" I ask, pulling up on my toes to offer him a kiss.

He leaps forward, turns, breaking my embrace.

"Geezuz, Deb, don't do that. You scared me. I didn't think you'd be back until later."

"I'm here now, and I missed you. Are . . . you . . . okay?" I touch his chest, then hold his face in my hands.

"Yes. Just got back from playing at a Barrington estate—the Goldmans' fiftieth wedding anniversary dinner party. Long evening.

Tired." Dennis averts his eyes as if he is focusing on a spider inching its way up the wet tile while he backs up against the wall.

He squeezes past me out of the shower, grabs a towel, and wraps it around his waist.

I'm confused. Barrington? It's just an hour's drive from here.

I shower quickly to catch Dennis in the bedroom and ask him why Carrie told me he was out of town when he was only in Barrington, but he is not in the room. I pull on a pair of sweatpants and an old T-shirt then plop in a stuffed chair by the window. There is just a sliver of a moon slicing the dark night. I think I could use a pile of Linney's crystals to rub in the palm of my hand right now, as I anticipate confronting Dennis about what happened while I was gone . . . and why he lied.

Noise turns my attention to the driveway below, where the garage lights are on. Dennis is rummaging through his car's trunk, then bangs it shut. He moves to the passenger side, opens the door, and pulls something from the car, then stuffs his finds in a pocket. The car door slams. He hurries back inside, into the kitchen. Before joining him downstairs, I put away my clothes in the closet, tossing most into the laundry basket, and I see it is full. And then I discover on the floor his carry-on, half-unzipped, tucked in a corner as if trying to hide itself underneath his gym bag, shoes, and workout clothes.

While walking downstairs to find Dennis, I question if I want to go there. I mean, do I want to get into something that might not have a good ending? He must have an explanation.

Dennis walks in the kitchen through the garage door, sees me, and freezes. He is unkempt as if he never did shower and change into fresh clothes.

"There you are. Did you forget some things in the car? I saw you in the driveway and thought you were bringing in a grocery bag of cheese, crackers, and a Beaujolais to go with it all . . . to surprise me."

I step closer to give him a peck on the cheek.

"I . . . I need you to sit, Deb, please."

He directs me out of the room and to the dining room table.

"What's going on?"

I hesitate to move. The scene is contradictory. I have been the one to direct him to come to the table, to encourage conversation and connection. And now it is Dennis. I swallow hard before pulling out a chair to sit on.

The linen tablecloth is fresh and crisp as I flatten my hand over it, connecting to its resiliency from its fibers. Melding my gaze with its weave, and pressing my fingertips into its creamy white smoothness, I wish for it to transfer its healing properties to me. This linen will always be the fabric of my life.

My gut tightens when Dennis sits. The circular table, uniting family and friends who sat there before, now feels like a circle that is breaking. No longer continuous but disconnecting. He doesn't speak at first but stares at the palms of his hands, as if his opening words are printed there. His jaw clenches before speaking.

"Deb, I . . . I want a divorce."

Then he sighs, as if relieved after making the request, calm as if asking for pocket money to run and get a coffee. I am unable to look directly at him, to search for a real truth. But what is the real truth? What is happening?

"Huh? What did you say? You could at least look at me if you're going to say something like *that*."

"A divorce, Deb, a divorce. You heard me." He hits his open hands on the table, and with the power of his legs, and a push off the table, he slides the chair back, catching the tablecloth. It pulls from its smooth layout and becomes misshapen.

I hit a fist on the linen to get his attention. Dennis's eyes blink as if trying to clear an unfamiliar image. For so long, I have been the one in compliance, making sacrifices to be at home, for him, to be a stepmother to his son, to be his everything, all the time.

"But you can't do this, here at this table, where we have come together as a family, where we connect." And now I raise my voice, or yelling is more like it. I break out in a sweat. Adrenaline dashes through me.

"You can't just go and disconnect that easily from what I've worked long and hard to connect." My voice cracks, and I shake.

"This is home; this is where we belong, Dennis. You think you can keep your secrets? Why, Dennis? Why didn't you answer my calls? Where were you? And I don't think it was in Barrington."

I change my tone of voice. There is anger with every word.

"You lied to me, Dennis."

He does not move or speak.

"And what exactly did you stuff in your pocket?" I stand and push the chair away with the backs of my knees and point a finger at his pants pocket. Losing patience, I lunge for his bulging pocket, and out pop a set of large gold hoop earrings and a lipstick tube in cappuccino that drop to the floor. I pick them up and throw them on the table.

"So *this* broke up our marriage?"

I point to his lover's accessories.

"I'm sorry, Deb, but . . ."

"Sorry? You're not sorry. You're damn happy you're out of this house, with me, to move on with someone else. You've been checked out and ready to move on for a while now. What about Charlie?"

"I haven't told him yet. I thought we could . . ."

"We? *Now* we're a 'we'? You're too late with that idea, Dennis." I chuckle and cross my arms.

He stands and backs away from the table. His staring face is impassive.

"Well, I guess there's nothing more that needs to be said now, is there?" he says.

"I guess not," I mumble.

I have never experienced losing at anything before. In fact, I understood that if I worked hard enough at anything, I could get what I wanted. And I proved that with the success of my career.

I notice where we are standing. We have taken steps away from the table and from each other.

"Get out, Dennis. Just get out of my sight," I say, waving him away and covering my face with my hands.

How quickly such a simple act of coming to a dinner table has lost its meaning.

I am walking away from a life into which I have poured everything I had. Funny how when we're happy, we're full throttle moving forward, casting aside any goals because something came along that wasn't part of the plan. When Dennis came into my life, then soon after, Charlie, there was a house that became a home, and then I became a wife and a mom. I pursued that life, and yes, I was happy. But marriage and motherhood weren't part of the plan. My weakness for not sticking to my plan got the best of me when I spent years defying my vulnerabilities.

From my bedroom window, I notice Dennis going into the garage, a man cave of a worn couch, a chair, a drum set and sax, and shelves of records and tapes, to spend the night. Good place for him there. He has his music, his work, his own private place to be. But where does that leave me? Where's my place to be now?

I don't see him for a couple of days, and I don't wonder where he is. I just don't care. Sitting at the dining room table, I fight weakness by clutching my trembling body. I don't want to admit this failure of us, of me. Ever. The phone rings, interrupting an attempt to find good memories of solace and understanding. It's Dennis asking me if it's okay for him to come over, which I laugh at the absurdity of asking permission to enter a house he owns, too. He wants to get his remaining clothes and box a few things that were originally his: pictures of Charlie, wineglasses, books.

I open the door. He is dressed well in tan slacks and a black button-down shirt that for once is tucked in all the way around his waist. I thought how attractive he looked that first lunch we had together at Maxine's and how I am still attracted to him now. He steps in and waves hello without making eye contact. I study every bit of his being as if to find answers to many of my questions.

I follow him up the stairs into the bedroom. Maybe we could talk this out, calmly. Maybe he really doesn't want—

"Thanks for . . . I'm sorry, Deb . . . I won't be long," is all he says.

"Who is she?" I ask, leaning on the bedroom doorframe, arms crossed and watching him yank clothes from hangers.

"Tracey." He mumbles this.

"Tracey? Tracey who?"

"Goodwin." He hurriedly tosses what remains of his belongings in the closet onto the bed.

What? *My* Tracey? *My* college friend Tracey? Jesus. Dear God. "How the hell could you do this to me?" I bury my head in my open hands and sit on the edge of the bed.

"It just happened. When we pitched CMG a while back and we . . . we hit it off. I had no idea you knew her."

He swipes a book of music, a pile of laundered underwear, and a couple pictures of him and Charlie off the top of his dresser and into a shallow box.

"She's your client, for God's sake," I say, running my hands through my hair. I sit on the bed with my elbows on my knees and stare at the floor, as if trying to arrange pieces of a puzzle that are scattered there. "Didn't she tell you she was my friend? Or even better yet, didn't you tell her you were married?"

"And when we met, I was your client."

"Don't change the subject, Dennis. Hardly the same thing here. Neither of us was married, nor stole our best friend."

And then it hits me.

"Wait just a minute." I sit up tall; the pieces come together.

"The conference. She was *supposed* to be there because she's CMG's sales manager and she needed someone for their event, and you naturally suggested K&M to her. But where were you . . . ?"

Dennis dashes into the bathroom, grabs his toiletry bag from the bathroom counter, and stuffs it with his toothbrush, toothpaste, and deodorant.

I stand with a clearer picture in my mind.

"Oh God. You went to San Francisco . . . to meet her."

"I'm sorry, Deb." He tosses a set of towels into the box.

"No, you're not sorry. You're an asshole, ruining people's lives," I scream, following him out of the bathroom and around the room as he pulls open dresser doors and throws pairs of socks and T-shirts into a duffel bag. "You're a pathetic piece of garbage who will never be what you think you are." I cut the air with both hands, pull up my sleeves, and jab a finger in Dennis's chest. My face heats up, and I can't get the words out fast enough. "I feel sad for Charlie. You had a chance at being number one in his life, and you blew it, Dennis. Hurry up and get out of here. I never want to see you again." I slam the closet and bathroom doors and stomp downstairs.

I'm not sure why I wanted to know who she was. Does it matter?

I retreat to the table in the dining room and watch Dennis skim down the stairs and out the door with an oversized, stuffed duffel bag around his shoulder, while carrying a clanking box. I then stare through the glass doors into the bruised night, searching for answers, but the dark is invisible. The front door closes. I touch the linen and recall this is where we once sat together, sharing our lives and planning for our futures. I never thought what we had would ever be gone. I trusted him. But I've learned now that trusting someone can be a weakness.

In defiance, I pack all that made the table our home: the linen tablecloth, empty pots where I once grew herbs, the box made of birch, candlesticks and holders, gifts from our wedding. I can't be here anymore. When I seal the box of connections to home, I close a life that I will store away until later, when it can be opened to free memories that are no longer weaknesses but strengths.

And then I put the house up for sale.

"Plenty of sun to flood this open floor plan," reads the *Highland Beacon*. After I put the house up for sale, uncontested by Dennis, I do a lot of driving. My dad used to tell us that when in doubt about making any important decisions or confused, just drive. Concentrating on something else removes the mind from indecision and immobility and clears a path to sound judgment. Since it came from a man who did nothing but drive to our vacation destinations when we were young, I understood his perspective. But after living in the city with Dennis and snaking through traffic and dodging distracted drivers, the last place I want to be sorting things out is in a car merging with chaos. I do it anyway. I am my father's kid.

I drive away from the city, north along Sheridan Road, with Lake Michigan hugging my side. It's always a source of orientation for me, as the lake remains east no matter where I stand. Knowing a large body of fresh water is always at my disposal is a connection to not only geographical navigation, but also to finding a place for me to be. When we were little, Ma would take us to the beach to burn off energy while we explored uncharted territory. Building sandcastles, running from waves, and picking up tiny shells after the waves retreated did the trick as far as Ma was concerned. Our naps for the remaining afternoon were longer than usual.

Unsure of how long I have been driving, I wonder if I am in Wisconsin. Maybe I should move there, land of cheese and brats, and don't forget the kraut. They've got their sports teams, too. But then I'd have to look for a different job, new friends, new bars, new restaurants, new everything. Not to say I couldn't follow through with the reinvention, but I can't give myself a good reason to do it. And then I spot it: FOR SALE.

The new construction of townhomes looks urban with a tidy, classical look of red brick and white trim. City living in the suburbs. Why not? I have missed the city and its energy, its opportunities to be busy with music, and art, and museums and zoos and parks, to belong. I pull over, stop in front of the unit, and watch a thirtysome-thing couple dressed in suits and shiny shoes walk out the front door. I hustle there to intercept a portly, balding man filling the doorway. His belly pulls on the buttons of his blue shirt.

"Hello, excuse me," I say, waving at him. "I wonder if I might be able to have a look?" He doesn't answer me. I speak louder. "I was driving by, and I saw the FOR SALE sign. Is it alright if I have a look before you leave?"

"Well, I s'pose," he says, adjusting his oversize wire-rimmed glasses as I push my way past his ample midsection and through the front door.

"Please, sign in," he says politely, motioning me into the kitchen. After I add my name to the visitor list, I take a casual walk around, noticing an open floor plan, bay windows, and sliding doors to the backyard, which are open, allowing breezes to cool the dining room. I go upstairs and see rooms with enough space to feel unencumbered. I nod my head in satisfaction as I come back down the dark hardwood stairs and meet the man. This is a place I could call home.

"Seems as though you've taken a liking to the place," he says, clutching a folder to his chest. Not sure if it was a question, but I turn it into a statement.

"I certainly have. I'd like to make an offer."

"Well, then, let me grab the paperwork."

It's freeing and new and feels alive while I stand here in an empty, open space, envisioning settling in with my own, new connections to home. And I don't have to move to Wisconsin.

I am so excited to have found a new place that I call Ma when I get home.

"I think I found a place, Ma, in Highland. I think it's the right one for me."

"Oh, that's great, dear," she says quietly.

Did I wake her? When I would call her with happy news—my job at K&M, my engagement, Charlie—I was used to her excitement matching mine. But she is groggy and doesn't offer conversation in reply. "I'll call you back later this week," I say. My happiness is subdued.

I think about Ma and Dad and when they first moved into the house on Birchwood Court. Did they know they'd be there forever? Did they think they'd ever have to move out of their first home because of something unforeseen? When Dennis and I moved into our home, I thought the same thing Ma must have—we were there for the long haul. This was where we were meant to be.

Things happen that you never anticipate. It's all about adapting and how you choose to handle the good . . . and the bad. For me, it's a day-to-day thing, one day falling into the folds of memories and starting a new home, alone.

I remember that next day, after Dennis told me he wanted a divorce, when I tossed into boxes photos of us, keepsakes from our travels, and anything else I considered to be memories of us and our life together. Not a trace of "D&D" remained, anywhere. Our table became bare of the very things that brought us to it. I was ready to leave as soon as I could. Running away was the only way to forget what I had to leave behind.

The first weeks in my new place are disorienting, but when I stand in the living room, I look left over my shoulder, out the sliding doors to the lawn, where there is not a willow tree but a birch tree, a sapling with more light than dark green slender leaves waving in the breezes, as if to say, "Hello." I look right, out the front bay window to a yard with curb appeal any homeowner would covet. I live sparsely, as I don't put up a fight with Dennis to take what he wants to make his love nest with Tracey homier. In fact, I am living simply, something that would be sure to please Linney.

The summer winds carry a sweet scent, and an emptiness fills the living room. There is no longer a second "D" sitting next to another "D." I am alone and starting to feel a little lonely.

⋙ Charlotte ⋘

Heat blankets the North Shore suburbs in late August. There is not much relief from the humidity at the beaches, and the shore of Lake Michigan is no exception. I don't understand how people can lie on a bumpy, hot bed of grit and roast like kebabs, turning faithfully to cook evenly. I'd rather sit in the shade, alone, with a view of green grass and chirpy birds, not a monochromatic beach panorama with biting flies and squawking seagulls.

I visit Ma and Dad for lunch on a Sunday.

Coming through the backyard gate from the driveway, I notice the foliage has withered. Flower bud heads flop, the daisies and cosmos have turned brown, and even the willow tree looks weak.

"Hi, Ma. What happened out here?"

I think I woke her from a nap, as I see her looking comfy, lounging on the chaise on the back porch dressed in roomy jeans and a long-sleeve shirt. She takes a minute to search for the voice that's calling her.

"Hi, dear. I didn't know you were coming."

She pulls herself up and adjusts the chair's back to more upright.

"I talked to Dad on Friday and told him I'd come for lunch. He said he'd tell you. Maybe he didn't?" I join her on the chaise, sitting on its foot end.

"Oh, I don't pay much attention to what he says anyway." She slaps the air.

"The yard, Ma. It doesn't look good. You and Dad put so much work into it. And the willow has never looked so sad. Everything's dry."

"I was counting on it raining yesterday. And it never did." She leans back and closes her eyes. "It's alright. Fall is just around the corner, and it'll be just a matter of time before this will die off."

"Hello, girls," Dad yells from the side gate kitchen. He's balancing a pizza box on one arm while watching his footing as he makes his way across the lawn. "I got pizza."

"Ma, I would have helped you with lunch. Dad didn't need to go out and get something."

"Your mother has taken a day off today. I'm cooking."

Ma perks up and joins Dad in the kitchen. I follow them and the inviting scent of a cheese and sausage pizza.

Dad's humor isn't fooling me. I'm serious. Ma doesn't do take-out, especially if any of her kids are coming over for a meal.

Dad dutifully tears a slice from the soggy-bottomed carton and places it on a plate for Ma. Dad and I follow, grabbing our own pieces, then find our seats at the table.

Ma beats us there and is already nibbling small bites, chewing as if she can't swallow. She sinks into her shoulders, becoming soft in her chair.

"Ma, I know you're not doing well. You need to see the doctor. I can take you . . . he can give you something . . ."

"I just need a little rest." Her cool hand pats mine.

Ma gets up and leaves the kitchen, walking as if in a fog. She is fading, slipping away.

I turn to my father and plead, "Dad, it's time. I need you and Ma to tell Deb and Rose and Linney what's happening. You can't let this go on. I can't keep this a secret from them any longer. It's not fair to them or to me."

Margaret

Oh, how I want to rid myself of these August days. Rushing winds stir nothing but heavy, heated air, and my endurance working in the yard slowly drips from me. And now, I think how it's not a curse at all, but a gift. How when a too-hot body responds by sweating to cool itself. How its internal workings are like a well-oiled machine in sync with checks and balances. Ordinarily, a hearty lunch would revive me, making me undeterred to work in the gardens in the afternoon. But now, sleep after lunch is required of me.

Soon, comfort and peace cradle me in the soft bevels of the bed where, in my room, the drawn sheers calm the day's sun. I roam my comfortable familiar, highlighting the pale green walls, a tall ficus in the corner, the vanity I inherited from my mother, a stuffed chair fitting just right in another corner, and Joe's valet next to it. My heaviness lightens, and the day slips away while I sleep.

Sometimes I can't stand to lie down, for when I do, my heart beats, and I flush with fear. The intruder, the "black beast," I call it, makes itself known to me. It is dark and scary and grows unwanted in my head. The doctors say they can't get at it safely to remove the growth. So, I do what I've done when one of the girls' hearts beat fast and her face became flushed. I sit with the troubled child in my lap in the chair next to the window. From there, I travel a backyard that has been forty years in the making, where stories were told, and memories were made over the years among family and friends. I can even measure the willow's growth from up here. I'm happy to see how life goes on, that the cycle of trees, left undisturbed, will outlive us all. How young life will always rejuvenate.

Aging can feel as if it is playing tricks on you. I'm no longer young with as much energy as I once had, yet not as old as I thought I'd ever be. When Linney was little, I could tell she would be the girl who would always have her youth. She never wanted to be indoors, even on a cold and snowy day in January. Romping in puddles, wearing her red rain boots, she would giggle while dancing with the splashes. My Linney never took anything too seriously as she never felt alone, but when she was barefoot, I could see her connection to this earth rising from the bottoms of her feet to the top of her head.

I hear from Charlotte that Rose got a part in a new production in the city. I'm sure she'll call with her news as soon as she has the time. It's nice to hear that Rose is committing to not only a new production, but also to writing a book. I hate to ask her how it's coming because I'm not sure she knows. And Debra keeps at it at Kinsey and Moore. And has she made partner? Oh, I can't remember. And

Charlotte, well, I know she believes I look at Deb as the one I rely on, but it is Charlotte who has been my strong one, a confidante, who is always at the ready for me as if she has a sixth sense.

This weekend, I get around to making space in the downstairs hall closets. I have Joe bring up from the basement Deb's box she was storing there to join the boxes from Rose and Linney, who have asked us to take them, too. The box reminds me of when Deb was packing her things in this house, ready to go off to college. I hugged her as if I were squeezing the last bit of girlhood out of her and making room for the woman she was becoming, in a life she was going to call her own.

Deb stopped by just a few weeks ago. When she walked in, she stood limp in the front foyer with a box in her hands, her head down. She whispered her first words, "Ma, I'm afraid I have . . ." I walked to her, concerned she wasn't feeling well, and then she dropped the box on the floor, and threw herself into my arms.

". . . Dennis and I are getting a divorce." I didn't believe the words that came out of her.

I hugged her tight, woman to woman. I thought of Charlie. How he followed her when he was little, wanting to hold her hand, or simply putting his pudgy palm on her thigh when both would be sitting on the couch. She stepped up in the mother department, always there for him when the going got tough. Don't know how she did it, with the work hours, and trying to give Charlie some sense of normalcy.

And then she broke from me, pushed away wet strands of hair from her tearstained face, and turned away.

She opened the front door and left the house quickly, as if fleeing.

I flip on the closet switch, bringing to light a darkness that appears to have neither a beginning nor an end. The closet is narrow and deep, and I'm afraid to go in there. Maybe it is the unknown of what lies ahead. When I push Rose's box to sit next to Deb's, I see a larger, unmarked box in the back, to the right of a stack of folded throw rugs and extra dog bedding.

I ask Joe to squeeze deep into there and pull out the mystery box.

"And what do you want with this?" he asks, backing out with it into the hall. I stare at the unknown at my feet.

"Well, I can't remember what's in it. Maybe it's junk I can throw out. Let's have a look."

I kneel, and Joe stoops to help me pull open the box's flaps.

"You've been doing a lot of culling lately. Hopefully, I'm not the next to be thrown out," he says with a wink.

"That's right. You could be next, mister, so don't go hiding in a corner in a dark closet, because I will find you."

I was close once back then, only it wasn't him but me who could have left. Having four little ones, I didn't get much help from Joe when he'd come home from work. I used to anticipate feeling relief, walking upstairs when Joe would get home, closing the bedroom door, sitting in the chaise, and looking outside to the backyard. I yearned for stillness and quiet and having a focus on a happy place outside I knew I could depend on, away from the inside's noise, confusion, and demands. Instead, Joe would walk into the kitchen from the garage door, set down his briefcase and car keys, take off his hat and coat and hang them on the hook in the mudroom, then go upstairs to wash up for dinner. He could go through this routine with freedom and without interruption or questioning. And like on cue and in reverse order, I dreamed of grabbing my coat, my purse, and my car keys, heading out the garage door to the car, and driving away. In my head, I planned my walkout, the timing to the minute in a rhythm any robber pulling off a bank heist would envy. I'd be methodical, quiet, and determined. But when I imagined sitting in the car and starting the engine, I knew only to back out of the drive-way. And then I would stop. Where would I go? What would I do? So, I would pull back into the garage and turn off the engine. And then I'd cry. I cried because I felt so invisible. I cried because every ounce of my being was needed until I was numb and couldn't feel how I needed more of me back. I cried because I had a husband who walked through the kitchen as if I were not there. I cried because I loved my children so very much but didn't have anything left for me or for my husband. So, I continued in the reverse order of my actions. In my mind, I went back inside, put back my coat and purse and keys. And then I took the chicken noodle casserole out of the oven for dinner.

"Oh, look, Joe. It's what I have saved from Deb and Dennis's engagement party and wedding. Now, stop with the look. I know what you're thinking."

"Never did like him. Could see right through him. He wanted to have someone around him personally and professionally, who was brighter, smarter, and stronger than him, so he could take all the credit and be the BMOC," Joe said with hands on hips. "And Deb couldn't see it. But we sure did."

"It didn't matter what we saw or thought. If she never married Dennis, she and Charlie would never have met and come to learn so much about each other."

"Deb realized it was okay to have people as a priority in her life. And when Dennis disappointed her, she had to reprioritize."

"But at least Charlie remained a priority."

I think about how vulnerable we all are. Deb, the least likely person Joe and I or her sisters would pick to say is vulnerable, came to be the most vulnerable. She's managed her life well, in strength and in courage.

When I moved out from where I grew up after marrying Joe, I took a few things that felt like home—a fancy alarm clock, a hard-covered pink journal my mother gave me when I was thirteen, and a houseplant that had overgrown its pot. I still have those connections from home, as they remind me of connections to my girls. I have the clock, though it's no longer working, but it reminds me of Deb and how she is driven by time; I have my journal, a book of writings by Rose since she has become a writer; and I have an overgrown houseplant, a growing thing I couldn't part with. When the plant looked as if it had nothing left, I took a snip of the root ball, including a single stem and four leaves, and repotted it. And it grew! It reminded me of reconnecting with another place and how four leaves are my four daughters.

Joe weaves the flaps closed and pushes it back into the closet next to Deb's other box, and then I turn off the light.

"Margaret, Linney is on the phone. She needs to talk to you," Joe yells to me from the kitchen. He settles the receiver on the counter and finishes drying his wet hands with a kitchen towel after cleaning up our breakfast dishes. Though it takes me a moment to get to my feet from sitting outside, I always have a sense of urgency to get to the phone when the girls call.

"Mom?" Her voice is weak, her tone sad.

"What is it, dear?" I hold the phone tight to my ear.

"I'm afraid I have some bad news . . . Bridget passed away. She's been sick for a while and never got better, and I suspected something was wrong when she wasn't coming into work some days, and she sounded so tired on the phone, and then showing me the books, the detailed finances . . ."

". . . it'll be okay, Linney," I say to calm her fast-talking upset through a burst of tears. I slide a kitchen chair to me and sit. "I'm so very sorry. You have gained all her knowledge and the memories of being such dear friends . . ."

". . . wait, Ma, there's more . . . she . . . she left the shop to me. Magnolia . . . it's mine."

I don't say anything at first as I'm not sure I've heard her right.

"It's yours? Magnolia is all yours?" I whisper.

"I don't know if I can do it. It's such a huge responsibility." Fear is in her trembling tone. "I'm lost, Ma. I can't think about taking over Magnolia right now. I'm empty without her."

"It's okay to feel the way you do. You're mourning. Bridget will always be with you when you walk through the doors of Magnolia; she will be holding them open for you. Now, go for a long walk. Take Dottie with you. She loves long walks like you. And when you do, listen. Listen closely to the trees, listen to the sounds the brush makes, feel the Queen Anne's lace tickling your calves, hear the thistle and honeysuckle and all the tall grasses rustling in this season's wind. It's all connected, Linney, and we're all connected to it. Find your place to be in all that you can see, feel, and touch. And you will be fine, Linney, just fine."

I hang up the phone and sit awhile in gratitude for Bridget and for the sense of place she has shown to Linney.

August humidity ebbs and flows as the month closes. I look forward to September, which can be an exceptionally lovely weather month for us. And it is also outstanding because that's when Joe and I married.

We planned a small wedding in the city and had a few friends over afterwards. We read the raised eyebrows as they suggested it might be a shotgun wedding. We left them guessing. But when Deb was born in March, they guessed no more.

And the rest, as they say, was history.

There's something about a certain time in your life when, suddenly, you realize there are more years gone than there are ahead of you. Sure, we know this logically, but when you're forced to recognize that you are aging faster than you expected, well, it makes you assess what kind of person you've been. I don't fear death. What I do fear is that I haven't been a good enough mother, or wife to Joe, or even good to myself. Did I live a life of kindness? Did I live out my purpose and serve it well?

It is time. I ask Joe to call the girls and tell them they need to come home.

I have always loved Sundays. They've meant walks in the park, finishing a book and starting a new one, baking cakes, and watching old movies. Sundays are God's day, not only to connect through prayer, but also to acknowledge ourselves and our physical and mental health in the name of our creator. Even when I was a single woman working hard as ever, Sunday was my day to exhale, only to start back up on a Monday morning. Maybe Charlotte got that from me. I had no sisters growing up who could stuff my hands with crystals and tell me to take a deep breath while rubbing the rocks together to soothe my anxious self.

And all the more reason to be present this Sunday, with Joe and our daughters, when I'll make chicken a la king, their Sunday favorite. I couldn't tell you how many tuna noodle casseroles or hamburger hot dishes I prepared, but I always had a hot meal ready for them that eased any anxieties the girls may have had. There is truth to calling it comfort food. It does remind you of home.

"Are you sure you want to do this? That's a lot of work. You'll be in the kitchen on your feet for a while," Joe says, watching me pull out mixing bowls.

"I wouldn't want it any other way, so go, shoo. Here's my grocery list, and don't come back until you've got everything on it."

Joe takes a moment in concentration to read through the list. His persistence and attention to detail in completing a grocery order are deserving of a gold star. He knows exactly what I'm looking for and won't come back with anything different.

The late afternoon sun strikes the kitchen windows, spotlighting the kitchen table where I remember the placement of our family: Deb to the right of her father, who is at one end of the table, as if next in command, directing table manners; Charlotte sitting to Joe's left, whispering "Organic titanic" to raise Linney's ire as she teases her sister while dangling her bare feet from the chair opposite; Rose, sitting to my right as if inside someone else's body, striking a pose with her jet-black hair cascading from well-chiseled cheekbones and eyes hiding behind bangs that always need trimming. So young, yet beyond their years in curiosity and determination to find their own sense of being. They'll be taking those same seats today, but now as adults who have come into their own.

Joe comes through the door from the garage, hustles into the kitchen, and drops full armloads of grocery bags onto the counter.

I'm grateful for his unpacking skills and his lining up on the counter all that I need, from chicken to puff pastry shells.

"You're at my heels now, Joe."

"Anything I can do? Don't be stubborn, and please let me help you."

He follows me around the kitchen as if we're waltzing, from the counter to the stove to the pantry.

"I'm not stubborn, and I'm fine. I'm feeling good today." Must be because the girls are coming, and I want to make something special for them, something they're familiar with, a reminder of being at home. My attention trails from chopping and mixing to the willow. Its plumes of grace are forever still in the settling of the day. I see the colors of the season have faded and the green carpet appears threadbare. It's the cyclical nature of things, the interconnections of the natural world that give us hope. In life, there's no real death, but a continuation of rebirths. I think of this especially now when I anticipate talking with my daughters. I go upstairs to my bedroom to change clothes, praying for fortitude with each step taken.

I plunk down on the bed like a bowling pin that's been struck. I guess I did do too much. I'll just take a moment to—

"Margaret, the girls, they'll be here any moment," Joe says, shaking me awake from a deep sleep. I hurry to dress in one of my favorite sundresses, a Monet of lilac, crimson, and blue flowers. When standing before the full-length mirror, I look like a hanger that keeps the dress from hitting the floor. My thin arms and shapeless body no longer fill out the dress as *it* is wearing me, and my thin hair has lost its bounce. I add a pop of cotton-candy-pink to my lips to offset my ashen color.

I hear Charlotte's voice first and meet her downstairs.

"Are you alright? Dad says to come home." She rushes into the kitchen with open arms and gives me a tender hug. Her concern doesn't stop me from pulling out the snack tray.

"Everything is fine. I want to have you over for a Sunday dinner, like we used to when you kids were little."

"What's this burst of nostalgia?" Deb interrupts, just arriving. "So, what did you make, anyway? Not that hamburger hot dish thing?" She plucks a Triscuit from the tray.

"I was lucky and young enough to not have experienced the 'goop,'" Charlotte says, popping a square of cheddar cheese into her mouth. "And who named it the 'goop,' anyway?"

"That'd be me," Linney adds, joining us from the screen doors. "The combination of elbow macaroni, ground beef, and tomato sauce topped with cheddar cheese and baked till it all bubbles made it all kind of 'goopy' when you scooped it out onto your plate."

Rose skims into the kitchen from the backyard and makes her way to me, giving me a gentle hug. "Are you all talking about food again?" Rose was my picky eater, with her concerns of quantity over quality. Just a few French fries, half a hamburger, and only half of the vanilla shake she'd eat at Jasper's diner in town. "It's all about the looks," she'd say, but then rethink it and finish all on her plate. She was already such a dramatic actress at the age of thirteen.

Puttering behind the counter feels like the old days when I cooked three meals a day like clockwork. Otherwise, I couldn't fit in the laundry, chauffeuring, grocery shopping, and house cleaning. Eventually, I'd mix up my hats or one would fall off or get lost, but they always would find their place, back on my head. The girls entertained themselves back then and now have picked up where they left off; I never do pay much attention to what they are talking about. It's sister-code where sentences are completed by someone else. Unless blood is being drawn from a limb or a face, I let the girls work out their differences. And they always do.

I peek out the window to see Joe shifting the picnic table to find its stable footing under the willow.

"Grab a plate, everyone, fill 'em up, and let's head on outside," I announce. Rose is a consummate plate designer of small lumps of food to remain inside the plate's rim; Linney takes her time to pick out mostly vegetables. I could name which plate belongs to which daughter by the way the meal sits on it.

My heart pounds as I near the table, anticipating my need to interrupt soon the family conversation. I pray for my nervous self to calm, and peace to wash away my shallow breath. As we commence with first bites, I look around the table at the faces of my daughters. The blue jay's cawing distracts me to find him in the willow, content, hiding behind the tree's flowing arms. The connections in the present moments are in front of me, and with the heavens above, I pray silently.

Joe has made a cozy spot under the willow for us to eat. Charlotte sits next to me, and Joe is on my other side. Deb, Linney, and Rose fill the bench seats. The girls chatter on about one thing or another, and I am delighted they are enjoying themselves, animated with laughter and chiding. My thoughts digress to the right time to tell them, but then I realize there is never going to be a right time. I shake the thoughts out of my head.

"Ma, are you and Dad going to get some landscape help for the fall cleanup? . . . Ma? Did you . . . hear me?" Deb asks.

"Girls, I have to tell you something." I look at Joe. He grabs my hand and smiles assuredly. I can't find the right words, or maybe I don't want to say it.

"I'm not well," I blurt, my nerves giving me a jump start. "And I'm not going to get any better."

It is as if a bolt of lightning hits the table, as utensils drop and eating ceases.

"Ma, what's wrong with you?" Deb asks, her brow tight as if she is trying to figure out a riddle I've posed.

"Let her talk, Deb, for God's sake," Rose says, putting her hand on my arm. "Ma, what's going on? What do you mean? You're sick?" A breeze comes through the yard, ushering the willow's branches in synchronized movement and thin clouds to filter a strong sunshine as if on cue.

"I have a brain growth thing, a tumor," I say, waving my hand over the right side of my head. "They can't get it out." I wiggle my fingers over the black beast as if performing some voodoo magic to make it disappear.

A stronger breeze blows a stack of paper napkins and plates off the table, sending them sailing to the ground. The willow's long limbs brush against our backs. Clouds like shades, now drawn to cover the sun. A chill waves through us.

Linney's shaky voice asks softly, "Are you in pain, Ma? Do you hurt at all?"

"Just headaches now and then. And I'm awfully tired from doing the smallest of things. Your father is here. That's all I need." I loop my arm through his and lay my head on his shoulder.

"But . . . there's got to be something that can be done. Have you gotten a second opinion? And we can get you some help. I can call and have someone come in and—"

"No need, Deb. There's nothing much that needs to be done," I say to slow her words.

The girls turn to Charlotte, who remains with her hands in her lap and eyes fixed ahead.

"You're awfully quiet, Charlotte. Did you know about this? How long have you—" Deb says, raising her voice and pointing a finger at her.

Joe interrupts. "Now, girls, it doesn't matter who knew what when. This is about your mother and her wishes. We're on her timetable, and this is when she wanted to let you all know."

Charlotte looks first at her dad's tear-filled eyes; then she turns to me. "I'm sorry, Ma." She leans against my shoulder. "I kept the secret, didn't I?" she whispers in my ear.

"I'm so sorry, Ma. Whatever you need, we're here," Deb's voice assures me.

"And we'll help you through the bad days," Linney adds. She bows her head and begins to cry. Rose's tears fall gently as she gets up from her seat and wraps her arms around my shoulders. Linney and Deb join in to make one perfectly warm and loving group hug.

Stillness comes over us as I think it's not about an absence, of death, of an ending, but the fullness, of us together, of the birth of a new season, of the life we have come to understand under the willow tree. I know it's a lot for the girls: it's on their faces, expressionless except for the tears that flow from their sad eyes.

"Don't worry, any of you," I say softly, looking them in the eye. "I'm at peace."

The winds turn calm, and the willow relaxes. A blue jay lets out another loud cawing, and the roses' perfume wafts nearby, mingling with the scent of wild prairie from over the fence. The only place I want to be is under the willow. I study the weave of its branches, noticing how smaller ones are soft and flexible, and how a subtle breeze can awaken the whole tree into motion. I note its trunk with a frost crack, likely from that winter years ago when the temperatures had dropped so quickly, the poor willow split. I think of how we believe we are firm and can withstand any challenge, but sometimes we can weaken and splinter when times get too tough. I think of this as a metaphor for Debra, Rose, Linney, and Charlotte. Despite their challenges in facing their life-changing decisions and finding who they're meant to be in this world, they have stood solid with the flowing grace of the willow. Speaking to them now, I am responsible for changing the course of their memories, and because of this, I weep.

I am drained; I can't speak, and neither can anyone else. Moments stop. Joe reaches for my hands and holds them tight. He is my rock, a pillar against my weakness. Our dinner plates remain half full as if frozen in time. I tell the girls we've had enough for one day and to go on home. We hug in silence to connect us.

Joe and I watch the girls file out of the backyard in slow motion and into the driveway to meet their cars. A soft rain falls. "Let's get you in the house. It's been a big day," Joe says. He knows what I was thinking. He stands close to me; I lean on him.

"What a life we've made with each other," I tell Joe, looking into his eyes while resting on our bed. His face is soft, his eyes gentle.

"I'm here, Margaret, with you all the way."

And I know life will go on.

September

Rose

I walk into Carmine's, a family-style Italian restaurant with ample seating and meal portions, to meet Ryan for dinner. He looks tidy with shirtsleeves that aren't rolled up this time under a dark chocolate blazer. We settle into a table for two, covered with a red-checkered tablecloth. Ryan orders a couple of glasses of Chianti. There's an awkward pause, and I drink water, sit forward to unstick my leather jacket from the back of the chair, and wait until he speaks first.

"You're a lot like Sheila. You love the married man but get frustrated with the situation with his wife. You're often bewildered, aren't you?"

"How do you know *that*? You don't even know me."

I pull a breadstick from a bundle propped in a tall glass.

"You seem to get frustrated if you don't get what you want."

"Who says I get what I want?"

I snap a bite out of the stick.

Our heads move closer to each other.

"You wouldn't be here having dinner with the artistic director if you knew you weren't going to get the part of Sheila."

"Good point." I wave the stick and pop the remaining stub in my mouth.

Our wines arrive. I take a taste; the red is dry on my tongue. I take a sip of water and peer over my glass. It's his fault for looking so appealing, reclining in his chair, lean legs spread to balance a muscular frame. Color fills my face when his dark eyes look through me.

"What are you staring at?" I ask him.

"A split personality. I'm trying to sift through and find the real character here, Rose Dowling."

"Do you think you'll ever find her?"

"I will by the end of the show's run. And to that, let's toast."

"You're early," he says on Saturday, handing me a cup of hot coffee. We're standing stage left at a makeshift refreshment table, where a commercial-size coffeepot, a stack of Styrofoam cups, and open boxes of assorted donuts sit haphazardly. Stage spotlights remain off; only dim, recessed lights illuminate the blacked-out theater.

"Do the first ones in get a free cup of coffee? Where is everyone, by the way?" I see I'm the first to show up for rehearsal, except for a couple of stagehands who are rearranging a set of furniture.

"They won't be here until this afternoon. I want time with just you this morning to read through some scenes and block."

"Are you suggesting I need extra attention because I don't know where to jump in? I'm a professional; I come prepared and ready to work. I suggest you don't underestimate me until you've seen me." My jaw tightens, and I cross my arms.

He shakes his head emphatically. "Look, please don't take that the wrong way. I want to get to know you. I haven't worked with anyone with your experience in a long time. It's . . . refreshing."

Is he blushing?

"My reputation is on the line here. If I don't give you what you're looking for, please feel free to let me go. I guarantee I take direction very well." I smile curtly and grab a cinnamon donut.

"I knew the minute we started talking that you're exactly what I'm looking for. I don't believe I will be letting you go anytime soon."

My return to the theater is magical. Writing can be a solitary endeavor, so walking onstage as Sheila is like returning home to the fold. I feel like a bright light in the dark of the theater, where it's my place to be, for now. Maybe it's that I have turned the page to a new chapter in my life, where I have grown into a more comfortable skin, a better view of the world and of myself.

Playing a role in a new play has connected me to the writing side. The experience has allowed me to fall into the familiar and to be comfortable again. I'm ready to finish my story, with clarity and understanding that I don't have to hide behind roles, becoming someone else, to avoid finding who I really am. I will never lose myself in the part I play, but rather, I will always be there even when my character no longer is.

On closing night, the day before my birthday, I walk behind the theater to the dressing rooms. I remember the first rehearsal here, when I expected a room with poor lighting, an unstable chair, and a cramped hair and makeup table . . . and no hangers. But this once-old cleaning closet, office, and storage room, now converted to a large space, is the cleanest, biggest dressing room I have ever been in. And there are plenty of hangers for all of us.

In the muted light of the room, a round scarlet bundle wrapped in tan paper, with a small note dangling from twine, brightens the middle of the table adorned by gold lipstick tubes and jars of crème. I step to the rose bouquet and bring it close to my face. The fragrance is intoxicating and adds to a high I am already feeling as showtime nears. "Happy birthday, my true Rose. Love, Ryan," reads the note. How does he know?

"I know it's tomorrow, but tonight is the last night of the show. We have two days of celebration," Ryan says from behind me, placing his hands on my shoulders. I turn to look at him and smile. "They're lovely. Thank you." I stand and we hug. I urgently turn my head to offer him my cheek when he goes in for a passionate kiss.

The morning after closing night is a hangover without the booze: we are drunk and giddy from the play's success. Okay, so there are a few bottles of the bubbly circulating at Byron's on Clark, where about a dozen of us manage to overtake the place.

"Anything lined up yet, Rose?" Ryan yells. We're sitting tightly among other cast members in a lumpy Naugahyde booth.

I half hear his question because I am too distracted by loud surrounding laughter and conversation. Our arms work not in sync but in opposition as we grab pizza slices from cartons, scoop Caesar salad from a giant wooden bowl, and fill glasses of red wine and beer.

"Lined up? You mean auditions? Roles?" I shout, taking a stab at my salad.

"Yes. I've got a couple of leads for you. Actually, you probably don't need my help, as the press took a hold of this run. You've made quite a name for yourself," he says, leaning within inches of my face.

As much as Ryan encourages me to take on additional roles, I can't, not because I don't want to. And I can't say I have outgrown the avocation. Outgrowing something implies you have become too big and can never slip back into what you were wearing. I can slip back into what I was wearing. I have proved it with the show's run. But maybe I have moved past a time in my life when I routinely filled someone else's shoes and became a different person.

"I'm done. I've got another project I've been working on while doing this show. And I'm going back to it full-time," I shout above the conversation noise.

"You can't be serious." He puts down his fork and shifts in his seat.

"Why wouldn't I be serious with you?" I twist my shoulders away from him, creating more space between our heads.

"You have to stay in the theater. Doors are opening . . . have opened for you. Chicago, and then who knows where. I chose you because you are everything the others aren't. We worked well together, a team. I could help you . . . manage your work . . ." His open hands beg for understanding.

"Ryan, I'm not interested. No. There's nothing more to say. Besides, this is not the time or place. We're here to celebrate what was, not the future."

I don't need to be surrounded by people who play characters, acting out scenes that aren't real. I am real now and asserting my position, one Ryan took as something long term, but was only a short-term opportunity for me.

It's getting late, and I'm ready to leave. I pull my shawl tightly around my shoulders and excuse myself from the booth.

"You leaving already?"

"Yes."

I raise my voice above the others who are sitting at our table and standing around it.

"This has been a memorable evening, everyone, and truly a wonderful ride. I wish you all the best, and I'll be watching to see what your next stops will be."

I turn to Ryan. "I'll see you sometime down the road. I'll be in the audience. Good luck to you," I shout, waving goodbye.

I don't deny my initial physical attraction to him. But my spirit told me it was time to break from old patterns. I'm not going to team up with Ryan, as I did with Julian, but with only myself.

The next morning, I take a mind-clearing walk to Wizard's Park, about four blocks straight east. I think of Linney and her walking practices, and of Dad and how he gets in the car and drives when needing to clear his mind, and of Ma, who sits under the willow to reconnect. Cooler, stronger east winds off the lake make my eyes tear and my nose run while I stare at the restless blue-gray lake ahead. The changes of seasons are in me, too. For a while, I was back where I once belonged, but writing this book is where I belong, too. I can leave the theater, for a time, anyway, and be okay doing something else.

The lake is endless and open; the water is like a chameleon, changing its mood and its colors from aqua to blue to green, meeting a thin line of dark gray horizon. The world, too, appears big, with its definition that is neither black nor white. And I recognize a new definition of my own place as I am making my way through it. Though lonely at times, I am reminded that I will be fine.

The following week, on a Saturday morning, I brew a pot of tea, sit at my kitchen table, and think of Linney. She's got a tea for every feeling and ailment. Upset stomach? Ginger. Can't sleep? Chamomile. I don't have a particular feeling, so I go with green. "Just green?" I can hear her say. I think how I've become a writer for me, and for this reason I continue working on my manuscript. And when I pick up where I left off, I realize I have been writing my story all along, honing my skills, gathering years' worth of experiences with a travelogue of places and people, and, in a covert way, learning my place to be.

Writing a story of myself may sound trite or self-indulgent, but I care. I care enough about myself to show the world the real Rose and no other character.

⚘ Charlotte ⚘

Rose calls me Sunday afternoon. Says she is going to see Deb's new place at six o'clock and wants me to join them. I'm excited to see my big sister's new place. Though I'm unsure of what to expect, with the monogram thing gone, one thing is for sure: she will make it her own. She won't need any initials telling visitors it is her home because her personality will come through in every room.

My sisters and I arrive at Deb's pretty much at the same time. That's one thing you could always say about us Dowling sisters. We're always punctual, never late.

The door is already open when I bring up the rear, peering inside over the shoulders of Rose, who is clutching a bottle of prosecco, and Linney, who stands in the doorway. "Are we going to have to check out your new place from out here?" I yell through the sister-wall in front of me.

"C'mon in, all of you." Deb ushers us in. She is dressed comfortably in wide-legged black pants and a long-sleeved gold tunic. Her chestnut mane is pulled back in a ponytail.

"Oh, this is a wonderful place for you," Linney says, taking off her sunglasses, turning her head to give a wide look about the place. Her green eyes are as big as her smile. "The light . . . it shines straight through." I watch Linney glide through the first floor and wave her hands as if ushering in an aura with the light. "The backyard . . . no willow, but a birch." Deb busts out a laugh.

"I'm so glad you're all here," Deb says, clapping her hands. "Have a look around."

Deb never said that to us before in her home with Dennis. Telling anyone to look around was like giving them permission to snoop in what was once their privacy. But now it's different. She's an open book, vulnerable.

Her new home is open and spacious, with adequate seating in the living room and just enough shelf space and tabletops to display photos, green growing things, and books on marketing and novels of historical fiction.

Deb escorts us around the first floor. She stares at a dining room table as if something doesn't look quite right. But we move along, and after a tour of the upstairs, an efficient floor of three neutral color-coordinated bedrooms and a complete bathroom, we convene in the kitchen just long enough for Deb to grab the prosecco.

Rose wrinkles her face. "Kinda sparse."

"Nothing wrong with that," Linney says. "Maybe you should look at following Deb's lead and give away all that stuff you've accumulated from your trips. Just how many tchotchkes does a girl need, anyway?"

"I'm not getting rid of anything. Those are my connections to the places I've been and to the people I've met. So, drop it, Lin."

"Okay, you guys. Perhaps you've forgotten we're grown now and have taken different paths," Deb says. "C'mon, let's sit; grab a glass."

We file into the new crème sectional and plop down, sitting L-shaped around a circular wooden coffee table. A cool cross-breeze slips through open windows, bringing with it a sweet fragrance of chrysanthemums as we adjust throw pillows and our legs. Deb gives each glass a good pour and starts the conversation.

"When we were all in our twenties, we couldn't possibly be bothered with each other. And now the Dowling women are grown up. When we were in middle school, we were so different. Charlotte, the baby, an attention-getter; Rose and her dressing up in Ma's clothes and costume jewelry, in her own world of make-believe; Linney digging, always out back, in the dirt and planting and replanting to find good homes for all God's things; and me, looking over all of you like a drill sergeant inspecting the troops. Now, different bodies, but still the same faces. You can tell we are connected by looking at each other's eyes and see Ma's spirit and Dad's loyal soul. And now we come together having found our own pockets of living. I miss my sisters. I miss the camaraderie."

It's quiet for a moment. We sip and then Rose breaks the silence. "What's next for you, Deb? Are you on speaking terms with Dennis? And Charlie? I bet you miss him terribly."

"The good news is my boss switched around my portfolio, so no more BMT Worldwide, which means no more 'T' either. Actually, I haven't seen him since he picked up the last of his things. As far as Charlie goes, well, he's a typical fifteen-year-old, hunkering down with Pokémon a lot lately in his bedroom."

"Okay, my turn. Calling on you, Rose," Deb says. Charlotte tells me you're sticking around here for a while. Any particular reason? The Irish guy didn't work out, huh?"

"No, the Irish guy didn't work out. Now, if everyone would please stop asking me about him. I've moved on and want to settle in at home . . . by myself. I don't regret any of my relationships or traveling to the places where I've started them. It's made me who I am today, kind of introspective," Rose says, taking a sip and tilting her head back, freeing her vision from her long bangs.

"Whoa . . . Rose? Is this the true you? This isn't a character seeping into your pores?" Linney says.

"Thanks, Linney, for your support, when I'm trying to get real with myself."

"I didn't mean anything bad, Rose. It's that I'm glad to see my real sister and not the chameleon-like drama queen otherwise known as an actress."

". . . and on that note, I think I'll open another bottle," Deb says. "There's something going on with you, though. I know you well enough to know that when you lift your eyebrows enough to hide them under your bangs, you're indeed hiding something."

"I've written a book, kind of like a memoir, I guess . . . There. I said it. Now no comments, okay?"

"Huh? A what?" Deb refills glasses. "And what *exactly* about your life are you writing about, anyway?"

"My travels. From the local theaters to world cities, and the people I've gotten to know."

Linney shifts to the end of her seat. "Oh, like a travelogue?"

"Um, not exactly. Things I've learned . . . about myself, through meeting others in foreign places."

"Oh, good Lord," I interrupt. "A drama queen who thinks she's *that* experienced, enough to write about places far from Chicago." I cross my arms and roll my eyes. "As long as it's not about us."

"You don't have to look so disgusted, Char," Linney says. "Rose has a few years on you." Linney winks and takes a sip.

"Well, that's fantastic!" Deb says.

"You've got my support, and I'm sure the rest of us support you, too," I say. "I've read all your articles and followed your travels. They're wonderful. And I bet it takes some real digging to look into all those experiences and what they, and the relationships, meant to you."

"Yeah. Can't wait to read it. Hurry up. I want to know your secrets." Linney giggles.

"Okay, Linney, your turn," Rose says.

"Well, I wanted to wait before telling you . . . when we could all be . . ."

"Do you need a drumroll or something?" I ask.

"What? What is it?" Rose says, moving to the edge of the seat.

"Well, I'm sure you heard that Bridget died last month . . ."

"Yes . . . Ma told us," Deb says. "We didn't want to bring it up to you until you were ready to say something."

"Well, it certainly wasn't *my* news to bring up," I mumble, bowing my head. I recall a similar time when I faced accusatory pointed fingers for not telling right away that Ma was sick.

"Well, Bridget left me Magnolia."

A chorus of "what?" resounds around the table as glasses are put down.

"I wake up each morning realizing I'm a business owner, and I go to bed thinking about it. I dwell on what to do to not lose money, how to attract new customers, and better yet, how to keep the ones we have . . . or had. I'll have to dip into the funds of what Bridget set aside for emergencies to pay the bills. I'm afraid I'm going to have to close Magnolia on Labor Day weekend, unless some miracle happens, and I can be assured of continued financial support in some way."

"Oh, Linney, I'm so sorry for all you're going through. I know how much the shop and Bridget mean to you. And now losing both," Deb says. Having that job and running the shop alongside a spirited mentor is all that Linney has come to know. "It'll all work out," Deb tells her. "Remember the time when we were kids, and Dad took a wrong turn on our cross-country trip back home, and we ended up having to go through Wyoming? We ended up stopping in Jackson Hole and at first thought it was going to be a real hole, but it actually was a cool place. He told us there are never any wrong turns in life and that you can end up where you least expected. Maybe this is a turning point for you, and you'll end up somewhere you didn't expect to be, and you will find your way."

"Let's hope it's not in some remote desert in the middle of the country, miles away from where she wants to be," Rose says, lifting her glass to toast.

I listen as my sisters catch up with each other, bantering back and forth about their jobs and relationships, my head bouncing from one sister to another. I shift on the couch, and my attention is

drawn outside, to a birch tree's slender leaves waving in the backyard. I think of the willow and of the memories made under it.

"Charlotte, you're awfully quiet. You okay?" Deb asks.

I sigh . . . and then I let it out. "You all go on about your lives.
But what about Ma? You're all so involved with yourselves, your jobs,
making money, and men. Well, let me tell you. The only involvement
I've had is with our mother. Not sure you've ever noticed while
you're too busy with a hotshot job in the city or traveling all over the
world and meeting one man after another, or all consumed with
running a shop, that you forgot who your family is, and that I've
been taking care of our mother. And because I help her often, I was
the one who took her to the doctor to find out she's going to die. I
had to keep this secret from all of you for months, carrying a lone
burden and not knowing what to do." I am flushed with heat. In a
crackling voice, I tell them, "I may not have a high-paying job or an
acting gig, or run a business, but I sure as hell have learned a sense
of responsibility. I've had to grow up a lot quicker than any of you. I
may be the youngest, but I've always known my place to be is at
home with our parents, unlike all of you, who consider your places
to be as far away from home as possible."

My words spark silence. The room holds still. After a beat, Deb
talks first.

"I didn't . . . I had no idea, Char, that this is all going on with
you. I'm sorry you've felt this way for a long time. I'm sorry you've
had the burden to keep silent about Ma's illness."

"We all have burdens," Rose whispers. "Until I started writing
this book and reflecting on my life's choices, I thought I was doing
and being exactly what I was meant to do and to be. That was the
easy, most convenient way of looking at it. I never questioned if I
should be somewhere else, or if I was called to be doing something
other than what I had known. Or . . . it's just how I deal with things. I

don't know, Charlotte, maybe I have split personalities or something."

"That's not funny," I bark.

"It's not meant to be funny. I'm sorry you've had resentment building up, and you couldn't tell us," Deb says, wrapping her arms around my stiffened shoulders.

"Yeah, like when? Was I supposed to call you, Deb, and interrupt you at work or at home with Dennis to talk? Or how about you, Linney—stop by the shop and ask to talk to you in the back office, taking you away from customers? Or how about you, Rose? Should I have flown to Ireland—or wait, you're not there because you just flew to London."

"You all have been about as unconnected to where you began in life as . . . as . . . oh, I don't know anymore."

I wave the air as if to clear it from my confusion, then drop my head and grab a stuffed pillow and hug it around my middle for comfort, as if to cover myself from vulnerabilities that were just let loose.

And then I fall apart. I become small on the couch, slumped, and I can feel my face becoming blotchy as tears tumble. My sisters rally to my side with hugs and pats on the back and "it'll be all rights."

"Charlotte, you're right," Rose says.

"There's nothing more to say," Linney adds.

"The youngest one is the most tuned in and connected of all of us," Deb says.

I am relieved from holding onto my emotions, as the old Charlotte had held them tight. The new Charlotte has learned to connect to her sisters, to be honest about her feelings. My sisters are family, and I now understand who will always be there for me.

☙ Margaret ❧

Winds blow in earnest through the old bedroom windows, and I shake along with the disturbed trees. I rest in the corner upon the chaise, where the back of the chair supports my head as it hurts, too, like an electrical current that has shorted down my spine with no ending. I peer at the gardens; once in sharp focus, they are now shriveled to a blurred version of themselves. I watch Joe give the thin lawn perhaps one last mow, recalling the sweet scent of cut grass that once wafted through open windows in summer, now stifled as the season's bounty draws to a close. I feel like the yard looks.

I'm relieved I don't have to keep my illness from anyone; relieved Charlotte no longer has to be the secret keeper. Now, I am simply at peace, catching the willow's smile in casual breezes as its stooped frame broadens to welcome all under its canopy.

"You okay there, Ma?" Charlotte whispers from the bedroom doorway.

"I'm just fine, dear. C'mon over here and sit." I move my feet aside to give her room to plop her bottom on the bed. Her once anxious demeanor seems to have given way to a more calm, mature self.

We don't talk at first. The quiet is our conversation, as I know what she is thinking. Her eyes catch the willow stirring outside, then shift to me, as if she is replaying memories of seeing her family sitting under the tree and listening to lessons about connections to all living things. It mirrors my thoughts, too. It doesn't seem long ago that we spent Sundays under the willow. What happened to all those years in the middle?

"The rose blooms looked big this year; they almost looked like the hydrangeas," she tells me.

I laugh at that one. They really didn't.

"How's Pearl working out?"

"She makes me tired just watching her efficiency. The laundry is done, and dinner made and ready for your father to heat up. She's all business, though. Not much conversation except when she has a question."

Having someone around to help takes a lot off Joe's mind. But it is a feat, convincing him he can't do all of it himself, especially when it comes to bathing and dressing me, tasks I do not look forward to. How the bathwater is like ice; how I dread taking off my clothes to face a body that isn't mine anymore, but rather a stack of bones and thin, ripply skin. How well I've come to know my body. But now, I think I don't know it at all. I am a frightening sight in the mirror. I inspect my feet, where the bones are no longer in command of my steps, then travel up to the top of my head, where I confront an uninvited beast that has taken up space, pushing out decades of knowledge and earned wisdom, infiltrating, then halting the flow of what makes me, me. And then there's fire. I envision heat and flames burning the offender, pushing it out of its comfortable place. I imagine the black beast retreating, shrinking, disappearing, and I hope to will it away. But neither my body nor my spirit is strong anymore. The fire extinguishes, and what remains is room for regrowth. That's what I want to do. I want to make room for new growth. I want to weave through the trees of connections and feel the security of the old growth of trees, of being part of something bigger, of seeing the light.

I don't remember much after that as I fall into a deep sleep.

PART
III

"*Walk tall as the trees, live strong as the mountains, be gentle as the spring winds, keep the warmth of the summer sun in your heart and the great spirit will always be with you.*"
—NATIVE AMERICAN PROVERB

Labor Day

⋙ Charlotte ⋘

I hold steady next to her hospital bed, my body pulled tight, my hands folded in prayer. I review her in stillness in the artificial light of the gray room. She is supposed to be my mother, a tall, hearty Irishwoman who dresses in cotton skirts and white blouses, and practical flat shoes, with wavy chestnut hair held off her face by an evergreen headband, her face full and pink with blushing life. But she is a body in form and structure I have not seen before. She appears at peace with a soft face and steady breathing, shrouded in cotton covers that outline her thin frame. Of all the years I have watched over her and Dad, I have never imagined my mother looking like something other. I sit and take Ma's frail hand and nestle it inside mine. I hope she can feel our connection.

"In the attic," she whispers, "the trunk." I see her lips part, then move, but I can barely hear what's passing through them. I lean my face closer to hers. She mouths, "Char, promise me . . . the trunk . . . you'll look in the attic."

"Ma, yes, I hear you. I'll find the trunk in the attic. Don't worry about a thing. I'll take care of it," I assure her with touches to her bony shoulder.

Dad is sitting with a staid face in a large corner recliner by a window where the blinds remain closed to the morning's rising sun.

He has been there all night. His plaid shirt is loose around his waist, his wiry salt-and-pepper hair uncombed. I don't think he's said a word since he first sat down there yesterday afternoon. I guess he doesn't need to. Ma has always been the pack leader, the one with the words. But I can read the words on his face. He just can't say them.

"Hang in there, Ma. It's Labor Day weekend, and you know how the Dowlings think of it as celebrating the past season," I tell her quietly, sitting on the edge of her bed. "And we've had our weekends, haven't we? But there is always Sunday, your day of rest, when you call us to the tree to our sit spot, to watch, to feel, to taste, and to hear a season in transition. Only, there's not much of a difference today. The day is warming like any summer day in July."

I reason that as long as I talk, Ma will stay awake, but she is slipping in and out of sleep; her now irregular breathing tells me so.

I study her small face, with indentations made by the oxygen mask and hard wrinkles created by the journey through her history. I open the nightstand drawer and grab a section of the newspaper to read to her. "It's—Saturday, Labor Day weekend," I remind Ma. "It's the close of summer. We've got work to do in the yard."

I bow my head as I can't hold back my tears any longer. I turn to look at Dad. His staring eyes seem to see a nothingness in the air.

I ask for his attention. "Dad, we need to call my sisters."

⋙ Debra ⋘

Charlie is staying with me this Labor Day weekend, and I thought we'd take a drive to the Skokie Lagoons, rent canoes, and then head to the Chicago Botanic Garden for a picnic. With the best days yet ahead this time of year here, I want to spend them outside, and with Charlie.

I know it's unusual to be in Charlie's life after the divorce, but Dennis can't be someone Charlie can count on anymore. He has hopped from the ad agency business over to the advertising and marketing department of one of his clients, and his professional and personal travels take him away from his son for weeks or months at a time. I told Charlie, after I married his father, that he can count on me to be there, always, despite his father's absences and his remarried mother, who relocated overseas and feels that checking in by phone periodically is a sufficient motherly obligation. My presence in Charlie's life remains uncontested by his parents, and I say we have a special relationship of which I am most proud.

"Hey, kiddo. Boy, you've sprouted since the last time I saw you, and that was just a month ago. And what's with the hair? Who knew you had such natural curls? You'll have to tell me what your secret is," I tell Charlie as he drops into the front seat of the car. His long, athletic legs are outgrowing the legs of his jeans, yet his shirt seems to always remain oversize. He gives me an eye roll in greeting.

"Oh, look, there's something growing out of your ears. Strings? You've got strings growing from your ears. What happens if I pull on them? Will the insides of your ears come out?"

He unenthusiastically plucks his earbuds from his ears, and again, the eye roll.

"Eager to see my new place? There's a bedroom for you with plenty of room to add your own stuff. I want it to be your space, ya know, to do whatever you fifteen-year-olds do in a closed bedroom . . . and I don't mean *that* kind of stuff."

Isn't this the child I helped to raise? Though I'm not sure I can call him a child anymore. He is growing into a man, a big person who will learn to drive, to vote, to drink, to date, to get a job. And all I want to do is to go kayaking with him.

I forget how long teenagers sleep in in the morning. It gives me time to make a breakfast of cinnamon rolls and a frittata. It has been a long time since I made a meal from scratch; I lost motivation since I have been cooking just for one. And now that it's not about me anymore, I have come full circle with coming to the table and sharing a meal. Though it's just Charlie and me, I realize we can still be a family.

After I set the table, it doesn't look quite right. I realize something is missing. My old linen tablecloth. Back then, it was a requirement to come to the table and to share a meal among all family. It was something that was a part of our lives. Not having it is a missing link in our family structure. But in its memory, now, I can see how far I've come.

I hear water running and thumping footsteps upstairs. Charlie is awake.

"I'm hoping it is the smell of my cinnamon rolls that woke you up and not my banging around to make us breakfast," I say to him, offering a good-morning squeeze around him as he stands in the kitchen. His dishwater-blond hair looks darker when wet. He smells of Ivory soap, just like that first day when I met him at the zoo.

"Smells good," he utters, diving for a seat at the round dinette table.

"I forget that in addition to teenagers sleeping late, their sentences are limited to two or maybe three words, if I'm lucky."

Charlie eats as if he hasn't eaten anything in days, one forkful after another with no breath in between. I grin as I watch him.

I join him, pouring myself a cup of coffee first.

"Hey, I'm glad you're no longer a picky eater." I think back to when he was a toddler and would separate the peas from the carrots on his tray table. I watch him before taking my first bite.

"You make good food," he mumbles in between mouthfuls.

"Why, thank you, young man. Glad you like it." I smile and give him a nudge with my elbow. He blushes.

Through a good home-cooked meal, I'm learning to increase our communication. Ma always had a hot meal for dinner before us at the table, one that she made from love, one that was a connection to the circle of comfort and familiarity around the table with family.

I put down my fork and take a full breath before speaking, laying my hands in my lap.

"I'm sorry you had to move from the only home you knew." I turn to him in apology and look down at my plate in shame, as if it were my fault and I am asking for forgiveness.

"You got bounced from your mom's house to your dad's. I understand your troubles over those years in finding where you felt you were supposed to be."

I want to embrace him, to reach out and hold on to this maturing boy, but I keep to myself to give him any space he might need.

With a disconnected dad and a stepmother who couldn't keep together all the moving parts of a marriage and family, the kid is doing well. I reassure Charlie that our splitting up was best for everyone.

"It's what was best for Dad, you mean." Charlie stops eating. I can't argue with him. He looks directly at me. There is sadness and even pain in his eyes as he gives me a quick glance before taking another bite.

"I'm here, Charlie. Always will be."

I wait for his reaction before I say or do anything. I want our conversation to be about him.

"I know," he says matter-of-factly, then takes a big bite from his cinnamon roll. And I wrap my arms around his broad shoulders and tell him he's the most special person in my life, and that I've loved him since the day I met him at the zoo. He leans his head into mine. It feels miraculous that our relationship has gone undeterred despite the changes in his life.

We finish breakfast, and I dump the dirty dishes into the sink.

"I'll clean up when we get back. Get ready. We'll be leaving soon."

I start packing for our morning at the lagoons when the phone rings.

"Deb, you need to get to the hospital," Charlotte says urgently.

⇝ Linney ⇜

Suddenly, Dottie barks, sticks her wet nose in the air, and howls at an intruding scent. I hear a racket and think it is our resident chipmunks using the downspouts as a treadmill. She rushes to Magnolia's front door and scratches it. I open it just enough to peek at who is there.

"Jesus, what do you think you're . . . Mr. Leone? What are you doing lurking around at this early morning hour?" I open the door wider to get a full look at him. He looks just like the last time I saw him—navy sport jacket, white shirt with cuffed sleeves, tan slacks—except his hair is longer, untidy, contradicting his otherwise finished appearance.

"You could use some new downspouts," he says, looking around the exterior of the shop. "And . . . gutters, too, if you don't mind me saying."

"Well, I do mind. You scared me. You make it a habit to trespass where you don't belong?"

"I'm not trespassing."

I roll my eyes.

"We don't open for another couple of hours. What is it you want?"

The brisk winds push their way through the door, challenging me to hold it steady. Swirls of dried leaves settle inside on the shop's floor.

"Can I come in, please? It's been a while since we saw each other."

I think about shutting the door in his face. And I also think about telling him he needs to make an appointment to see me. But since neither is going to completely rid me of him, I let him in.

"Follow me into the office, please," I tell him as I lead him down the hall. "You've got a knack for sneaking up on people." Dottie gives him a good sniff around the ankles while we walk.

"Please, sit."

I sit tall opposite him with my hands firmly folded in front of me, bracing for what is to come next. I notice the jar of crystals sitting in the middle of the table; the sun beams at just the right angle to illuminate the cuts of the minerals. The sight is calming.

"I didn't mean to be a cause for alarm. Actually, I didn't know if this place would still be open. I heard about Bridget, and I'm sorry about that. What will happen to Magnolia?"

I eye him warily, wondering if he is asking out of genuine concern for the shop or his own personal interests. "Why do you ask?"

"I'm still interested in this place and was wondering . . ." He leans closer, pushing a musky scent of cologne to my nose.

"Well, you can stop wondering because I'm still interested in this place, too. Bridget left Magnolia to me, and I'm not letting any person or rich investors talk me into anything otherwise," I tell him assuredly. I realize I'm sitting in Bridget's chair. She is here with me.

"Tell you what, Ms. Dowling. Can I call you Linney? Seems like we should be on first- name terms after all this time."

"Go on."

"I'd like to make you an offer."

He runs his hands through his black hair, taming errant strands.

I interrupt with a wave of my hand to cut him off.

"I've already heard your offer and have not forgotten it, as you have reminded me more than once. As I told you before and, now . . ."

"I see how understandably connected you are to this place." His voice quiets.

". . . and what would be in it for me, Mr. Leone?"

"Would you be interested in, let's say, yoga classes here, and wellness workshops? How about selling flowers and organic skin-care items or whatever the hell it is you organic types are into." He slides back in his chair and crosses one leg over the other. "I'll take a modest portion of the sales, and you keep the rest. You have free rein over the shop, to manage your own business, whatever you'd like to make it."

"What's the catch? And what would be in it for *you*?" I ask.

"No catch at all. I trust you'll take care of my business as if it were your own. And—"

"But you'll still be the sole owner. *That's* the catch, isn't it?" I ask.

"And I'll get to see you . . . more often."

I squint at him and cross my arms. He grins and cocks his head to one side. *Is he flirting with me?* I must admit, his attractiveness eases my wariness.

"Mr. Leone, this is not a game here. We are talking about a serious business transaction."

"Miss Dowling, if you can't have fun while conducting business, then, well, why are you doing it in the first place?" His eyes move around the room, from Bridget's desk to the walls of landscape paintings, to a seating area at the other end of the room, then back on me. "You look as if you have fun here maintaining the business of

Magnolia. You've turned it into quite a personal, homey spot." He grows a smile.

"Mr. Leone, I'll need . . . some time."

I slide off my sandals and run my bare feet in the rug.

I consider if our relationship doesn't need to remain so businesslike. I'm getting tired of our confrontations being adversarial—there must be a better way to make this work. I realize this is something Bridget would have considered.

"Take all the time you need. How about spending some of it over dinner? Tonight, with me?"

"But how will that look, having a social evening with your potential employer?"

"I won't tell, if you don't tell you're having dinner with your boss. And it's Alex."

I think how Mr. Leone has returned like a lost ship in the night to make me an offer that is appealing. The shop still needs repairs . . . the money . . . which Magnolia doesn't have. But then I would be turning Bridget's Magnolia into something . . . of mine. And I think that Bridget would be just fine with that. But what if I fail?

At midday, I take a break with a cup of tea and yogurt topped with homemade granola and sit a while at Bridget's desk. I look for some direction out in the gardens. I think of Deb. She'd know what to do when it comes to these business things, and I give her a call. I think never in all our growing-up years I'd asked her for advice because she would give it unsolicited anyway.

"I'm so glad you all came over the other night," she says, squealing between words. "I had no idea Charlotte was feeling this way. Did you? I guess we've all been so busy going about our own business that we've lost sight that our business is our family, and that we should have—"

"Deb, sorry, can you stop a minute? I need your advice. You remember the guy who wanted to talk to Bridget about buying Magnolia? Well, he showed up at the shop this morning. Said he heard about Bridget in the papers. He made me a new offer that, frankly, I don't think I can walk away from. He's pretty convincing, but I don't want to be taken advantage of."

"And . . ."

"He'd buy Magnolia, and I could stay. I would be free to do whatever I want with the shop. I could have yoga classes, create a wellness shop, and sell a few things. Said he'd be investing in the place and in me."

"So, what's the problem? Sounds like a great deal. You'll have a job, you won't lose Magnolia, and you'd make it your own."

"And he wants to have dinner with me, tonight, to talk more about it."

"And is *that* the problem? The seeing him part?"

"He's pushy. Like he expects each time to get what he wants. And it goes against my nature. Expectations are a funny thing. I've never had any, and I've been quite content without them."

"You don't have to marry him. He'll just be the person who owns the place. Go to dinner. Enjoy his company outside of work. Your life can't be all business, Linney. Do you even have any friends, any social time outside of that place?"

I don't answer her. Isn't she supposed to make me feel better? Making me look like a lonesome loser is more like it.

"Just because I'm a year shy of my fourth decade, with neither a man in my life nor any women friends, and I haven't met your expectations, doesn't make me a lesser person."

"When Dennis and I married, I expected to be a ready-made

family. I expected the connections to zap together right away, to feel
I belonged and that we were a unit in harmony and rhythm, like a
superpower that could never be powered down. We charged our unit
at the table. Meeting each night was what families did, and we did it,
too. It was what I expected. My expectations defined me, and when
they were no longer met, what was I supposed to do? Linney, you're
a tough cookie. You're doing just fine on your own, with the help of
your sisters now and then."

We laugh. It's been a while since she and I laughed together;
maybe at each other, but never really together, like friends.

"And it's not going to be all business all the time, ya know," she
says.

That night, Alex and I relax at our table for two at Avanzare. The
place is fancier than I'm used to, with white tablecloths, delicate
stemware, and a shiny silverware set with many pieces. Now I have a
good look at him, his dark almond eyes, Roman nose, and smile that
activates his dimples. There's a European elegance to his simple
dress of black slacks and starched white shirt. Violins in the background play quietly from overhead speakers, enough not to drown
out our conversation.

"Like I was saying, Alex, thank you for your offer." I wring my
hands in anticipation while shifting to calm an unsettledness. "I've
thought about what you said, and I think it best . . ."

He refills our glasses with more sparkling wine. Between this
second glass of sparkly and the candlelight, I am beginning to think
I, myself, am shining, lit up, and not in a good way. I can't remember
the last time I had a glass of alcohol. The tiny bubbles pop and float
up my nose and down my throat.

". . . I think it's in my best interest and in Magnolia's that I accept your offer." I open my twisted hands flat on the table. My silver bangles clash and jingle as if a closing to the open offer. "I will manage Magnolia's rehab and the startup of a new business. And, of course, I expect the terms put into a contract where we both sign in agreement."

That's one from Deb. I wouldn't have thought in a million years about putting the arrangement in writing with our signatures. I think how there's much I have yet to learn.

"Well, I'm glad. Let's toast to our new venture. To Linney and Alex. May they become successful together and live happily ever after."

There's a new, different sparkle in his eyes as he reaches across the table to embrace the top of my hand with his.

I don't remember the last time I had a reason to giggle. Not laughing because something was funny but to giggle in a silly, carefree way because, well, I am happy. I think of how much I've been missing from not being in the company of friends or someone I am attracted to. Though Alex has grated on me since day one, the irritation has weakened. We're partners now, in business and in friendship.

Alex stops by the shop every couple of days, and when he doesn't, he calls. I look forward to his "check-in," as he calls it, with the new manager of the new store. I appreciate his active presence in my daily work, and it gives me a chance to ask him a lot of questions while the contract is quickly drawn.

One morning the following week, I hear whistling. Dottie does, too, and her ears prick up. Together, we shift our heads from side to side to figure out the source. A knock on the door. I open it, and it is Alex.

"This is it, Linney, the official papers," he says, waving the thing in my face as if I don't notice it. He is more casually dressed—hooded sweatshirt, jogging pants, and very white Nikes on his feet—than I am used to seeing him.

"Well, then, let's make it official."

With pep in our step, we walk down the hall to the office. My hands twitch with nerves, and I can't sit any closer to the edge of my chair, as for sure I'd fall off. Alex slides the bundle of papers from the envelope and pushes one stack to me, keeping the other for himself. "Let's go over these, shall we, now that our attorneys have reviewed them?" he says. Together, we page through the terms, and I am satisfied with them.

While I ink my signature not only on a black line, but also to a new business endeavor, I think of Bridget. I do miss her, but I know she is proud of me, starting a new shop I can make my own, carrying on just as she did when she started Magnolia.

I sit back in Bridget's chair, now mine, relaxed. While he gathers the papers and slides them into an envelope, I ask him, "Now that we've settled our new joint venture, how about spending some of the Labor Day weekend with me? We'll have a walk on the beach, drop in a yoga class at Gilson Park, grab lunch at Jackie's Bistro, and go for a bike ride. Perhaps it's time you get out yourself, Mr. Alex, and enjoy life outside instead of inside behind a desk, giving direction. Let me direct the day."

"I see you're quite a go-getter. I like that. But how about the beach walk first, for starters, and then see what happens after that, shall we?"

"Sure. Whatever you'd like to do . . . boss man."

I give him a poke in his side. He wiggles and laughs. I join him with a hearty laugh, too.

"Now that you're making commitments in business, perhaps making personal commitments is next for you. Can you make personal commitments, too?" he asks. I think my naivete at this boy-girl dance is showing. I straighten up, contemplating his question. I assume it's rhetorical, but I play an answer in my head anyway.

I sober.

"I think I already have. Bridget's death, your offer to me, changing ownership and management of Magnolia, dinner . . . it's all very personal."

"Well, then, Linney, let's look forward to our time together over the holiday weekend," he says as I walk him out the front door. "I'll call you tomorrow, and we can firm up our plans."

I close the door, then face the shop. I peruse every table, wall shelf, and nook holding the familiar items of Magnolia, where once broken pieces of her connections have now found their fittings. Alex is an answer to my moving forward with new ventures in my life, professionally and personally, as I begin to have closure with Bridget's death. I am satisfied I made the best decision for Magnolia and for me.

I get home later that afternoon, and my inner dialogue whirls . . . it all happened fast . . .

The phone rings.

"You need to get to the hospital," Charlotte tells me.

Rose

Well, it's done. Thank God I know what it means to work under a deadline, as I imposed one on myself. I wanted to get a final draft of my book completed by the end of the year, but I finish early. Editing my own articles is one thing; it's what I've learned over the years, but finalizing my own story is a personal testament to my learned wisdom. It's one accomplishment I can speak of.

A bright sky calls me from my cocoon inside to the outside world. I hitch on my sandals, grab a baseball cap and sunglasses, and start out for a walk. The lower sun in the late season filters through trees which have slowed their growth. I meet the end of the street and turn east, a habit I've fallen into since I've been actually living here. Exploring my neighborhood and points beyond is an exercise in connecting.

My desire to act and to be Sheila ran its course, and I'm ready to be rid of her. I no longer feel I need to take on a new role to figure out who I need to become. Using these past weeks to work on my book has been an opportunity to see who I am, and that is someone I like just fine.

But I do miss Ryan. How odd for me to say that I miss anyone. I wonder if this unusual feeling is because I've changed. I've gone from feeling just fine without male companionship to feeling a void, a lack of connection to someone. I remember Ma telling us when we used to sit under the willow on summer afternoons that everything has its own time, from a rosebud unraveling her petals to a friend-ship evolving into a deeper relationship. You can't hurry any of it or slow it down. Know that it will eventually be what it is meant to be.

I stop at Grinds, the coffee shop Ryan and I frequented near the theater. A college student wearing a Northwestern T-shirt sits alone at a table with thick textbooks, flicking his Bic pen on an open blank notebook. At the next table, an older gentleman wears green sus-penders over a Grateful Dead shirt and contemplates while looking out the window. It is quiet except for the occasional whirring of a coffee grinder. The roasted bean aroma gently stirs from activated ceiling fans.

While I order a cappuccino then dig in my wallet for a few dollar bills and some change, a man's voice yells from behind me. Its commanding tone and volume startle me.

"Double espresso."

"You back, so soon?" the barista asks the man. She is an attractive middle-aged woman, heavyset with an ample bosom. Her deep-set brown eyes are striking as is her toothy white smile, one that would light up anyone who greets her. I lean aside to allow for the two-way conversation, still searching for additional bills in the pocket of my shoulder bag.

The barista laughs flirtatiously, and the man matches her with his own chuckle. She takes my payment, and I step to the other end of the counter and wait for my coffee while scanning the packaged coffee and mugs on the shop's shelves and the local artwork in bright colors on the wall.

I remember first sitting with Ryan over there, at that table. It wobbled as soon as we sat, and we both bent down to stuff a sugar packet under the leg, and clunked heads. I took that to mean we were both too headstrong and that could be a conflict between us. But I wanted the part; I wanted it to be like coming home. It was, for a while.

"I'm a man on a mission . . ."

"I like that." She giggles.

"Only for coffee . . . for now, that's my mission. And I have you to thank for helping me to complete it."

My memory stops. That voice . . . he sounds like . . .

"Ryan?" I say loudly over the milk steamer.

"Rose?"

"Excuse me, you owe me, mister," the barista interrupts, holding out her hand.

"Oh, yes, sorry . . ."

Ryan finishes paying and joins me, kissing me on the cheek in greeting.

"How're things? It's been a while."

"Things are good." I nod and smile.

I feel my cheeks flush. He looks different. His hair is cut shorter; his face is clean-shaven. Dressed in cargo shorts and a wrinkleless T-shirt, he shows his athletic build well. I see him with a fresh pair of eyes.

I ask him, "You suppose your barista girlfriend will get jealous if we walk out of here together and take a walk? That is, if you've got some time for me."

"For you, I have all the time . . . Sheila." He grabs his coffee and opens the front door. I slip through between it and him, and when I do, our eyes lock. "And she's not my girlfriend, by the way."

We stroll for most of the morning passing bungalows and two-flats nestled on tree-lined streets. We talk easily of where we've been and what we've been up to.

"Look, I didn't really like how it all ended, at Byron's. I was a little . . . I apologize for . . ."

"Hey, nothing more needs to be said. That was the past."

We walk a few paces noting the subtle changes in the season.

"So, what are you doing this weekend?" he asks, as if wanting to carry on this conversation further at another time.

"Spending it with an old creative director."

I thread my arm through his, and he leans into me.

"Are you making that a question or a statement?"

"I do believe it's a statement."

I stop, take his hands in mine, then look into his eyes.

"I look forward to it . . . shouldn't you be at rehearsals by now?"

"Oh geez." He checks his watch for the time. "I sure do," he says, skipping backwards. "I'll see you, soon." He turns and hustles back to the theater.

The last time I was with Ryan, I needed to finish my man-uscript, and I also had one last production run left in me. I had to finish both before I could make any new commitments. Well, both are completed, and now the timing is right.

Early the next morning, very early, the "new" Rose calls Ryan. He has been on my mind.

I think of the "old" Rose, someone who would quickly dispense with a relationship, who was eager for the next character, who lived in a place she'd never been. And then I think of the "new" Rose, who is finding happiness in what is and not what is yet to become, and who wants to see Ryan again.

"I like the new Rose," he says. "You've grown a second skin of fine silk, smooth and shiny and resilient." I freeze. My limbs tense. His words remind me of Julian and the silk tapestry he had given me. I will never forget Julian and our years together. The only thing I regret of our relationship was that maybe I used him. He was someone at the right place and the right time for me to advance my interests and secure my insecurities.

"Hey, it's the start of the holiday weekend. Meet me at Grinds?" I ask.

"I'd like that. See you soon."

I slip on my sneakers, grab a sweatshirt and my shoulder bag, and head out the door. I notice the swollen rain clouds hanging over the lake, but I don't care if a storm is approaching—my morning is a sunny one no matter what.

My timing matches Ryan's as I turn the corner and see him nearing the coffee shop. He waits for me at the door. He looks fresh and attractive, dressed in washed denim jeans and a V-neck navy sweater over a white shirt. His short-cropped hair is clumped with still-wet strands.

We greet in hugs and cheek pecks, and then he bows, opening the door for me.

"After you, madame."

"Why, thank you, kind sir." We laugh at our playfulness. "I'll order. Grab us that corner window seat . . . our table," he tells me.

While I wait for him and our cappuccinos, my phone rings.

"Rose, you need to get to the hospital," Charlotte says.

❧ Charlotte ❧

Ma dies on Sunday, her day of rest, with her daughters and husband beside her. And she wouldn't have wanted it any other way. The corners of her mouth have a slight upturn that tells us she is relieved of her suffering, at peace, and is finally in the arms of Jesus.

We linger in stillness in a tight corner of the room where lights and monitors have been silenced. The air is heavy with grief. We say our personal prayers gathered at her bedside, and then pray together, vowing to Ma that we'll always carry with us the wisdom of the willow. Each of us touches her gently, then releases herself from her, knowing she is at rest. Dad steps to her and lingers, gently touching her cold cheek, smoothing her hair. He kisses her softly. He, too, must let her go, only in body, but not in spirit.

And then it's time to go. We file out of her room, and don't look back.

I can't even describe what it feels like to leave Ma there, and all of us go home. Because home has changed now.

We drive Dad to the house, keeping quiet during the ride. He stares out the window on a chilly, gray, cloud-streaked sky, looking at each house, as if searching for something he has lost. We follow him into the house, where it is dark and dank. Deb, Linney, and

Rose stop at the den's doorway, an opening to Dad's comfort space, while he heads for his chair in a cozy corner as if anticipating Ma's usual four o'clock delivery of a bottle of Miller. His face tightens; his eyes circle the unlit room. He looks confused, frightened, as if he is in an unfamiliar space.

I turn on a desk lamp and rely on the lowering of the fading light slipping through the clouds to cast unobtrusively in the room.

"Don't worry, Dad, we'll take care of everything," I tell him, kneeling beside his old, lumpy chair and taking his hand. It is a scene of Dowling sisters standing before our father: Deb, with hands on hips, looking poised with directions on what to do next; Rose sighing in sadness; and Linney bowing her head in prayer and quiet contemplation.

I then look at Dad and remember a time when I thought he loomed larger than life. I must have been five or six. Dad fired up the lawn mower out back before the sun rose too high, and the heat of the summer day settled in quickly. He traversed in concentration the green carpet of grass in even rows, back and forth. My eyes jumped ahead of him to see a small ball of unidentifiable gray fur fitting snuggly between two bulging roots of the willow. The wiggly thing emerged, and out popped a pair of white and gray cotton clumps. I screamed. Dad was looking so intently at the mower moving in front of him that he didn't realize he would soon plow right into the baby bunnies. I ran as fast as I could and stood in front of the mower, almost getting run over myself. Dad stopped and shut off the machine. "What are you doing, Char? I nearly ran you over with this thing," he said, raising his voice and a hand. I couldn't talk, but I pointed under the willow. "You were headed right for them, and you would have killed 'em," I screamed through tears. And I never saw Dad jump as fast as he did then. He upended Ma's gardening tool caddy, grabbed the furry balls, placed them in the emptied container, then rushed to the row of hedges along the fence, where he gently placed them on a bed of grass clippings and leaves under the shade of the branches. Dad strutted back, proud of his ability to avoid a near horrific accident and save our beloved bunnies. I clapped in delight and hugged Dad's thighs. He was a savior in a time of distress. He was my hero that summer, and I never doubted his ability to save any day.

My sisters stay well after dinner, lingering around a quiet kitchen table with Dad.

"C'mon, Dad, let's get you upstairs and into bed," I say.

I don't see my father, the savior, but a man who looks as if he no longer has a purpose. A man who has lost his wife.

Inside the church, the air is cool and a dry, dusty scent mingles with burning incense as Ma's friends file into the narrow pews. I notice the shine of it all, the linoleum, the wooden pews, the stained glass, and I think how Ma must have felt welcome and at home when she would slip away in the early mornings for an hour to attend Mass here.

My eyes tear and my skin tingles when the organ keys strike re- fined notes in long, dramatic tones. The stained-glass windows on the church's side walls beam from the late-morning sun tagging them to shine. With Dad sitting in the middle of two daughters on each side, we fit snugly together in the first pew. The readings from the Bible and songs sung by the choir are familiar. I recall one Sunday morning, weeks before Ma died, when she handed me a file folder. "What's this?" I asked. "For my funeral. For a change, you won't have to do a thing. I talked to Father O'Brien, and I'm good to go. And don't tell your father. These religious things aren't for him," she said. Neither Dad nor my sisters knew that Ma had planned her own funeral Mass.

"It's time, let's go," I say to Dad and my sisters as Father O'Brien signals us to exit the pew.

As the procession to the cemetery begins, hunched-over bodies move sluggishly through the church, stirring incense-laden air. From the church's high ceiling, the acoustics echo, becoming louder with each note played. The organ notes lurk in dark corners as our plodding steps contribute to a scene of death and finality.

"Oh God, make that horrible organ music stop," I whisper to Deb, with a tissue blotting my eyes and nose.

"They won't play it much longer. It'll be okay," she says, taking my hand. "It'll all be okay."

Strangers' feet align along the sidewalk, creating a corridor to lead the Dowlings to the grave site. Arriving at the plot of soft dug-out earth, we bow our heads as if acknowledging the depth to which Ma will be buried. It first strikes me as odd, how we place our dead loved ones in a box with a tufted silk lining and bury the shiny, adorned wooden casket deep into the ground. How primitive, how dramatic. Not to take away from the seriousness of putting Ma to rest, but just because she is to be buried six feet under doesn't mean her spirit has to be. I feel her with us: she is embracing her family, telling us everything will be okay.

We wrap our arms around Dad and around each other, seeking warmth from the chilly winds and connection with each other, praying with Father O'Brien while he says his last words.

Our hearts are broken, and our spirits tremble. We are the Dowlings, now minus one.

The remaining weeks of the month bleed, one into the other. My schedule of stopping by the house doesn't change. I figure the routine comforts Dad; he knows he can depend on a visit from me. He's doing okay, barely. Dishes in the sink need filing into the dishwasher, and I see there are a couple of loads of laundry stacked on top of the washer, and his den is the only room that needs tidying of newspapers, bills, and *National Geographic* magazines. Ma believed the den is Dad's man cave, while he believes the other rooms in the house are Ma's—"she spaces" he calls them. He doesn't want to step into a "she space" without her. The yard isn't the same either. With no recent rain, spent blooms hang their heavy heads, dry leaves quiver on the oaks, and once a carpet of green grass is now patched with brown, a landscape reflective of our emotions. The backyard looks like the state of the Dowlings—loss of life. But the willow tree, always the exception, canopies all who seek a sit spot under her. We learned about life under the willow, where Ma dispensed the wisdom of the tree and some of her own.

I stop by the house the next morning and find Dad at the kitchen table with a cup of coffee and an uneaten slice of toast smeared with marmalade in front of him. I sit with him, and together we stare out at the willow, its thin branches weighted from overnight spitting rain, drops falling from leaves as if they are weeping. Dad sits heavy with memories, perhaps replaying a scene from summer when the rose blooms burst with scent, hydrangea flower heads bent in fullness, and grass grew into a thick emerald carpet. And Ma, sitting under the willow with me and Linney and Rose, while Deb, with one hand on her hip, told us we shouldn't be sitting but working on our chores. Ma was the only one working, weeding and deadheading the flowering pots, while the rest of us took in the heat of a summer afternoon, spotting birds and watching bees and butterflies find their landing spots. It is a time gone by, yet it feels like yesterday as I recall those memories.

There's a silence in this kitchen we have never heard before.

"It'll be alright, Dad," I tell him, squeezing his hand. "We'll all be alright," he whispers, his eyes filling with tears. I don't know what is to become of our home on Birchwood Court, as the loss of one inhabitant turns the Dowling home into just . . . a house. It doesn't feel like our home anymore. But for now, I keep an eye on our willow.

PART
IV

"Weeping may endure for the night,
but joy comes in the morning."

—PSALM 30:5

OCTOBER

✦ Charlotte ✦

The week after Ma's death, I realize I have a lot of time for myself, unscheduled and free. I am idle on my couch in the largest room I have, a sitting space with an additional two stuffed chairs and an unused table that Ma had given me from the house when I moved in. An all-purpose heavy wood table is centered in front of a floor-to-ceiling window. A few of my favorite photos I have taken over the years of my sisters and our willow hang framed on pebble cream walls. Over the years, I have made this space my home, and realize I have an opportunity to live my life in a way I didn't consider while Ma was ill.

I stare out the window from my third-floor apartment and spot a sliver of the lake in the distance between two other apartment buildings. In the stillness of the teal water and the quiet in the room, I can still hear all the don'ts from my sisters, and not many dos. From Deb, don't sacrifice your job under any circumstances; and from Rose, do what you think is right to follow your creative spirit, and that includes your relationships; and from Linney, don't be afraid to step through a door of an opportunity that invites you to a new place to be. But now, I understand the conclusions as more than simple advice. They are life lessons that would never have been learned if my sisters were not faced with life-changing decisions.

Rose would still be acting if she didn't decide to walk away from it and from Julian to write and pursue it as a career, just as she walked away from Michael and Ireland. And Linney's initial decision to hold on to Magnolia, proving to Mr. Leone how much she valued Magnolia, prompted him to offer her a way to keep the shop and to be free of the very financial burden that tempted her to give it up. And with Deb, it wasn't about losing her husband to her best friend, but in deciding to no longer be with them when she has become a better, stronger person. But no matter what, we remain daughters of Margaret and Joe, our teachers in finding our places to be.

I think how it was just last Saturday when all who loved Ma came together and celebrated her life in church, and, as she would say, gathered "to be present with the Lord in body and spirit." When I close my eyes and think about that day, just for a moment, I hear Ma's voice: "Attic, trunk, promise me."

I shoot up from the couch as if an alarm has gone off. The idea of doing what Ma asked me to do in her final breaths makes me hurry in obligation. I grab my bag and a jacket and dash out to the car. Trying to keep my eyes on the road, I am distracted when driving through town. It looks . . . different. I remember life here when I was growing up. The Commons, a strip mall, used to be over there, that entire block, with the four-way intersection fencing it in. *This was the center of town, where we all belonged.*

On the corner across from Deer Park State Bank was the old Franklins Pharmacy with its skinny, short aisles tight with rows of shelves, where I passed as a grade-schooler dressed in a plaid uniform and white blouse. The stop with Dad at the shiny white counter on Saturday mornings was customary. I waited by his side, holding on to his pants pocket while he talked to a man who blended in behind a white counter, dressed in a white short-sleeved shirt with buttons down the collar.

The grocery store was over there, where the parcel pickup man spoke in lively conversation and always with a smile, never hidden by his thick chocolate-brown mustache. Always dressed in a white button-down shirt with its tail not quite tucked in, and a dark tie that was always a little loose, he looked hurried while bagging groceries at the end of the checkout lane. "What a polite young man," Ma would always say when we'd pull away from the loading zone after he packed the groceries into the station wagon. Everyone called him by his name, and that seemed to please him. We raided the dime store for school supplies each September. My sisters and I held our lists, ready to check off the requirements as we plucked spiral notebooks and pens and rulers, and placed them into our wire baskets that we balanced in the crooks of our arms. After shopping, we got a milkshake or a Black Cow (root-beer float) in the diner section, and then went off to visit the parakeets in the cages aligning the wall. Linney followed the birdseed remnants on the scuffed linoleum at her feet and listened to their tweety calls to find them. After we slurped the last drops of our treat, Ma would take us a few doors down to the Gift Lantern. With its carpeted blue floor and glass-topped wood cabinets, fancy, sparkly things caught Ma's attention. She bought each of us our first pair of pierced earrings there, solid gold balls (really, they were more like dots) of various sizes. Then we went next door to Junior Miss, to try on a new outfit for my seventh-grade school dance. The saleslady said she thought I was wearing my big sister's clothes. No, I wasn't wearing a thing of Deb's. They were mine, albeit a little too grown-up looking, but Ma got them anyway just for me.

I remember the Commons, a small neighborhood place where everyone shopped, greeting their neighbors as they got in and out of their Country Squire station wagons. I smile as if I've visited an old friend and we have picked up where we left off after a long absence. It was where I could always find home.

I pull into the driveway and quickly notice the house looks tired; sad, too. Void of vibrant summer color, I am reminded it has lost its primary caretaker.

Standing in the foyer, I usually listen for Ma's footsteps and wait for her to find me in greeting, but the silence is palpable, except for the constant ticks of the swinging pendulum of the grandfather clock.

I visit Dad's den, the first room to the left, as the first place I check to find him, but he is not there. I continue down the hall to the kitchen and find him sitting at the table. I greet Dad with a kiss and a hug.

"Dad, how about lunch? I can fix you something," I say, sitting next to him. The kitchen, tidy and clean, looks as if it hasn't been used. He has kept it her way. He isn't in his usual seat, facing Ma so he could watch her work at the counter, but instead, he's where he has a full view of the backyard. His eyes are fixed on the willow, and I do not disturb him. I scuttle to the fridge and find a still-good quart of milk, a jar of marmalade, two sticks of butter, and a loaf of bread. The near-empty cupboards don't give me much to work with either. Jars of peanut butter (Linney's favorite), Pringles (Deb's go-to), and Cadbury chocolates (Rose's fix) are about all that remain on the shelves. Ma always had our favorites on hand as if we were still living at home. She left them there for us as her way of letting us know we were always welcome back. And then I spot a box of cookies.

"Dad, look what I found. Ya know, Ma left these for us." I pour us each a glass of milk and bring them and the box to the table. Mom always kept a supply of Lorna Doone shortbread cookies on the counter. At the noon hour, she granted herself a time-out from chores and errands to watch the news on television while eating a ham sandwich. She'd cap it off with a cup of coffee and shortbreads suitable for dunking.

He would ignore her efforts to chase soggy bits of cookie on the bottom of her coffee cup while he worked the crossword puzzle, sighing each time he had to erase. Time stalls as I relive moments when she and Dad sat together, right here at the table for lunch.

"It's okay, Dad, to talk about Ma. She left all this in the cupboard for us so we could remember her and talk about her. We have good memories, and it's okay to tell each other stories. She's always with us."

"Yes . . . she is," he says, looking outside and spotting a pair of cardinals, one a red male, the other a tan female, pecking at seed on the feeder. "Look, out there," he says, drawing my attention to the feeder. "Now, aren't they a little bit of heaven that's come visiting?" I remember Ma telling us that when we spot a cardinal, we are sure to know that it is a messenger from heaven, of love and of hope. "And the willow will always connect us to her and to home."

After we finish, I clean up the kitchen. I keep an eye on Dad, who is strolling subdued in the backyard during his post-lunch check, with Jingle at his side. He digs his hands into his pockets and, with his head bowed in a concentrated look, walks the circumference of the yard. In spring, he'd eye the azaleas, gently pinching the tip of a stem to determine how far along its bud is progressing to flowerhood. He'd continue in his hunched-over saunter, looking for spring flowers emerging from their bulb hibernation. He'd take close to a half hour checking the foliage, making mental notes of to-dos while kicking piles of dried leaves. He paused where perennials had been cut down for winter, as if trying to remember what grew there.

"Dad, I'm going up into the attic for a while. You okay?" I yell out to him from an open kitchen sliding door. A rush of cold air chills the space we just warmed with our memories.

"I'm fine, Charlotte. I'm fine. Now, go; go do what you need to do." I watch him pull up the collar of his denim jacket and settle into a chair under the willow before he leaves my sight. I take the stairs up and around the corner to another set of narrow stairs to the attic. The steps creak in conversation as if awakened from a dormant sleep. My feet make prints in the dust and I wonder how recently the attic saw visitors. Ma used to tell me the attic could provide enough stories to create its own family with all the stuff up there. I wonder what was here; she never told me, and I didn't ask. I love the mystery and intrigue.

Surveying the dark space, I follow a line of someone else's memories—an old dresser, wooden toys, golf clubs, and rusted toolboxes of various sizes—and drop in on a time gone by. *Was this what Ma was talking about?* I approach a far corner, but I can't see if it is empty or if something is in the space. And then I spot something big and dark. A trunk! For sure, this was what Ma was telling me about in her weakened breath. I grab a leather side handle and drag it to the center of the room, into a spotlight coming from a window below a triangular roofline. I kneel before running my hands along the scratched, dark wood, down the vertical metal bands. There is no lock, and with effort, I lift the top. Inside, there are items from our past, the dolls my sisters and I played with, and here are Deb's books, and Rose's diaries, Linney's glass marbles. These, too, made up a timeline of our growing up. *Was this what Ma was telling me to look for? Is there more?*

I move the treasures aside and discover a box. I lug it out of the trunk and drop it onto the floor, scattering dust. I sneeze. I lift the box's stiff lids and pull out pieces of fabrics that look new. A white envelope flies into the air and lands in my lap. It is simply addressed, "Charlotte." I put it and the fabrics back into the box and head downstairs, careful not to stumble. I pass Dad's den, hear a subdued snore, and see the crossword puzzle fallen in his lap. In my adrenaline-filled state, I hurry into the kitchen, drop the box on the table, and then call my sisters and tell them they need to come home.

At the kitchen table, I wait, staring at the closed treasure. I lose track of time, lost in my thoughts, when I hear cars pull up in the driveway, one after the other.

Then the sliding door opens.

"Why have you called us here?" Deb asks. Her palms are open in demand of an explanation. She takes a seat at the table. Linney, standing behind her and hesitant to enter, says, "It's about Dad, isn't it? Is he here? Where is he, Char?" And Rose follows, immediately sits down as if she is ready for a show to begin—sitting tall, hands clasped in front on the table.

"I called you over because before Ma died, she asked me to go into the attic and to look for a trunk. I didn't know what she was talking about, so I kind of forgot about it. I thought she was dreaming or thinking back to an old memory."

"Get on with it, will you, please," Deb says.

"This morning, I remembered Ma telling me in the hospital about a trunk in the attic, so I hurried over here. At first, I couldn't find it. It was dark and old and stained, and come to think of it, so was the attic. Actually, I don't think I'd ever been up there before to see it . . ."

"God, Char, get to it, please," Rose pleads.

"There was this big old trunk with our old things, some dolls and diaries and books and photos. Maybe these were what I was supposed to find, but maybe not. Like I said, it was dark, and I found things only with the feel of my hands. And then I found another box with this envelope on top of it." I show them the envelope in my shaky hands, the white paper now damp from my sweaty fingers. "I hauled the box downstairs to have a better look, and this is what I found."

I stand up, release the box's flaps, and pull out the fabrics, holding up each one, one of cotton, one of silk, and the last of linen, separating them from each other as I lay them on the table.

"Oh my God, my linen tablecloth. This is mine. It was on our dining room table in my home with Dennis. It was our connection to each other, our place to be." Deb cries and grabs the cloth, holding it to her chest.

"*That's* where it was. I forgot about the box of things I brought over here. I thought I had lost that cotton rug. It meant so much to me when it was under the farmhouse table at Magnolia." Linney squeals in delight, grabbing the heavy folds of cotton.

"Oh my. *This* is from a while ago," Rose whispers, remembering when Julian gave her the tapestry. "The silk has held its luster and shine." She holds it up to the light. The tapestry looks different; it has aged. Maybe the colors and threading that held the abstract design of shapes have settled in, creating a new picture from an old perspective.

"Julian once told me the silk's luster and reflector of light reminded him of me, and now it reminds me of Julian because of its patchwork of art, of single images fitting just so like puzzle pieces to form a single picture. 'We've come to fit so well with each other,' he'd whisper into my ear before I would open my eyes in the early mornings."

I watch my sisters mesmerized by what they hold, by their memories, as if cradling the very fabric of their lives. But the middle of the table is empty. I am reunited with connections that have meaning for my sisters. But there isn't a thing for me.

"Charlotte, the envelope," Deb says, pointing to it. "Open it."

I am so involved with my thoughts of not having something for me, that I forget that the envelope in Ma's very handwriting is in my hands. I eagerly open it and read.

My dearest girls,

Over the years, your father and I have watched you grow into your best selves. You have had your ups and downs while finding your unique posts in life. I know it wasn't easy for you, Deb, being the oldest. Oh, how I relied on you to set a good example for your sisters, and you always did a great job! You learned fast how to take charge, and because of that, today, you are a strong businesswoman. You claimed the linen tablecloth, also an example of strength and durability, and made this a connection to bring to your table for your family. And, Rose, when you showed me that silk tapestry that Julian gave you, my eyes lit up, as I saw you in its shimmering light. He knew you so well as he gave you a mirror to yourself. Silk—strong, light, and breathable—reflects light and you, Rose, always reflective in your acting career. You chased the theater to find your place to be, only to reveal a softness within you in writing. My dearest Linney, with your aversion to having your feet covered. I know why. Feeling a cotton rug under your feet is comforting to you, like home. I can understand how its softness is appealing as you were never one for the hard edges of a confrontation. You handled Mr. Leone and his offer with such grace, and with each breath you took, you relied on feeling its strength, insulating you from the chill of a floor. Grounding yourself on the rug in Magnolia's office was a way of telling yourself that everything will work out. And it did! And, Charlotte, my youngest, who has given me a great gift of knowing when I needed you nearby. I asked you, a great keeper of secrets, to keep my illness to yourself, though I know you were torn between telling your sisters, as you always did as a child, and honoring my request, as you were asked as an adult. You are free now, Charlotte, to fulfill your own needs, to be at home. Thank you for remembering the trunk, for bringing the fabric of your lives back to where they belong.

I hope your father and I have shown you the importance of life, in gifts of connection and home. What better way, I thought, than to sit you down, outside under the willow, your classroom, where powers of observation are in the stillness of present moments. I hope I have given you home. And now that you are grown, reclaim your rug, your tablecloth, your tapestry as they are once again yours. Our willow is old and has outgrown its space, but remember it when holding the fabrics of your lives.

My love to you,
Ma

We stare at our past in our hands as we imagine our futures.

One might think I was left out because I did not have a treasure of my own. But I did. My fortune was in an envelope, speaking Ma's words for her, and in her calling me her secret keeper.

My sisters and I meet at the house the last weekend of October, before the first flurries of snow escape from winter clouds. Dad fires up the grill and pulls the picnic bench near our willow. He is dressed in his usual banged-up jeans and L.L. Bean work boots, with a red plaid flannel shirt under a canvas jacket. This is his outdoor work uniform. Ma said that with wearing the same thing when working outside, he's limited to wrecking only a few pieces of clothing at a time. We spread a blanket and sit in a circle, first remembering Ma as the circle is open, and then closing it in remembrance of her.

It is quiet at first, as I glance among the Dowling generation with bowed heads, until Deb speaks up.

"As my mother and the mother to the three of you, and by the grace of God, she managed to raise four girls who have grown into their own, starting with a piece of her at our births as the seed that, when ready, took root, and sprouted with a uniqueness defined as genuine. I have Ma's strength and adaptability. Rose, you're like me in that way—strong. You don't unravel easily, and you do reflect the light wherever you go. Linney, do you remember when you were about seven or eight, riding your bike on our way home on a summer night? You'd follow the fireflies by the flashes of light as if they were fireworks on the Fourth of July. To you, they weren't just fireflies— they were summer, riding bikes after dark, and sitting by campfires into the night. I wish I had a little of you, Linney, of your softness and breathability. Charlotte, you are no longer my baby sister, but a young woman who is on her own path to her place to belong. Your loyalty to Ma has been irrefutable."

We talk of memories and life lessons, of Ma's favorite flowers, of anticipating the bees and monarchs, of waiting for the blue jays and cardinals to feed in the corner once again. Whenever we're together, we're home. And life will go on, as there is nothing to stop it. We have our memories. We have the fabrics of our lives.

"How can we live without our lives? How will we know
it's us without our past? . . . How if you wake up in the
night and know—and know the willow tree's not
there? Can you live without the willow tree?
Well, no, you can't. The willow tree is you."

—JOHN STEINBECK

ACKNOWLEDGMENTS

It seems like forever that I have been a writer of memoir and personal essay; I considered writing fiction to be daunting. Creating stories of the imagination was intimidating as I relied on my reflections and meanings of personal experiences. But it wasn't until I understood that I could still infuse my writerly self equally into alternative narratives.

And so *The Wisdom of the Willow* was born, a reflective story of learning from the natural world, and a willow tree, a symbol of fertility, new life, thriving in challenging conditions

Thank you to Brooke Warner, publisher of She Writes Press, for giving me every reason to return to She Writes Press with this second book! I am full of gratitude. And Lauren Wise, Associate Publisher, gracious recipient of all questions, large and small, who kept the pages turning with grace and fortitude on my editorial schedule.

I am thrilled and thankful for Annie Tucker and her prudent developmental editing. I couldn't have imagined working with anyone else on a second book project.

And many thanks to Marcia Trahan for copyediting this book. Over many years, I have valued her professional keen eye and flawless edits to make my work smooth and resonate. And so it does with this book!

And to the engaging and effervescent team at PR by the Book. Thank you for your enthusiasm and dedication to promoting my first novel. You're the best!

And to Mike. I am forever grateful for your unwavering patience and understanding as I continue to write and publish what's on my mind and in my soul.

ABOUT THE AUTHOR

NANCY CHADWICK grew up in a northern suburb of Chicago. She got her first job at Leo Burnett advertising agency in Chicago. After a decade there, and later, another decade in corporate banking, she quit and began to write full time, finding inspiration from her years living in Chicago and in San Francisco. Her essays have appeared in *The Magic of Memoir: Inspiration for the Writing Journey, Adelaide Literary Magazine*, Turning Points – The Art of Friction, blogs by Off Campus Writers' Workshop, the Chicago Writers Association Write City, and *Brevity*. She and her husband reside in a northern suburb of Chicago.

SELECTED TITLES FROM SHE WRITES PRESS

She Writes Press is an independent publishing company founded to serve women writers everywhere. Visit us at www.shewritespress.com.

The Best Part of Us by Sally Cole-Misch. $16.95, 978-1-63152-741-8. Beth cherished her childhood summers on her family's beautiful northern Canadian island—until their ownership was questioned and a horrible storm forced them to leave. Fourteen years later, after she's created a new life in urban Chicago, far from the natural world, her grandfather asks her to return to the island to see if that was lost still remains.

The Lockhart Women by Mary Camarillo. $16.95, 978-1-64742-100-7. After Brenda Lockhart's husband announces he's leaving her for an older, less attractive woman, she—devastated and lonely—becomes addicted to the media frenzy surrounding the murder of Nicole Brown, which took place the same night her husband dropped his bombshell. In the ensuing months, her whole family falls apart—but ultimately comes together again in unexpected ways.

Ferry to Cooperation Island by Carol Newman Cronin. $16.95, 978-1-63152-864-4. Former ferry captain James Malloy is a loner—but in order to save his New England island home from developers, he'll have to join forces with the woman who stole his job.

Moon Water by Pam Webber. $16.95, 978-1-63152-675-6. Nettie, a gritty sixteen-year-old, is already reeling from a series of sucker punches when an old medicine woman for the Monacan Indians gives her a cryptic message about a coming darkness: a blood moon whose veiled danger threatens Nettie and those she loves. To survive, Nettie and her best friend, Win, will have to scour the perilous mountains for Nature's ancient but perfect elements and build a mysterious dreamcatcher.

Gravity is Heartless: The Heartless Series, Book One by Sarah Lahey. $16.95, 978-1-63152-872-9. Earth, 2050. Quinn Buyers is a climate scientist who'd rather be studying the clouds than getting ready for her wedding day. But when an unexpected tragedy causes her to lose everything, including her famous scientist mother, she embarks upon a quest for answers that takes her across the globe—and uncovers friends, loss, and love in the most unexpected of places along the way.